I0565815

BORDERLINE
JUSTICE

BORDERLINE JUSTICE

THE ROGER BRINKMAN SERIES
#3

TIM W. JAMES

IRON SPIKE
PRESS

Jackson, WY

Copyright © 2024 Tim W. James

Borderline Justice Tim W. James © 2024

All rights reserved. No part of this publication may be distributed, reproduced, or transmitted in any form or by any means, including recording, photocopying, or other electronic or mechanical methods, without the prior written permission of the publisher, except in the case of brief quotations embodied in critical reviews and certain other non-commercial uses permitted by copyright law.

This is a work of fiction. Names, characters, businesses, places, events, locales, and incidents are either the products of the author's imagination or used in a fictitious manner. Any resemblance to actual persons, living or dead, or actual events is purely coincidental.

For permission requests, write to the publisher, addressed
Attention: Permissions Coordinator
Sastrugi Press, P.O. Box 1297, Jackson, WY 83001, United States.
www.sastrugipress.com

Library of Congress Cataloging-in-Publication Data available

ISBN-13: 978-1-64922-281-7 (Paperback)

Cover design copyright © Sastrugi Press LLC.

Iron Spike Press is an imprint of Sastrugi Press LLC.

10 9 8 7 6 5 4 3 2 1

Dedication

The first born in any family is traditionally one of rank and privilege. It can also be one of honor and respect but that usually has to be earned. Gerald Merritt Linsdau was all that and more.

Jerry was born December 12th, 1937 in Oshkosh, Wisconsin. He departed to be with his Lord and Savior, Jesus Christ, July 20th, 2024.

The oldest of four boys, Jerry moved with the family to Ocala, Florida. During that time, he followed his father to Wyoming for temporary work in the timber business. Later, the entire family moved to Wyoming about the time Jerry entered high school.

Jerry was an excellent student and athlete and was named All State for football his senior year. After high school, he entered the United States Navy and served as an electricians mate on board ship. After being honorably discharged, he returned to Wyoming and worked for the state's Game and Fish Department until his retirement.

Jerry fulfilled his role as big brother with distinction. He married Linda Robertson-Slagle and became parents to Leah Linsdau, who later married Jeff Cooley. Jerry's granddaughters, Kami and Kadi Cooley, were excellent students and athletes in their own right. Kami is married and a librarian, while Kadi practices medicine as an orthopedic surgeon.

After retirement, Jerry took up golf and rapidly progressed. He would challenge his younger brother to a match whenever they spent time together. It took Jerry several matches before he finally beat his brother, but he never lost a match after that.

After the death of Merritt and Dorothy Linsdau, Jerry became the touchstone for his younger brothers and remains so in their hearts.

Jerry was a devout Christian and member of the Immanuel Lutheran Church in Powell, Wyoming. He led a humble life but his influence will live on. There are things men strive for in life and never attain. What Gerald Merritt Linsdau achieved was not only a life well lived, but he also gave definition to what it means to be the first-born son.

Godspeed.

Chapter 1
Galveston

United States Marshal Nik Brinkman was summoned to Judge Jedediah Conklin's office for what he believed would be a briefing on what was to become of Captain Cutlass Baudelaire and his fellow pirates. Baudelaire and those aboard his ship were accused of assisting in the theft of about one million dollars worth of silver bound for the United States Treasury.

Baudelaire had used his ship, Tiburon, in a celebration of Galveston's famed pirate, Jean Lafitte. Baudelaire claimed he had served under Lafitte before the infamous buccaneer was driven off Galveston Island.

His ship just happened to "run into" the barge that was carrying the silver shipment to Galveston to deposit it in the First United States Bank established there. Baudelaire's ship was seized, but the silver shipment was not on board. It was carried away by a hot-air balloon, mistaken to be part of the Lafitte Celebration.

Nik had heard that Baudelaire was seeking clemency by turning state's evidence. The marshal remembered the Jean Lafitte impersonator as colorful and not such a bad sort. The worst of the bunch was Al Nelson. Nelson, a former sailor, had been selected to serve onboard that barge commissioned to ferry the silver across Galveston Bay to the bank. When it was learned that Nelson was part of the heist, the former seaman jumped ship and was never found.

"You wanted to see me?" Nik said, peeking his head into Conklin's office.

"Yes, Marshal, come in, come in," the judge beckoned. "Have a seat, Nik, we have some things to discuss."

Conklin's white hair seemed whiter and thinner since Nik had first met him following Nik's arrival in Galveston to take over as chief marshal of the area's United States Marshals Service. Conklin's muttonchops were thinning, but he had not lost his taste for cigars. In fact, Nik could not remember visiting the judge's office without seeing a stogy lit and sitting in the judge's ashtray.

Nik also noticed a colorful bird perched on a stand in the corner of the office. "Did you acquire a new pet?" Nik asked.

"That's Maggie, Baudelaire's pet parrot," Conklin said. "Now that the pirate is awaiting trial, I'm babysitting his bird while Cutlass remains incarcerated. Very interesting animal, I must admit."

"Awk, Cutlass is in jail," Maggie cried out.

"I'm sorry I didn't have more information on Baudelaire and his disastrous involvement in trying to steal that silver shipment," Nik started, taking a seat before the judge's desk, "I would never have dreamed…"

"Save your breath, Nik. Baudelaire's singing far better than that bird of his," the judge said.

"So, he decided on a plea deal?" Nik asked.

"For the calamity, yes, however there is the issue of the lost deputy, a Casey Wyatt, I believe," Conklin said, reaching out to tap the ash from his cigar into the ashtray. He picked up the cigar, drew in on it, turned his head to one side and blew out a plume of bluish smoke. The judge then leaned over his desk toward Nik. "Baudelaire may have to do time for manslaughter. His sidekick may also be sentenced, but oddly, the other men are keeping quiet on this. So, it may be a bigger deal than we thought."

"How so?" Nik inquired, leaning in the direction of the judge.

"The name King Victor popped up and Baudelaire identified him as Judge Victor Kensington," Conklin said.

"Judge Kensington," Nik nearly blurted out. "I know him. I went after him when I was a deputy marshal out of Wichita. Did Baudelaire say Kensington was behind this?"

"Apparently," Conklin continued. "He said Kensington is running some kind of racket out of Mexico, somewhere on the Yucatan

Peninsula. He indicated there were others, but we're going to have to run a background check on them."

"One of them wouldn't happen to be Curtis Packard, would it?" Nik asked.

"That was one of the names, along with a General Porfirio Diaz. Do you know him?"

"No, I've never heard of the general, but we believed that Kensington and Packard were allies during our investigation of Kensington," Nik answered. "However, we were never able to pin anything on the sheriff."

"So, Packard was a sheriff?"

"Yes, he was the sheriff of Clarksville, Texas, where my brother and I found him and Judge Kensington working together. Though, at the time, they weren't breaking any laws, but they were dealing with an outlaw gang we eventually broke up," Nik stated.

"Was that the Sulphur River Bunch I read about in the newspaper?" Conklin asked.

"That's the one," Nik answered.

"Well, Nik, that brings me to my next point, which is a big one," Conklin began. "Nik, that silver shipment was destined for the United States mint in order to coin money, putting it on par value with gold. With this currency crisis we have going on, the farmer's union is pressuring Washington to do something and do it soon. The loss of that shipment was a huge setback."

Nik leaned back in his chair and placed his thumbs behind his gun belt.

"Nik, we feel that silver shipment is somewhere in northern Mexico."

"That would kinda make sense, if Kensington is in Mexico like we believe," Nik replied.

"That's the catch, here," Conklin added. "To our knowledge, Kensington lives somewhere on the Yucatan Peninsula in southern Mexico, not up north where our informants have suggested."

"What informants?" Nik inquired.

"As you know, Marshal, that silver shipment was carried off by a hot-air balloon."

"And you think that balloon carried that silver into northern Mexico?" Nik queried.

"Don't get ahead of me," Conklin cautioned. "The U.S. Navy pursued that balloon and came across a Mexican naval ship anchored off the Mexican Coast just a few miles below where the Rio Grande flows into the gulf. General Diaz was onboard that vessel, along with a small crew. Oddly enough, Diaz inquired of the Navy captain if he had seen a red hot-air balloon. When the captain told him that balloon had gone inland near Corpus Christi, the captain said the news severely agitated the general. The captain said Diaz became anxious to sail back to port in Mexico."

"So, you believe Diaz was waiting for that silver shipment to be delivered to him?" Nik said, leaning forward.

"Yes," the judge replied. "What we don't know was the destination of that balloon. We received reports of a red balloon flying over parts of Duval, Encinal, and Webb counties. It appeared headed for Mexico. Where in Mexico we don't know, but that's what we'd like you to find out, Nik."

Nik squirmed a little in his chair, somewhat apprehensive as to what Conklin might say next.

"Marshal, on behalf of the Federal Government, including the Marshals Service, we'd like you to go into Mexico and find that silver."

"It's that important?" Nik queried.

"Considering the counterfeiting problem we've had here, it makes it bigger than just important," the judge said. "You have been authorized to head up a task force to go into Mexico and find that silver shipment. All we really know is that it was headed toward the Sierra Madre Oriental Mountain Range."

"How do you propose we do this?" Nik asked, taken aback by Conklin's request.

"Your authorization allows you to take a small detachment of soldiers to complete this search. However, it is important they go with you as surveyors, not soldiers," Conklin said. "We don't want Mexico to think we're trying to invade their country and start another war."

"I'll need an interpreter, sir, I don't speak Spanish."

"You are also authorized to select the civilian help you need, just don't go overboard," the judge advised. "The soldiers are already paid for. You'll have to negotiate for the rest."

"It has been suggested you enter the country from the New Mexico Territory," the judge advised. "That area is half Mexican anyway."

"And Apache," Nik interjected.

"Yes, and Apache, which is why we have suggested taking soldiers," Conklin continued. "The military has suggested departing out of Fort McRae. President Grant is sending a wire to the commandant there to authorize the use of soldiers."

"Fort McRae is where my brother is staying," Nik said, surprised by the suggestion.

"Your brother... he helped you here to break up that counterfeit ring, right?"

"Yes, but I can't recruit him for this," Nik cautioned. "I'm already guilty of putting him way too deep into harm's way. But he could be valuable in helping me select my task force."

"How long do you estimate this will take?" Nik asked.

"I wish I could tell you, Nik. It may take quite a while, so you may have to purchase supplies along the way. That will be taken care of by the federal government," Conklin added. "We need that silver, Nik. I'm counting on you."

"I'll do my best, judge," Nik said, looking at Conklin. "I'd like to offer you something more solid than that, but until I've recruited the men necessary for this I won't know where we stand."

"Oh, as for the U.S. Marshals Service, they've been contacted and will send us a temporary replacement," Conklin said. "Until then, I think your deputy will have to handle things."

"Ambrose is more than capable, and I might know some others that can help," Nik said, referring to his hired deputy and volunteer assistants. "I'll speak to them."

"I knew we could count on you, considering the job you did on that counterfeit case," the judge said. "Let me know when you can get started."

Nik returned to his office, where Ambrose was busy going through warrants and wanted posters.

"Ambrose, I've got to ask you for a big favor," Nik started. "I'm going to need you to run the office for a time. I have been given an assignment that's going to take me out of the country, and I don't know for how long."

"I can handle the small stuff, but I would hate to be in charge of what we went through with the counterfeit case and the stolen silver shipment," Ambrose said, looking a little concerned.

"Judge Conklin has asked the U.S. Marshals Service to send a temporary replacement for me, but the judge isn't sure when he will arrive," Nik said. "In the meantime, I'm going to ask Abel Mosely and Isaiah Boatman to assist you."

"You know I'll do my best, boss," Ambrose said, putting down the papers he was going through. "But as fond as I am of those two fellas, they're likely not as spry as they used to be."

"Get Sheriff Duke Atkins to help you if things heat up," Nik replied. "I would not like to see those Abel and Isaiah in a shootout of any kind. Just ask them to give you a hand with the routine work, okay?"

"Sure. Where are you headed?"

"Mexico, to look for that stolen silver," Nik said. "That robbery apparently put Washington back on its heels, as far as the national currency is concerned. This counterfeiting issue didn't help any, either."

"Mexico? They have their problems down there as well," Ambrose said. "Are you sure you want to do this?"

"It's my duty, Ambrose. When and wherever I'm called, I go."

"Did the service know what they were getting when they hired you?" Ambrose inquired, implying the racial prejudice.

"Abraham Lincoln opened this door for me," Nik said. "I have to deal with the bigotry wherever I go, but the service has always been fair to me."

"Do you think we'll ever be put on the level that white folks enjoy?" Ambrose asked in a serious tone.

"Only time can answer that one, my friend," Nik said. "All we can do is perform at the best of our ability and stand our ground when required. You, of all people, have been blessed with the physical ability to do that."

"I just don't want to have to fight all the time, Nik," Ambrose said, now comfortable answering his boss by name. "I don't expect special favors, but I would like respect."

"I can't imagine you not getting it, but I understand what you're saying," Nik offered. "Just continue as you are and I believe the folks in this area will give you all the respect you need."

Nik sat down behind his desk and began jotting down some notes.

"What are you going to tell Esther?" Ambrose casually inquired.

Nik looked up as if hit in the face with a splash of cold water. He stared at Ambrose for almost a minute before responding.

"I don't know, Ambrose," Nik said in a flat monotone. "I haven't been in this position before."

"What if she gives me an ultimatum not to go?" he added, his voice rising.

"She's not going to do that," the deputy said, trying to comfort Nik. "You two are in love. If she can't handle this, she had no business getting involved with you, you being a chief marshal and all. I can't imagine she's going to like it, but she's been through tougher situations than this."

"I, I guess you're right," Nik said, calming a little. "I'm trying to figure out how to put this hunting party together and hadn't given any thought to telling Esther about it. All of a sudden I can't think straight."

"Set some time aside, get a buggy and go out and tell her," Ambrose advised. "She'll understand and then you can put your mind straight on how to do this."

"You make it sound so simple," Nik said, with a stupefied look on his face. "How do you know this? Have you ever had a girl?"

"No, but I see what's going on when it comes to lots of folks," Ambrose said. "You have to give folks more credit."

"Sometimes I think I may be the wrong one in charge here," Nik said with a grin. "I know you're going to be just fine during my absence. I believe I'll be okay too. Now I have to get Esther to be all right with this."

"I told you how to do it…" Ambrose began.

"Okay, okay, I get your point," Nik said. "Look, I'm going to have to go to the library and find a map of the area where I'll be going. She's going to want to know that. If you need me that's where I'll be," Nik concluded.

Chapter 2
Fort McRae

"We have certainly appreciated your presence here at Fort McRae," Captain E. P. Horne said, as he stood in the doorway of Roger Brinkman's quarters. "You've brought purpose and encouragement to my men."

"It has been my pleasure, Captain," Roger replied. "For an itinerant clergy, I couldn't ask for better accommodations and a captive congregation, so to speak."

"Just so you know, rumor has come down that McRae may be in the conversation to be decommissioned," Horne continued. "Not within the next year or so, but one never knows when Congress decides to cut its losses."

"I wouldn't call this a loss, Captain. You and your soldiers have done an amazing job of bringing relative peace and security to this region."

"I often wonder what will happen to these men if we are decommed," the captain continued. "I think a number of them will return to civilian life. Chasing Indians can get old."

"By the by, I have a letter here for you. I think it's from a relative, a Nik Brinkman?"

"That's my brother," Roger replied. "I've been expecting to hear from him since I wrote him after I got back from Galveston. I figured I'd be getting a wedding invitation soon but I didn't think he'd wait this long."

"Well, I'll let you find out what he has to say," Horne said. "I have to select some men to investigate a possible Apache attack near Chuchilo Negro."

"Well, if I don't see you for a while, be careful," Roger said. "I've got to start my next missionary sweep to shore up my flock, so to speak. I should be back in about two weeks."

"Do you want me to assign a few soldiers to go with you?" Horner asked.

"I appreciate it, but I'm better off going on my own. I'm less threatening that way," Roger said.

"Just be sure to take something to defend yourself with," Horne stated. "Things are still a little uneasy, and I hear that Victorio has moved off the reservation in the Arizona Territory."

"I never leave home, or the fort, without it, Captain," Roger said, smiling while patting his holstered pistol. "Some of my parishioners still frown when they see me wearing it, but I try to put them at ease by removing it when conducting services."

As the captain touched the brim of his hat in a gesture of farewell, Roger sat down to read Nik's letter. When he tore open the envelope, he discovered another envelope inside with Pricilla Wiggins name on it. Roger chuckled to himself as he set that letter aside and began to read his brother's epistle.

"Dear Roger,

I regret that we had so little time to spend together during your visit. As a former deputy marshal, you know how unpredictable life can be. I also regret using you to spy on Sheriff Ellsworth and Ron Lester. It was confirmed that Lester was a customs agent, albeit a crooked one. According to Sebastian Mason, he was suspected of being crooked when he worked for the Treasury Department, too.

All is well since your departure. Thank you for baptizing Esther and I. I feel as if Pa's hand reached out, courtesy of the Good Lord, to get it done through you.

Esther and I are getting along fine and have been talking about marriage, but there's been a bit of a holdup. As you may know, that shipment of silver is still missing, and Lester is nowhere to be found. We, on the side of the law think he's in Mexico, which brings me to another matter.

Judge Conklin, on orders from Washington, D.C., would like the United States Marshals Service to retrieve that silver, if we can find it. The loss of that silver has forced the farmers to put a noose around Congress's neck concerning the coinage of more currency. Apparently, the balloon that carried away the silver was last seen headed across the Rio Grande into Mexico. The best guess is that the balloon had lost its guidance system, or the pilot, and was blown off course. They believe it came down somewhere in the Sierra Madre Mountains.

For that reason, the judge has suggested entering Mexico from the New Mexico Territory to look for the silver. Therefore, I will be coming to Fort McRae to set up a task force to help with that search. Your suggestions and guidance would be helpful but you would not have to be involved beyond that. I would ask that you let the company commander know of the plans. He will be getting official word from President Grant to assist us in this matter. I will send a wire to let you know when to expect me.

Again, I want to thank you for making that trip to Galveston and doing all that you did for us. I hope to see you again soon.

Your Brother,

Nik

P.S. There should be a second letter in the envelope from a Miss Pricilla Wiggins. I believe she is the woman you met on your trip down here.

God Speed"

Roger sat on his bunk and leaned his pillow against the wall. He picked up Pricilla's letter and rested his back against it while tearing the envelope open.

"Dear Pastor Roger Brinkman,"
A bit formal, Roger thought.

"I hope this letter reaches you. I sent it in care of U.S. Marshal Nik Brinkman in Galveston and asked him to send it on to you.

Mother and I made it back to Philadelphia just fine and have begun blending back into the life we knew before leaving for California. Being back here is very little different from what it was when we first left. I had looked so forward to getting back, after experiencing the untamed state of California. We did get a letter from my father, whom I believe will be joining us before long. I think his hopes of finding gold turned out to be more of a dream than a reality.

I must admit that I truly enjoyed our time in Texas, though most of it was on the sea. I grew instantly fond of Galveston and since our return wished we had never left there. I mentioned it to mother and she just laughed, saying I liked it because of you. I must confess that you did make our journey home far more pleasant, in spite of being together only a short time.

Your brother, Nik, is a delightful man. I do hope you and he had a good time visiting and he received the baptism he so longed for. I hope the pirate incident was settled and perhaps the man who came up missing was found alive and well.

I blush a little when I write this, but that trip onboard the Texas Belle under a full moon and our embrace on the dock at Galveston are things I cannot get out of my mind. I hope I am not being too forward, but the bores in Philadelphia do not appeal to me in the way our time together did.

But enough of that, please let me know how you are doing. After all, you did imply that you would possibly answer my letter, providing you get it.

Take Care,

Pricilla Wiggins"

Roger let out a big sigh, recalling the visions Pricilla mentioned. As much as he enjoyed her company, the New Mexico Territory was more of a place for a woman like Sally Zimmerman. Sally demonstrates a toughness required to survive in the West and still be able to provide her husband with the gentleness a man needs.

Roger looked about his quarters and nearly broke out in a laugh trying to imagine what Pricilla would think trying to make a home of the place.

Roger folded the letters back up, put them away, and went in search of the captain.

After explaining to Captain Horne as to the contents of Nik's letter, the captain ordered his sergeant to seek out potential volunteers. Meanwhile, knowing Nik would need a suitable guide, Roger decided to give his friend Carlos Sanchez Santana a visit.

"So good to see you, Señor Brinkman," Carlos said, emerging from his cabin located in Alamocita, located about six miles north of Fort McRae. "Are we having services tonight?"

"I came to ask you to inform the locals that I will be preaching at Fort McRae this Sunday," Roger stated. "I plan to begin my circuit after that and will stop in to visit any parishioners needing my assistance when I pass through again."

"You know you are welcome anytime. I will pass the word along," Carlos said. "It is wonderful to have you back, although Señor Zimmerman has been filling in for you admirably."

"Like you, Carlos, Paul is a Godsend," Roger said. "However, there is another reason for my visit."

"I am at your service, Pastor Brinkman."

"I know you speak fluent Spanish and even some Apache," Roger started. "I am looking for someone to assist my brother on an excursion into Mexico. I do not know the extent of the journey but am trying to find help for my brother in advance. Would you be interested?"

"I would do most anything for you, Pastor, but it would not be a good thing for me to do," Carlos answered. "My responsibilities here are too great for now. Will you be leaving again?"

"My brother did not request I accompany him, but he is trying to put together a task force," Roger said. "Is there any chance you know of someone else who could serve as an interpreter? I'm not sure what the compensation would be, but the expedition is being backed by the Federal Government."

"If she will do it, I know of one that would be much better than I," Carlos offered.

"She?" Roger replied. "I don't know if this would be the kind of thing a woman would want to do."

"This woman would be better than any man I know in these parts," Carlos continued. "She is a mestizo Apache shaman. I swear, she speaks with God's tongue."

It took Roger a moment to digest Carlos's comment, but he knew it wasn't a personal attack against him. "Can you tell me a little more about her?"

"Her name is Morgana Maria Cabazon, and she claims to be the granddaughter of Cochise," Carlos began.

"The Apache Chief?" Roger exclaimed, raising an eyebrow.

"Si, she claims to be the daughter of one of the chief's two daughters born to an unknown woman."

"But does she speak the language of Mexico?" Roger queried.

"Si, although that is a mix of mestizo and Indian," Carlos said, "and that is good. In Mexico, perfect Spanish is not always so good."

"I am intrigued," Roger replied. "Do you think she is strong enough to take such a journey into Mexico?"

"I would say she is stronger to do so than Carlos, Señor. She is both young and strong."

"All I can do is introduce her to Nik and let him decide," Roger said. "However, I would like to meet and talk to her before making up my mind on this. Can you put me in touch with her?"

"Most certainly, Señor Brinkman, I will speak with her and make arrangements. I will let you know Sunday at the fort."

"I knew I could count on you, Carlos," Roger said, smiling and extending his hand to his friend. "However, if you should change your mind about this, you know you are my first choice."

"I do not like to disappoint, but such a journey is not for Carlos," he responded. "Fort McRae is far enough for me," Carlos concluded with a laugh.

Chapter 3
The Proposal

U.S. Marshal Nik Brinkman rose early the next morning with a knot in his stomach, ate a light breakfast and headed for the Galveston Livery Stable. He rented a suitable horse and carriage and set out for the Galveston Ferry. After crossing over the bay to the Texas mainland, he selected the most direct route to the Covington Plantation.

Arriving at the estate around mid-morning, Nik pulled up to the paddock where Isaiah Boatman was busy cleaning the horses' stalls.

"Good day, Marshal. What brings you out here this early?" Isaiah called out, setting aside his shovel and approaching the buggy.

"I am sorry to come unannounced," Nik answered, "but I have some news that I think is important, especially for Esther."

"Not anything bad, I hope," Isaiah, Esther's father, said.

"Nothing tragic, Isaiah," Nik responded, "but important enough that I come in person to let you know."

"Well, let me put your horse away and then come on into the house and you can let us know what it is. Miss Tillie and Esther are working inside today."

"Before we do that," Nik began, "I need to talk to you personally about this."

Isaiah Boatman broke into a smile and remarked, "If this is to officially ask for Esther's hand in marriage, I think you already know the answer to that. You have my most assured and humble blessings that a father can offer."

"You can't know how good that makes me feel, Isaiah," Nik said.

"But there is a little more to the story."

Isaiah stood silent for a moment letting his expression invite Nik to continue.

"Isaiah, I have to go away for a spell, and I do not know when I will be back," Nik said. "And it's not just the uncertainty that bothers me, but it's the patience I have to ask of Esther and the anxiety the journey may bring."

"Sounds serious, Marshall," Isaiah replied. "Do you want to go in and inform everyone about this?"

"No, I have to speak to Esther alone on this because she is likely to be the one most affected by it," Nik continued. "That's why I brought the buggy. I had hoped a short ride alone with her would help lessen the impact of what I have to say and help me figure out exactly how to say it."

"I guess it isn't necessary to unhitch your horse then," Isaiah said.

"Not unless Esther cannot breakaway at this time," Nik said with anticipation.

"If this is as serious as you make it seem, I don't think there'll be any objection from Esther or Miss Tillie," Isaiah assured.

"Then let's proceed," Nik said.

The two men entered the plantation house and Isaiah asked the two women inside to join them.

"Nik, I didn't know you were coming today," Esther said, somewhat flustered by his presence. "If you'd have let me know …"

"Please, Esther, this is all my fault, but I felt it important I come and see you," Nik started.

"Why, Marshal, this is a pleasant surprise," Tillie Covington said, entering the room where the others were gathered. "What brings you out here this time of day?"

"Madame Tillie, so good to see you, but I must request you give Esther and I some time to talk," Nik replied. "I know this is un-expected and I will explain everything later. I brought a buggy so Esther and I could take a short ride because the news I bring will, I believe, affect her the most."

"Do I need to make us a picnic lunch?" Esther interjected, somewhat shaken by the urgency of Nik's request.

"No, I fear I've made this a little too much of a mystery and have upset all of you by it," Nik said. "It is my awkwardness that has made it so. Please forgive me, but this is largely about my job and it is important that I relate it to Esther first, and then I can do a better job of discussing this with all of you."

"If it's just a ride you want to take, I'll grab my bonnet and we can get this thing off your chest as soon as possible," Esther said, trying to read Nik's face.

"That would be terrific, Esther," Nik said. "Folks, I appreciate your indulgence here. Esther, I'll go fetch the buggy and bring it up here while you get what you need," Nik concluded.

After Nik had retrieved the buggy and got down to assist Esther, she began to feel the anxiety of the situation. As soon as she was seated and Nik climbed in beside her, she said, "Nik, if this is about not wanting to marry me, it isn't necessary we take a buggy ride."

Nik looked at her with an expression mixed with confusion and hurt, "Oh, no, Esther, quite the contrary," Nik answered. "You are the most important person in the world to me. As I said, I may be going about this all wrong, but I've never been in this situation before. Please, be patient and indulge me."

Esther was at a loss for words and merely turned and looked straight ahead while Nik drove the buggy into a shady grove of trees and stopped. He turned to Esther and took her hand.

"Esther, my love, I hope you take this in the sincerest way I have to say it ... but I have something for you."

Nik let go of Esther's hand and pulled out of his shirt pocket the gold locket he had purchased from Abel Mosely.

"Esther, I want you to have this," Nik said.

Esther took the locket and let the gold chain fall across her hand. "This is lovely, Nik. Is this what this is all about?"

"Not quite. I hope by now you know how much I love you and will accept this necklace as a token of that. We have talked about marriage but have not finalized anything. I'm trying to do that," Nik said.

"This is fine, but perhaps I'm being old fashioned, but shouldn't you be doing this with a ring?" Esther said, trying to choose her words politely.

"Look inside," Nik said.

When Esther opened the locket, she found a gold ring inside.

"Oh, Nik, this is lovely. I will marry you," Esther said, turning to Nik with tears welling up in her eyes, "but shouldn't you be asking for my hand in marriage and placing this on my finger?"

"I can't do that right now, Esther," Nik replied, reaching for her hand again. "Now I have to tell you why I've done my part this way."

Nik paused, looked away for a moment and then turned back to her. "Esther, I have to go away for awhile and I do not know for how long. I want you to have this as a token of my love … and commitment … that I hope you will keep until I return to put that ring on your finger."

"Where are you going?" Esther asked, with some of the joy draining from her face.

"I have to go into Mexico and try to retrieve the lost silver shipment believed to be somewhere in the mountains of that country. Because we do not know exactly where it is, it may take us some time before we find it."

"Is it really that important to find it?" Esther inquired without really thinking about her question. "Who is going with you?"

"I will have some soldiers and a guide with me on the expedition, but that's about all I know for now," Nik said, bracing for his next statement. "And because I don't know what I'll be facing, I wanted you to have the ring … even if … even if I don't return to put it on your hand. That way you'll have the locket and the ring to remember me by but not have to wear it."

Esther's face changed dramatically as she looked at Nik, "Nik, that's just dumb. If you really want to marry me, put the damn ring on my finger and I'll wait until they bury me with it."

"I just didn't want you to get tied up with a promise I couldn't keep," Nik said, feeling a little dumbfounded by Esther's response.

"Nik Brinkman, I love you for who you are, and this silly thing you're trying to do. You may be naïve, but you are the dearest, most loving man I've ever met. Have you spoken to my father about this?"

"Yes, and he's given me his blessing," Nik said.

"Then let's get out of this buggy and you can propose proper like and put this ring on my finger," Esther demanded. "After that, you can head off to Mexico, or wherever, and do what you have to do. And when you return, I'll be here and we'll get married before they send you someplace else."

As Nik was scrambling to get out of the carriage, he turned and said, "If they do that, you're coming with me."

They met in front of the horse, where Nik got down on one knee and proposed proper-like to Esther. They kissed, got back in the buggy and returned to the plantation.

After announcing their engagement, Tillie sent Isaiah into the wine cellar to fetch two bottles of Champaign. During the celebration, Nik related his assignment to find the lost silver in Mexico.

"How do they know the silver is there?" Isaiah asked.

"They don't, for sure," Nik said. "But they believe the balloon that carried the silver was supposed to drop it onto a ship waiting for it off the coast of Mexico. However, it's believed the balloon was blown off course and there were reports of it crossing the Rio Grande and heading for the Sierra Madre Oriental Mountains."

"So, they don't really know any of this for sure," Tillie responded. "What kind of goose chase are they sending you on?"

"I admit it is sketchy, and that's why we're going to enter Mexico out of the New Mexico Territory. I've already alerted my brother, Roger, who is putting together an expedition task force to assist in the search."

"Is Roger going with you?" Esther inquired.

"I can't ask him to do that," Nik said. "Not after what I talked him into doing concerning that counterfeit case."

"You seem to underestimate him," Isaiah said. "He strikes me as a very capable lawman, in spite of his calling as a preacher man."

"Don't think I wouldn't love to have him come along," Nik replied. "But he has a job to do for the Lord, and I and this mission do not take precedence over that."

"So, when do you have to leave?" Tillie asked.

"As soon as possible, it's going to take me a while to get to Fort McRae in the New Mexico Territory. Besides, they don't know who else may be in search of that silver. The thought is that silver was originally supposed to go to the Yucatan Peninsula, not the Sierra Madre Mountains."

After the celebration, Nik and Esther went for a short walk.

"How do you intend to get to the New Mexico Territory?" Esther asked.

"I'll take the train through Houston as far as it will go and then a stagecoach into Dallas. The Butterfield Line runs from there to El Paso," Nik said. "I'm making arrangements for soldiers to meet me there. I think Roger is going to find me a guide and interpreter, since he's far more familiar with that part of the country than I am."

"If you let me know when you're leaving and could stop in Houston, we could see each other again before you go." Esther said, trying not to seem overanxious.

"I can do that and would like that very much," Nik replied. "We could spend the day together, and I could leave Houston the next day."

After returning to the Covington Mansion, Nik bid everyone farewell and returned to Galveston, both happier and a bit sadder. It had been a while since he'd felt so deeply emotional, not since that fateful day in Bordertown, Missouri.

The following day, he returned to Judge Conklin's office, where Senator Ashley Maxwell was also waiting. Nik laid out his plans to the two men and they all agreed as to how to proceed. Senator Maxwell then presented a federal voucher to Nik, signed by the U.S. Congress and President Grant, to finance the expedition.

"Right now, we do not know how much this venture is going to cost," Maxwell began, "so, use your discretion. If the expedition becomes too expensive, or too dangerous, it is up to you to continue or not."

"You say the military will cover the cost of the soldiers I'll have?" Nik posed. "I presume they have limits as well?"

"There was a great deal of opposition to funding this operation, Marshal." Maxwell answered. "Many in Congress saw no reason to try and recover this silver, but the Farmers Union applied enough pressure to get it approved. Just do your best and try not to break the U.S. Treasury or lose too many men."

"You have my word on it, Senator," Nik said. Gentlemen, I appreciate your trust in me."

"This could do a great deal for your people should you succeed, Marshal." Maxwell said. "Don't let your kind down."

Nik wasn't fond of the senator's remark, but he knew who he was dealing with. He also realized a successful mission would go a long way in easing some of the prejudiced that remained in spite of the war.

Nik received a wire from Chief Marshal Ned Borchers that he was sending a deputy marshal to assist Ambrose in Nik's absence. Nik also informed his deputy that Isaiah Boatman and Abel Mosely were at the ready to help, as well.

Now, there was nothing left but to make ready for the trip.

The day Nik arrived at the Houston Train Depot, Esther had a buggy waiting and the two rode off together. The first stop was the Cotton Gin in Freedman Town where Nik reserved a room. Nik showed his fiancé where the counterfeit printing press was kept and the sheriff's office, now occupied by a new group of honest lawmen, or so he hoped.

They also stopped at Rudy's barbecue for a late lunch.

"What time do you have to start back?" Nik regretfully asked.

"I don't want to go back," Esther said. "I want to spend as much time with you as I can."

"I would not feel comfortable with you going home at night," Nik said.

"I will leave in the morning," Esther said, her emotions palpable.

"I'm sorry, I did not think to reserve you a room at the Cotton Gin," Nik said. "I could probably still do that."

"That's not what I mean," Esther responded. "I meant I want to spend as much time with you as I can. I don't know when I'll see you again, or even if I will ever see you again. I hope you can understand."

Nik was frozen in thought at Esther's words. He was silent for a brief period and then said, "I ah … I ah, think I understand perfectly."

When Nik awoke the next morning, he was disappointed to find that Esther had already gone. As he stared at her pillow imagining her head still lying there, he noticed a note was pinned to it. He anxiously read it.

"To You, My Love,

I knew I could not bear to say goodbye to you one more time. Please forgive me, but I left early and by the time you read this I'll be at home or close to it.

It is very difficult for me to write this, so I'll keep it short.

Please ask Roger to go with you. It's the only way I'll know you'll have far more than my prayers traveling with you.

All My Love,

Esther"

Nik could not hold back his tears. He eventually gathered himself, his things, and left for the Houston Train Depot.

Chapter 4
The Recruitment

Pastor Roger Brinkman was beginning to feel like he was back in the army again. Only this time, he felt like he was in it for the right reason.

Fort McRae, located in the New Mexico Territory, had become home to him. The officers and enlisted men of the 125th Calvary Buffalo Soldiers looked upon him as their liaison with God, giving them peace and comfort in a land that offered little of it.

His Sunday services were attended by all, with the exception of those on patrol or sentry duty. It also brought parishioners from the area surrounding the fort creating a harmonious bond between the military and the community. There were even attendees from a nearby Mescalero Apache Tribe.

Roger had gone to Carlos Sanchez Santana, an elder in the pastor's circuit church, asking him to help his brother, Nik. Nik Brinkman was seeking those willing to help search for a silver shipment believed to be lost in the Sierra Madre Mountains of Mexico. Carlos, a native of Mexico, had suggested Roger contact Morgana Maria Cabezon, a mestizo shaman.

After the Sunday service, Carlos approached Roger.

"Pastor Brinkman," Carlos began, "Senorita Cabezon said she would be willing to speak to you today, if you wish to visit her."

"Wonderful, how do I find her?" Roger asked.

"Just come to my place and I will take you to see her. She lives near the edge of my property in a cave. She is a private person but is a great help to me," Carlos said. "She communes with nature each morning but can see you this afternoon. Are you all right with that?"

"That suits me fine. I had planned to set out on my circuit this afternoon anyway," Roger replied. "If you don't mind, depending on the length of our meeting, I just might spend the night with you and the Santana family."

"You are always welcome to stay with us, Señor Brinkman," Carlos answered. "We would be honored to have you as our guest for the night."

Several soldiers were patiently waiting for Roger to finish speaking with Carlos and stepped forward when Santana retreated.

"Pastor Brinkman," a lieutenant said, approaching Roger. "I'm Walter Gateway. I'm responding to your request for volunteers to assist your brother, a U.S. Marshal, I believe, in a search to recover a stolen silver shipment. I believe these soldiers with me, are also interested in joining in that search."

Roger looked over the five soldiers and smiled.

"Gentlemen, I'm pleased you have come forward like this," Roger said. "However, Peter, I would have to get permission from your parents for you to do this."

Roger was speaking to Peter Zimmerman, the son of Paul and Sally Zimmerman, two of his devoted parishioners from nearby Palamos.

"But, sir," Peter protested. "I'm a United States Army soldier now. I do as I am told and do not require parental approval."

"Yes, but this is a little different, Peter. This isn't official military business."

"Excuse me, Private," Lieutenant Gateway cut in, "the pastor is correct. This isn't a direct military order. It is a request for volunteers and we do not want to upset the local community by sending their sons out on unofficial business."

Roger was pleased to hear the lieutenant speak up. Gateway was young and spoke with an authority that belied his years. His clean-shaven face spoke of his discipline as an officer, but his countenance indicated a soldier with experience, not often found in someone his age.

"The lieutenant is right," Roger chimed in. "However, if your folks say it is okay with them, I'm sure my brother would be happy to have someone as eager as you."

"As for you other soldiers, I assume you are interested in doing this as well?"

Among the men was Sergeant Beaumont Davis, otherwise known as Beau. Davis was a middle-aged man with a history of fighting in countless battles, both in the Civil War and Indian Wars. He was tougher looking than Gateway but had a reputation of following orders to the letter. He and Gateway had fought together and had a close relationship.

Private Carter Townsend was only slightly older than Peter Zimmerman. However, as a Buffalo Soldier, he had seen action and performed valiantly. His goal was to become an officer, like Gateway, and was unafraid to volunteer for most anything.

The oldest of the soldiers was Private Kelly Laumpagh. Laumpagh had held a higher rank among the Buffalo Soldiers but struggled with alcoholism leading to a reduction in rank. Yet his combat record was unquestioned and he hoped joining the mission to Mexico might help him get back on the right track.

"Gentlemen, I am overjoyed you would come forward like this, even you, Peter," Roger started. "But mine is not the last word on this. My brother, when he gets here, will make the final decision as to who, how, and when this expedition will take place. I expect his journey from Galveston, Texas to take a few weeks so please go about your normal duties until then. I will keep you posted if I receive any further word."

Roger returned to his quarters and began packing his gear to begin another circuit mission. Something told him he best try to recruit elders to fill in for him in the event he found himself included in Nik's quest to find the silver. He tried dismissing the possibility but it nagged him just the same.

When he reached the homestead of Carlos Santana, he was greeted by his friend and family. Mrs. Anna Santana reminded him of Sally Zimmerman, although Anna was of Mexican descent. Their four children ranged in age from sixteen to six. The oldest, Carlos Jr., helped with the farm work and Ronna, the oldest daughter, helped her mother around the house and in caring for the two younger children.

Carlos readied his horse and rode out with Roger to meet Morgana Maria Cabezon, the mestizo shaman. After a twenty-minute ride, they approached a stone bluff that was fronted by a row of pine trees and brush. Carlos stopped and dismounted, indicating that Roger do the same.

"We must go on foot from here," Carlos said. "We will have to make our way through the brush to get to Morgana's place. She will be waiting for us."

The two men tied up their horses and followed an almost obscure path that led to a small open area at the base of the bluff. There, on a ledge sitting facing them was Morgana Maria Cabezon. She waved her left hand and Carlos nodded.

"This way, Señor Brinkman," Carlos instructed, leading Roger toward a small bush where his friend pulled part of it back and waved for Roger to proceed. "This path will lead you to where you can ascend to the bluff where Morgana is sitting."

"Are you coming?" Roger asked.

"No, I must return home," Carlos said. "After you have spoken with Morgana, she will send you back to my place where we will have dinner waiting."

Roger nodded and ducked behind the bush to find another path that led to what resembled a stairwell leading up the bluff. With minimal effort, Roger pulled himself up to the level where Morgana was sitting with her legs crossed in a meditation position.

"Welcome," she said. "Please, sit by me and tell me what it is that you want."

Roger made an awkward attempt to mimic Morgana's posture but found his legs didn't work quite like the shaman's. He eventually curled one leg under him and the other he propped over it with his hand on top of his knee, bracing himself with the other hand on the ground.

"Ahh, Miss Morgana, is that what I should call you?"

"My name is Morgana Maria Cabezon," she said. "Address me as you wish. Since there are only two of us, I will know who you are speaking to."

Roger was surprised by Morgana's appearance. He had imagined an older woman, although Carlos had told him she was young. Her long black hair flowed down her back, her skin was brown and her face was strikingly handsome. She was pretty but did not appear delicate. Her hands were distinctly that of a woman but bore the calluses of one who works. Roger noticed a small opening behind the ledge that he assumed was her home.

"I've come to ask for your help," Roger began, "My broth ..."

"You want me to lead you into Mexico, is that it?" Morgana interrupted.

"Well, I was going to say my brother is the one ..."

"He is a U.S. Marshal, is he not?" Morgana again cut in. "He searches for silver in the Oriental Range of the Sierra Madre."

"I guess Carlos has filled you in about this?" Roger questioned.

"To some extent," Morgana said. "Following his words, I consulted the spirits and have a good idea of what he is up against and what he will need."

"That's terrific, Morgana, will you do it?"

"Why would I want to do this, Señor Brinkman?"

Roger was a bit stumped by Morgana's question. He had planned what he was going to say but wasn't prepared for her to fill in the details for him. He had experienced communicating with a shaman before and decided it was better to let her take the lead.

"I could appeal to you with money," Roger said. "But I doubt that would interest you. I assume you know that I am a spiritual person, somewhat like you."

"Not like me, Preacher-man," Morgana said. "You are a speaker. I am a listener."

"I guess I never thought of it quite that way, but I need you for all the reasons I cannot fulfill," Roger responded. "You are from the land where my brother is going, I am not. You know the culture and speak the language of those who abide there. You also have visions that I don't that can help lead my brother and his men safely to their destination and back, I hope."

"You have visions, Preacher-man. I can sense that."

"Mine are a bit different," Roger said. "I have nothing that would help my brother where this mission is concerned."

"Don't doubt yourself, Preacher-man, You have more to offer than perhaps I do."

"I've never been to Mexico, you are from there," Roger said.

"I do know Mexico but you know what favors your brother and his men," Morgana said. "If you do not wish to make this journey, why should I be inclined to do so?"

Roger thought a moment of where the conversation was leading. He felt he was in over his head but decided he was at a moment of either sinking or swimming.

"Would you go if I go?" the words almost froze in Roger's throat, but he was compelled to say them anyway.

Morgana, who had been facing the land below the bluff during this time, turned and looked straight at Roger.

"Together, we may just be able to complete this mission of your brothers and get most everyone back safely," Morgana said.

"Most?" Roger reiterated.

"I cannot guarantee everyone's safety, as I'm sure you cannot," Morgana stated. "But the chances of this mission being a success depend a great deal on your spirits as well as mine."

"I was afraid you would say that," Roger mumbled.

"Are you afraid, Preacher-man?" Morgana asked. "You do not impress me that way."

"It's not fear that holds me back, it is those I am obligated to in my ministry here," Roger said. "I have been away and only recently returned."

"Have you not already given them what they need?" Morgana asked. "Cannot they follow those words in your absence?"

Roger paused and looked out over the high desert area surrounding the bluff. "I guess if that is what it's going to take, I have no other choice but join the party as well."

"When would we have to leave?" Morgana asked.

"I think sometime during the next three weeks, does that work for you?" Roger answered.

"I could be ready now," Morgana said. "But I do believe you have work to do in preparing your ... flock, I believe is how you refer to your charges."

"Perhaps I need to give them more credit than I do," Roger answered with a slight sigh. "It's a tough land requiring tough choices."

"So, when I get back, we will prepare to help my brother together?"

"I will be here, Preacher-man," Morgana replied. "As I said, I am ready to go now."

Roger made his way back down from the bluff and eventually found his way back to his horse. As he was about to mount up, he heard a voice."

"I guess that shaman helped you make up your mind, right Roger?"

Roger looked across Brinker II's saddle to see a man dressed in black wearing a sombrero leaning against a nearby tree. Roger also noticed the silver conchos on his pant legs and jacket sleeves.

"Wait a minute," Roger exclaimed. "Didn't I see you on the train out of Galveston a while back?"

"That's certainly possible, I do get around," the man said, laughing. "You'll love Mexico, amigo. It is very pleasant this time of year."

Roger placed his foot into his stirrup and swung up into the saddle, "Say, maybe you'd like to come along ...." As he looked over at the tree where the stranger stood, there was no one there. He turned Brinker II around and set off in the direction of the Santana homestead.

Chapter 5
The Texas Rangers

After boarding the train in Houston, United States Marshal Nik Brinkman sat quietly in the last car as The Houston Tap and Brazoria began to chug away from the depot on its way to Richmond, Texas.

He had sent a wire to Fort McCrae asking Roger to meet him in El Paso, Texas, at the end of the month. Nik had hoped to enter Mexico in early to mid-spring to give his team the better part of the summer to complete their expedition and be home by fall.

Two men entered the front of Nik's car and quickly sat down. Nik wasn't sure if they were avoiding him, sitting near the back of the car, or did not see him. Although uncertain, he thought he'd seen a badge on one of the men when the man sat down. He soon dismissed any concerns he had about the two men and settled back to watch the southern Texas landscape pass by.

After arriving in Richmond, Nik rose from his seat and made his exit from the back of the car. After descending onto the depot platform, he turned to notice the two men also leaving the train from the same exit. This time, he could see for certain that one was wearing a badge.

Nik made his way toward the front of the train, where the porter was carrying off luggage. He spotted his bag, retrieved it and checked in with the station ticket agent.

"Where do I catch the stage to El Paso," Nik asked the attendant.

"Won't be leaving 'til morning. It stops in front of the Richmond Hotel," the clerk said. "The livery stable is just down the way from there."

Nik tapped the edge of his hat in gratitude and turned to see those same men waiting to speak with the attendant as well. Again, they made no attempt to acknowledge him, but made the same inquiry about the stage line to El Paso and got the same answer, except for the livery stable remark.

Nik had federal authorization to stay at each local accommodation along the way, but knew his quarters would not match that of white travelers. However, he had vowed not to trouble himself with such details and just keep his mouth shut, for the most part.

"I'm the U.S. Marshal from Galveston," Nik said, approaching the Richmond Hotel front desk. The clerk looked at him as if he didn't understand what Nik said. Nik reached into his jacket pocket and produced the federal authorization letter. He tossed it on the counter for the clerk to read. The registrar looked up, still appearing as if he could not comprehend what he had heard.

"Yes, sir, Marshal," the clerk said. "We have a room reserved for you. It's just up the stairs and at the end of the hallway to your left."

"Much obliged," Nik replied, reaching down to pick up his bag. He noticed the two men from the train entering the hotel lobby, as he proceeded to the stairs. He noticed one of the men following him with his eyes as he reached the end of the stairs and turned left. He could not hear what the conversation between the other man and the clerk.

He entered his room and chuckled to himself. The room had likely been made up to lodge a white man. Nik was pleased that advance reservations did not make mention of his "color."

After sitting down on the bed, he heard the sounds of the other two men approaching their room. Nik stepped out into the hallway as they approached.

"Gentlemen, I could not help but notice you on the train earlier today. It seems you are going everywhere that I'm headed. May I ask your business?" Nik did his best to sound cordial and non-confrontational.

"We're Texas Rangers," the lead man said, showing no signs of concern. "We're on assignment."

"I'm pleased to meet you. I'm U.S. Marshal Nik Brinkman, at your service," Nik said, extending his hand.

"So, you're the U.S. Marshal we've been hearing about," the second man said. "Apparently the U.S. Marshal Service is making an effort similar to the Rangers."

"Pleased to meet you, Marshal," the second man continued, grabbing Nik's hand. "I'm Captain Stevens, Geoff Stevens."

Nik smiled as he shook Stevens' hand, "Likewise, I'm sure. What similar effort is the service making?"

Stevens turned to introduce his companion, Captain McNelly. "Hiring Negroes, former slaves," the captain then replied.

"Leonard," the other Texas Ranger said, extending his hand to Nik, "Leonard McNelly."

"Have you suffered any racial problems since taking over in Galveston?" Stevens asked.

"Not for the most part," Nik said, relinquishing his grip on McNelly's hand. "Galveston has made a lot of progress in that area. I'm sorry I can't say the same for the rest of Texas."

"We've got coloreds in out outfit, as well. Damn good men, if you don't mind my saying so," Stevens added. "But the diehard Confederate politicians are trying to do away with the Rangers because of our hiring practices."

"You mean," Nik started, "because you have black lawmen in your ranks the state is trying to disband the Rangers?"

"We're hoping the effort gets defeated," McNelly said. "Texas needs Rangers just like the country needs its marshals. Not sure what colored skin has to do with it."

"The one exception is red skin," Stevens cut in, "it's part of our latest assignment. The Comanche and Apache have been raising hell in the unsettled territories of western Texas so we're riding the stage to help with security."

"How far are you going?" Nik asked.

"I get off at San Antonio," McNelly said. "Another Ranger will replace me and continue onto El Paso with Geoff."

"The state of Texas may have a problem with Rangers, but I'm quite happy to have you two along as fellow passengers," Nik said.

"I guess we'll see you again in the morning," McNelly said, swinging open the door to their room. "Or maybe at dinner, the food here is pretty good. Why don't you join us?"

"It would be my pleasure, gentlemen," Nik replied. "My room is right next door. Give me a knock before you head downstairs."

"We'll do that," Stevens said, as the two men disappeared inside their room.

Nik returned to his accommodations. He wasn't tired, so he pulled out the chair that accompanied the small desk in his room and sat down. He opened the drawer, pulled out a sheet of paper and began composing a letter to Esther. After writing two sentences, he crumpled up the paper and threw it in the wastebasket.

He was motivated by all the wonderful things he wanted to say to Esther, but all the issues crowding his mind made it impossible to put the good things into words. He thought about Roger and felt a little ashamed thinking his brother might not recruit people qualified to fulfill his mission. He shook his head and mumbled to himself, "Roger will pick people better qualified than I would."

Then he thought of the Rangers next door and their concern for their organization possibly being disbanded for hiring black men. But he was aware of the hate against his race, driving one man to kill a sitting president. The battles continue and now against the Indians as well.

And then there was Esther, raped by a white man. Nik wondered if he raped her because he was attracted to her? Not likely, he thought, rape is violent and certainly not an act of admiration.

Nik was shaken out of his thoughts by a loud knock at the door. "Dinner's being served if you're hungry," a voice shouted through the door.

Nik jumped to his feet, grabbed his hat and stepped into the hall way where the two Rangers were waiting for him. The trio descended the stairs and entered the hotel's dining room. A few eyes widened at Nik's presence, but no words were spoken. Nik wondered if their silence wasn't because of his companions. They selected a table and sat down.

A man in an apron approached. "May I get you gentlemen something to drink before serving your meal?" he asked.

"Whiskey for my partner and I," McNelly said. "Nik, what are you having?"

"Oh, I'm sorry," the waiter said, "we don't serve …" McNelly buried his elbow into the man's stomach, bending him over. The captain grabbed the attendant by his apron and pulled him close. "Nik, what will you have," McNelly asked.

"Ah, whiskey would be fine, thank you," Nik replied.

"You heard the man," McNelly growled in the man's ear. "And our friend's dinner better be every bit as good as ours. Any questions?"

"No, sir …," the man wheezed, "right away, sir." The waiter turned without unbending and headed for the bar.

"I'm sorry about that, gentlemen," Nik said.

"Not at all, Nik," McNelly said. "I just wish I could do the same thing to those politicians threatening the Texas Rangers. I'm just sorry it takes something like that to get folks to listen to reason."

"It's hard enough just upholding the law," Stevens said, with a laugh. "Without having to deal with individuals who think like that fellow does."

No further incident interrupted the men as they traded stories over their dinner, one in which Nik's meal was just as inviting as the one served to the Rangers.

Following another round of drinks after eating, the three men retired to their rooms for the night. Nik again sat down at the desk and began to write.

"Dear Esther,
    We've both been through a lot in our young lives and know there is a nagging wound in this great country of ours. But let me tell you about two men I've had the pleasure of meeting, both are Texas Rangers …"

After describing his experience to Esther, he closed the letter and folded it.

After mailing the letter the next day, Nik and the two Texas Rangers boarded the stagecoach, Winchesters in hand, for San Antonio. Ranger Geoff Stevens rode as shotgun for the driver and the stage line's regular shotgun perched on top of the stage amongst the luggage. There was also a rancher heading back to San Antonio, who rode inside with Nik and Captain McNelly.

"Are you gentlemen both Texas Rangers?" the rancher asked.

"I'm a United States Marshal," Nik replied. "The gentleman next to you is Texas Ranger Captain Leonard McNelly."

"Pleased to meet you both," the rancher said, casting a glance out of the window on his side of the coach. Turning back to the men he said, "I'm Howard Vogelhorn. I have a ranch just outside of San Antonio. It's nice to have so much protection on this stage. There seems to be an endless supply of Indians and outlaws to contend with during these trips."

"That's why we're here," McNelly said. "The man up top riding shotgun is my partner. The marshal, here, is on different business."

"Really, so what is the purpose of your business?" Vogelhorn asked.

"I'm heading up a task force to try and find a shipment of silver that was stolen," Nik answered, not wanting to give away too much information.

"Silver, seems like a lot of trouble where silver is concerned," the rancher replied. "Now, a gold shipment I could understand."

"Depends on the government," Nik said. "There is some talk that silver will be as valuable as gold one day."

"I don't see how that's possible. Gold's value is known around the world, not so for silver," Vogelhorn offered.

"Again, you'd have to speak to a congressman about that," Nik said, "seems there's something about needing silver for coinage."

"Coinage, eh," Vogelhorn snorted. "I would say they have to do something about the money situation, too much Confederate money, and counterfeit too. A man can't run a decent business with all that uncertainty."

"I just hope finding that silver will help," Captain McNelly rejoined, "Do you think you can do that, Nik?"

"I have to confess, Leonard, I only know where to begin. Where the search will take us is still a guess."

"Where do you think the sliver is?" the rancher cut in.

"We think it may be in Mexico," Nik said, guarding his words.

"Mexico, that's a pretty big place," Vogelhorn added.

"We have a few leads but nothing substantial at this point," Nik said. "We just hope someone in Mexico can give us something more solid."

"In that case, your best bet is the Apache or bandits, and I wouldn't want to have to deal with either one," Vogelhorn said, with a slight chuckle.

The conversation tapered off, and before long the stage was pulling into San Antonio, Vogelhorn's destination. San Antonio was also as far as McNelly would be going. He would take another stage west to Eagle Pass and Fort Duncan.

Joining the party heading for El Paso was a man of Chinese descent. Although he wasn't officially a Texas Ranger, the Rangers did employ his services.

"Nik, this is Chili Buck," Ranger Stevens said before boarding. "Chili is a nickname. His mother was Chinese"

"Do you mind if I call you Chili?" Nik asked, reaching to shake his hand.

"Name is Shi Lei Buck," Chili said, bowing rather than shaking Nik's hand. "Chili is fine, everyone calls me that. Buck was my father, whom I never knew."

"Sorry to hear that," Nik said, mimicking a slight bow. "I did not have much of a chance to know my real father, either."

"Chili will ride shotgun and I will take Leonard's place in the coach," Stevens said. "There's a second lieutenant who will be riding with us, heading for Fort Chadbourne."

The second lieutenant did not look like someone fresh out of West Point. His uniform was a bit unkempt and his boots were the color of dust. He wore a sidearm that gave him the appearance of a hired gun and he carried his carbine in one hand, as well. He was young and looked clean-shaven because the few whiskers he had didn't offer that much to shave.

"Lieutenant, you will be riding with Texas Ranger Geoff Stevens and U.S. Marshall Nik Brinkman," the driver called out from his seat above the horses. Stevens nodded and Nik touched his hat when their names were called out. "Board up, we're burnin' daylight."

"Is the marshal riding in the coach?" the lieutenant drawled.

"That's where most marshals ride," the driver answered. "If that bothers you, you can trot along behind the coach."

"Don't seem right," the lieutenant said.

"If it helps, I'll sit next to Nik," Stevens said, giving the officer a look of disgust. "You can curl up in the corner and suck your thumb if you like."

"You're talking to an Army officer, sir," the lieutenant snapped.

"And you're annoying a captain of the Texas Rangers. Now get your ass on that stage," Stevens ordered. Nik looked over at Stevens and almost broke into laughter.

The three passengers rode along for several miles without speaking a word. The lieutenant kept his eyes trained out the window, not wanting to look at Nik.

"What's your name, lieutenant," Stevens asked.

"What's it to ya'?" the soldier remarked.

"Not much, but we need to know in case we have to contact your next of kin," Stevens said.

"My name's on the Wells Fargo manifest," the lieutenant answered and then fell silent for a long while. "Butler, Caleb Butler," he said out of the blue.

"You don't make friends easy, do you, Caleb," Stevens responded.

"Depends," Butler said, taking his eyes off Stevens and again staring out the window.

"You look a bit slovenly to be a lieutenant in the Army," Stevens said. "How did you obtain your rank?"

"It was my condition for joining," Butler said.

"The army took you on as a lieutenant. How did you pull that off?" Stevens continued.

"I was a decorated captain in the Confederate Army. When this army looked at my record, they agreed to my terms," Butler answered.

"I figured you for a Rebel," Stevens said. "How about you, Nik, were you inclined to think that same thing?"

"Seems about right, Geoff," Nik said, turning slowly toward the Texas Ranger. "My brother was one."

"No kidding, your brother?" Stevens said, as Butler turned his gaze on the two men.

"He was under the impression Union soldiers killed our Ma, Pa, and sister, so he joined the Southern Army. It was a mistake, though."

"I don't believe that," Butler unexpectedly cut in. "Coloreds weren't allowed to fight in the Confederate Army."

"Who said he was colored?" Nik responded, with a sly smile.

"You just said he was your brother," Butler snapped. "Either you're lying or you're crazy."

"For all you know, I could be either or neither," Nik said. "It really doesn't matter to me what you think."

"So, your brother was white?" Stevens inquired.

"Still is, at least he was the last time I looked," Nik answered, smiling broadly at the captain. "And we're real close, too. We grew up that way and have stayed that way in spite of fighting on opposite sides in the war." Nik turned his gaze upon the lieutenant.

Butler quickly turned his head to stare out the coach window, not wanting to look into Nik's eyes.

"Where did you grow up?" Stevens continued.

"Bordertown, Missouri," Nik answered. "Oh, some treated Roger and I differently, but for the most part, we were seen as equals."

Butler let out a sudden sigh, as if to object to Nik's last remark. Nik continued to stare at him, while maintaining his grin.

After a brief stage stop, the coach pulled into Fredericksburg for an overnight stay. Early the next morning, the stage pulled out for Fort Mason with its three passengers, the driver, and Chili riding shotgun.

Chapter 6
Trouble on the Trail

The day was pleasant enough as the stagecoach pulled out of Fredericksburg for Fort Mason, although there were dark clouds building on the southern horizon. If a storm was brewing, it was hoped they would arrive at the fort before foul weather did.

The ride became more uncomfortable as the driver drove his team hard to try and reach the next stage stop ahead of the pending inclement weather. The front wheel of the coach hit a pothole, throwing Nik nearly on top of the lieutenant. Butler's eyes widened anticipating the worst, when Nik twisted and landed backward into the space next to the soldier. Nik began laughing out loud at the near "catastrophe."

"Can you slow it down?" Captain Stevens called out to the driver. "We're being twisted into pretzels back here."

"Sorry, sir, but I'm trying to stay ahead of that storm behind us," the driver called back. Chili had put his rifle below his feet to hang on with one hand and hold onto the driver with the other.

Stevens poked his head out the window and looked back to see gray sheets of rain in the distance backlit by lightning flashes.

From his position next to Butler, Nik could see what Geoff was talking about. He picked up his rifle, which had fallen to the floor when the bump in the road sent him flying.

About a mile ahead of the stagecoach was a fairly steep climb and the driver hoped to crest that hill before the road softened. As the stage approached the incline, rain began to fall.

"Captain, you and the other passengers may want to get out until we crest this hill," the driver yelled as the rainfall intensified and he pulled his team to a halt. "With less weight, I may be able to make it."

The stagecoach doors flew open and the three men piled out. The driver snapped the reins and put his tiring team back into a gallop. At first, Nik, the ranger, and the lieutenant stood and watched.

Then Nik called out as he started to run after the coach, "Come on, we need to get behind and push if he doesn't make it!"

The other two men followed as the stagecoach began its climb. The going was good at first, but as the horses began to slip, their progress slowed.

"Captain, get on that wheel. I'll get on the other," Nik shouted. "Butler, grab a big rock and prepare to chock the wheel to keep it from rolling backward."

Butler stopped in his tracks, not wanting to follow the orders of a black man.

"Lieutenant, if you don't grab a rock, I'm going to bounce one off your head," Stevens yelled. Reluctantly, Butler went to the side of the road and found a suitable rock.

With less than one hundred feet to go to the top of the hill, the coach was nearing a standstill. Chili quickly jumped down to help push the coach. The efforts of the three men helped to move the coach forward, one complete turn of a wheel at a time.

"Butler," Stevens called back. "Put that rock directly behind Nik's wheel and help us push!"

The lieutenant moved faster now, as water began to flow down the hill, causing both men and animals to slip. The driver jumped down and ran to the front of the team, grabbed hold of the horses, dug in the heels of his boots and pulled.

As the men neared exhaustion, Stevens again yelled: "Lieutenant, get that rock and bring it up here so we can rest."

With the rock in place, the driver came back to the rear of the coach. As the rain continued to fall, he encouraged the men to continue.

"It's not far now. We can make it," he said. "I'll continue to pull and you men push and then replace the rock. We can do this!"

Oblivious of the rain and lightning, the men slowly moved the stage up the hill until it was securely at the top. They all then fell to the ground, exhausted.

"Great work, men," the driver said, returning to where the men lay. "We'll have to wait until the rain lets up before we proceed. Downhill is not so steep, but the road needs to dry some so the stage doesn't slip off to the side. Soaked to the skin and breathing heavily, the four men on the ground simply nodded and smiled, knowing they had made it. Almost on cue, the rain stopped and the sun broke through the departing clouds."

Late that evening, they pulled into the stage stop. The caretaker came out holding a lantern.

"Curly, you made it," the man with the lantern called out to the driver. "I was beginning to wonder, with that storm and all."

"We had a bit of an adventure back on the hill, but these men helped pull her through," Curly replied, tossing down luggage to the men below. "We'll have to stay here 'til morning."

"I'm Zeke, gentlemen. I'm afraid all I have is a dry floor to sleep on and a few blankets. Heck, you can sleep on the tables if you want," the caretaker said. "You best get out of those wet clothes. I'll rustle up some grub for you."

"Thanks, Zeke," the driver said. "We could use it."

Nik and Geoff forfeited their blankets to Curly and Chili. The lieutenant decided to keep his.

"Let Curly and Chili have the blankets," Geoff said. "They have to stay awake and drive the stage tomorrow—we don't," he emphasized, casting a dirty look at Lieutenant Butler.

Meanwhile, Zeke set up several glasses of whiskey and broke out some bread and cheese.

"Here, fellas, this ought to warm you while I make up some sandwiches," he said. "I got some cider to go along with the food, as well. Wish I had more to offer ya."

"Right now, Zeke, this is like a little slice of heaven," Nik said, finishing his glass of whiskey with a smile.

"Just happy to help, in any way I can," Zeke said, smiling back.

The next day, the sun was back out. Zeke and Curly harnessed a new team of horses and after a breakfast of bacon, biscuits, and coffee, the overland was ready for the road again.

"Any reports of trouble on this leg to Fort Mason, Zeke?" Curly asked before climbing up to the driver's seat.

"Not really," the caretaker answered. "There was a report of a lone masked highwayman trying to hold up the stage several weeks back but he turned and rode off when the shotgun sent a load of buckshot after him."

"Did he wound him?"

"Not that anyone could tell," Zeke continued. "They say he appeared more scared than hurt when he rode off and no blood was found where he and his horse were standing."

"I'll keep my eyes open," Chili chimed in. "However, it doesn't sound like he's much to worry about."

"Apparently not," the stationmaster concluded. "But that's about the only trouble I've heard about."

With the passengers inside, Curly and Chili climbed up to the driver's seat and soon the stage was on its way. There was a branch of the Colorado River to cross and fear it might be swollen after the storm, but the crossing was made without trouble. After a full day's ride, the coach arrived at Fort Mason, where they would spend the night before continuing on to Fort Chadbourne.

"There are stops in Concho County and Runnels County before we arrive at Chadbourne. It's a three-day trip through open country," Curly said, as the men made their way to the billets where they would stay for the night. "If we meet any trouble, it's during that run it's likely to occur."

"How rough does it get?" Nik asked.

"It can get a little rough if it's an Indian attack," Curly answered. "Bandits don't usually bother us going north, it's the turnaround after we've picked up a strong box from Wells Fargo."

"So, the money goes south?" Nik inquired.

"Wells Fargo bought the old Butterfield Overland Stage and that runs through Phantom Hill, north of Chadbourne. The Army runs a buckboard between Chadbourne and Phantom Hill, delivering water up north and bringing the gold back. We then load the gold and make a run for it."

"That's one of the reasons Chili and I are on this stage," Ranger Stevens added. "The gold is coming out of California and the New Mexico and Colorado territories, much of it headed for Galveston since they put that U.S. Bank in."

"I knew the First U.S. Bank of Galveston was getting gold from somewhere, and now I know where," Nik said.

"You would think a U.S. marshal would know that," Lieutenant Butler said with a smirk.

"My jurisdiction doesn't cover gold deliveries of this magnitude," Nik said. "We don't have the manpower. It's the Texas Rangers and U.S. Army that protects these shipments."

"As an Army officer, I would think you would know that," Nik shot back, much to the delight of Geoff Stevens and Chili Buck.

Butler approached the post commander and requested separate accommodation. He was given space in the officers' quarters, where he would spend the night.

The trip from Fort Mason to the Concho County stage stop was made without incident, but after crossing the Concho River the second day, the passengers heard a rifle shot and the sound of Curly bringing the stagecoach's team of horses to a halt.

"Show yourself," they heard Chili call out.

"Not 'til you drop your sidearm and get down from that stage," a voice announced from behind a stand of brush alongside the road. No one from inside the stagecoach could see who was speaking. They could tell that Chili was climbing down from his position next to Curly.

"Tell the passengers to get out of the coach and put their valuables on the ground."

"I can't do that," Chili responded. "They're too afraid of outlaws to come out. You're going to have to come and get 'em out."

"I've got you right in my sights. If you don't get the passengers out, I'm going to shoot you," the voice continued.

Chili walked over to the stage door and in a low voice said, "What do you want to do?"

"Why don't we throw the door open and come out shooting?" Stevens said in a hoarse whisper.

"One of us could get shot that way," Nik said. "Why don't you both put your guns away, get out and pretend to put whatever you have onto the ground. Take your time, because I'm going to go out the opposite door and work my way behind that bush where this person is hiding, whoever it is."

"Chili, keep talking to him and tell him there's a woman on board too afraid to do what he says. Do whatever you have to do to stall him."

"That's a dumb plan," Butler said. "Hell, I can probably pick him off from inside here."

"And get Chili shot in the process?" Nik said, raising the volume of his whisper. "Either do as I say or stay in here and pretend you're the woman too afraid to get out."

"Do as he says, Lieutenant," Stevens growled. "Pretend you deserve to wear that uniform."

Butler scowled, set his carbine aside, and moved toward the door. Stevens followed and Nik slid over to exit the other side of the coach.

"And put your hands up," the voice shouted, as Butler and Stevens emerged from the coach. "Put whatever money and jewelry and things on the ground and turn around. And keep your hands up."

"Do we look like we have a lot of money?" Stevens called out. "You can bet the soldier here doesn't."

"Just do as I say. And you too, shotgun and driver," the voice answered.

Meanwhile, Nik found where he could cross the road unseen and slip behind the stage robber. He moved up behind some rocks directly above the bush where the voice was coming from. As he drew closer, he could see it was one man, not very big, calling out the orders.

Nik drew his pistol, slipped out from behind the rocks and quietly approached the thief, putting the barrel of his pistol up against his head.

"If you want to keep that head on your shoulders, you'd better drop that gun," Nik demanded. "And don't turn around."

The robber complied, stood up, and raised his hands.

"It's okay, fellas. I have him and we're coming out," Nik called out to his companions. Nik put his hand on the bandit's shoulder and pushed him out in the open.

"Why, he's just a kid," Stevens said. "Not even as old as Butler, here."

"What?" Nik said, moving in front of the outlaw.

It was obvious the would-be stage robber was barely a teenager. He was wearing overalls, with a shoulder strap missing. His hat was made of straw and his shoes were worn to the point that he had tied cloth around them to keep them on.

"What are you doing trying to hold up a stagecoach, son?" Nik asked.

"I need the money," he answered.

"There are better ways to do it than nearly getting yourself killed," Stevens said. "Why, we were ready to start shooting until the marshal talked us out of it. He may have saved your life."

"Then shoot me, if you're going to," the youthful highwayman said. "I ain't got no other way to make money I know of."

"Where is your home?" Nik asked. "Do you live around here?"

"I used to. We had a homestead not too far from here, but Indians killed my Pa and took my Ma," he began. "I tried to make a go of the place but couldn't grow nothin'. I knew the stage ran by here and thought maybe I could make some money robbin' it."

"Say, were you the one that tried to hold up the stage a while back, but rode off when the shotgun fired on you?" Chili asked.

"Yeah, that was me," the boy said, looking down at his tattered shoes.

"So, where's your horse?" Nik asked.

"I couldn't feed him so I run him off. Otherwise, I would have killed him and eaten him, and I didn't want to do that. He was a good horse."

"I don't think there's anything we can do but take this lad with us," Nik said. "Maybe they know something about his mother at Fort Chadbourne and can take care of him until he's able to find some other way to support himself."

"Why don't you arrest him?" Butler asked. "He's a menace, out here holding up stages."

"Butler, you're hopeless," Stevens said. "I think that's a good idea Nik. Let's just put him on the stage and look after him until we get to Chadbourne."

"What's your name, son," Nik asked. "Toby, Toby Stoner," the boy replied.

Meanwhile, Curly and Chili had removed the rocks and brush that the boy had placed in the roadway to stop the stage.

"I've got no objection," Curly said. "He's a bit of a mess, but if you fellas can put up with him there's no charge to take him to Chadbourne. We'd best be going though, it's getting late."

It was well after midnight when they reached the Runnels County stage stop. Although the group got a late start out of Runnels, the next morning they started on the final run to Fort Chadbourne.

"Do you intend to have me put in jail?" Toby asked, looking at both Nik and Ranger Stevens.

"It all depends," Stevens responded. "Different parts of Texas prosecute juveniles differently. You may go to jail, or the judge may give you a spanking and let you go with a stern warning."

"Am I a juv … juv,"

"Juvenile," Nik cut in. "That means you're still too young to be called an adult man. Putting boys in jail with adult prisoners has not worked out so well."

"Typically, you'd be put in custody of local law to handle your case," Stevens said. "The marshal and I are not authorized to do any more than bring you to justice, whatever that might be."

"Why didn't you just shoot him?" Lieutenant Butler commented. "I can't see that he's going to grow up to be of much use to anybody."

"You did," Nik said. "Maybe he'll become an officer, like you."

"That's ridiculous," Butler shot back. "The only thing he'd be good for in the Army would be target practice."

"Is that right?" Toby said, again looking at Nik and Stevens.

"The lieutenant is just letting off hot air," Stevens said. "Like him, we'll drop you off at Fort Chadbourne and see what the commandant there wants to do with you. He may just send you back to Fredericksburg or San Antonio on the stage and let the law there deal with you."

"And with Butler's attitude, he may send him back with you," Stevens said with a laugh, joined in by Nik.

"If your circumstances are true, Toby, both your attempts to hold up the stagecoach failed and you didn't hurt anybody. They may just try and find a foster home for you."

"Foster home, what's that?" Toby asked.

"A good home where they can teach you some manners and maybe send you to West Point," Nik added, to Stevens' amusement.

As the evening shadows began to cover the landscape, the stage pulled into Fort Chadbourne.

Chapter 7
Roger's Circuit on Hold— Again

"Taking off again so soon?" Paul Zimmerman commented, following Roger Brinkman's request that Paul take over the ministry in the Palamos region of the New Mexico Territory while he ventured into Mexico. "Why Mexico?"

"My brother, the U.S. marshal, has been given an assignment that takes him there," Roger answered. "He asked me to recruit men who are familiar with that country. Since many who live in these parts are native to Mexico, he asked for my help in forming a task force to go with him."

"And you agreed to go too?" Zimmerman again questioned.

"It wasn't supposed to be that way. In fact, Nik, my brother, rejected the idea of me going because of my experience in Galveston."

"We prayed for your return," Paul said. "I guess we can continue praying you will again. How dangerous is this mission?"

"That I don't know," Roger said. "I would like to say it was just a friendly visit, but I don't know how the folks in Mexico will feel about it."

"Have you got the other areas of your circuit covered?" Paul asked.

"I took the liberty of going into Albuquerque to talk to the pastor up there. He is going to send one of his assistant pastors to cover my circuit while I'm gone," Roger added. "So, you won't have to act alone this time."

"I'm sure we all appreciate that," Paul said, leading Brinker II into his corral. "Do you know the name of this assistant pastor?"

"The lead pastor said the assistant's name was Thomas Lindell. Apparently, he wants to eventually become an itinerant preacher also."

"We'll miss you, Pastor B, but we'll welcome Pastor Lindell and see to it he gets a clear understanding of what he's getting into."

"I was afraid you might say that," Roger commented with a laugh. "Just don't discourage him."

"Who else do you have going on this trip?" Paul asked.

"I'm glad you asked," Roger responded. "I need to get your approval on something, both you and Sally."

"What's on your mind?" Paul said, grabbing Roger's arm and leading him in the direction of the house.

"I'll tell you inside so Sally can hear," Roger said, following Paul's lead.

Once inside, Roger asked Paul and Sally to sit down at the table. Roger pulled up a chair on the opposite side and explained about the expedition into Mexico.

"What you may not know, is Peter has volunteered for this mission," Roger stated. "I made it clear to him, and I got the post commander to agree, that he had to have your permission to go."

"How dangerous is it?" Sally asked sternly.

"Honestly, I don't know" Roger began. "Peter is a soldier now and probably knows more about this territory than I do, having grown up here."

"I can also add there are other capable soldiers that have volunteered as well, including a lieutenant, Walter Gateway, and Sergeant Beau Davis. Gateway and Davis have chased Apache renegades into Mexico before and know that territory very well."

"I'm sorry, Pastor, but that doesn't sound very encouraging," Sally said, staring at Roger. "I know my son is a soldier and will likely have to fight renegades in the New Mexico Territory, but this Mexico thing sounds much too uncertain."

"How badly does he want to go?" Paul asked.

"If ...," Roger said, hesitating, "if you say no it's going to embarrass him in front of the other soldiers."

"I do not see that as a reason ..." Sally started. Roger quickly held up his hands to interrupt her speech.

"I only tell you that so you will know how Peter is going to take this if you say no. However, if it is what you wish, that is what will stand."

"Let me also say that Peter wants to be the expedition's cook."

"The cook?" Sally and Paul said almost simultaneously.

Roger continued, "Granted, that does not guarantee his safety, but I can say he will be well protected by everyone making that journey."

"I can say that Peter was helpful around the kitchen, but he didn't say anything about wanting to be a cook," Sally interjected.

"Who knew?" Roger said. "He told me he's thinking of making a career of it while in the military."

"And you're going with them?" Sally added, trying to mitigate the churning in her stomach.

"Unless my brother won't allow it. But I won't know that until I reach El Paso," Roger answered. "Right now, I have been preparing myself, and the circuit, for that eventuality."

"Promise me this, then," Sally said, turning to Paul for approval. "If your brother refuses to let you go, then you bring Peter back here with you."

Roger slowly nodded his head, looking back and forth between Sally and Paul. "You have my word on it," he said.

"Then it's settled, Pastor," Paul said. "As always, our prayers will be with you and everyone on that mission. If you do go, just promise you will look after Peter."

"I could not imagine doing otherwise," Roger answered.

Roger stayed the night at the Zimmermans' and left in the morning for Fort McRae.

Roger confirmed with Post Commander Horne that the Zimmermans had agreed to let their son volunteer for the Mexico expedition. He then informed Peter Zimmerman of the situation. Peter was a little disappointed that his parents were allowed to have a say, but he knew Pastor Brinkman would not break his word to them.

Together, Roger and Captain Horne made preparations for the departure of the task force. To complete the entourage, Roger rode out to Carlos Santana's place to ensure that Morgana Cabezon would join them.

"So, you will be joining the expedition," Morgana said rhetorically. "That is good."

"If my brother will let me," Roger replied. "I really don't think he will say no, but he has regrets about involving me in an investigation we resolved in Galveston."

"So, you still assist in serving the law as well as your Lord," Morgana said, as she gathered her belongings to join the expedition.

"I would have stayed a U.S. marshal if I had not had a higher calling," Roger said. "I don't like to think that the law and my faith contradict one another. However, I do prefer to avoid physical violence if I can."

Morgana shouldered her bag and motioned for Roger to lead the way. She glanced back at her dwelling, silently whispered a few words, and then followed.

After arriving back at Fort McRae, Roger introduced Morgana to Captain Horne. Horne sent word for the six volunteers to meet in his office for a briefing.

"Gentlemen, Pastor Brinkman and I will fill you in on what little we know about this journey you've been asked to volunteer for. Pastor Brinkman," the captain said, surrendering the floor to Roger.

"The plan has changed somewhat from when we last spoke. We will start out for El Paso, Texas, in the morning. Our route will take us along the edge of the Sierra de Caballo Mountains to San Inedo, where we'll camp for the night," Roger began. "Then we'll cross the Jornade del Muertos to Fort Sheldon. It'll be a two-day ride from there along the Colorado River to Fort Bliss near El Paso."

"Thank you, Pastor," Horne said, rising from his chair. "Zimmerman and Townsend will man the chuck wagon. Nantan will assist in Apache relations, and Laumpagh will help provide security. Lieutenant, you and Davis are in charge of the men, but remember, you will all be traveling as civilians, not soldiers. As I understand it, you will be issued civilian clothes when you reach El Paso, right, Pastor?"

"Those are the instructions I have, Captain," Roger replied. "Gentlemen, I also want to introduce you to Morgana Cabezon. She and I will be the front for this mission under the supervision of my brother, U.S. Marshal Nik Brinkman."

"To my knowledge, we are the only real civilians in this group so, please, follow our lead if we run into any trouble."

"May I ask Miss Cabezon's role in this?" Lieutenant Gateway asked.

"Morgana is mestizo-Apache," Roger said. "She is a shaman from Mexico and knows the terrain and languages spoken there. Please treat her with the utmost respect for our survival may very well depend on her."

Gateway seemed less than satisfied with Roger's answer but did not comment further. Sergeant Davis cast a glance his way, but the two men remained silent.

"With that, men, you're dismissed to gather your gear and ready yourselves to pull out in the morning after chow," Horne announced. "Zimmerman, you, Townsend, and Laumpagh get the wagon loaded and ready. A fresh team of horses will be supplied for departure. Davis, please see to it their task is properly carried out."

"Yes, sir," Davis replied, leaning forward to get up. The rest followed and left the captain's quarters.

"Well, Pastor, Miss Cabezon, are you ready for this?" Horne said. Roger looked over at Morgana.

"It is my country where we are going," Morgana responded. "I am probably the least anxious of anyone among those going. But I am anxious to learn of this Great Spirit that Pastor Brinkman serves."

"In my humble opinion," Horne started, "I would say you could not be in more capable hands where that is concerned."

"Nor the two of us under my brother's command," Roger said, nodding to the captain. "This is truly a unique group we've assembled here."

While Roger gathered his things, Captain Horne gave Morgana a tour of the fort and showed her to her quarters.

"Where have I heard that name before?" Sergeant Davis said to Lieutenant Gateway.

"Are you speaking of Cabezon?" Gateway asked.

"Yes, she seems awfully young to be chosen to go on this mission," Davis replied.

"I have to admit that her last name sounds familiar, but I can't place it," Gateway said. "I guess we'll just have to trust Brinkman's intuition."

"Do you have everything you need?" said a soldier standing in the doorway of Roger's room.

"I could say I have my Bible and therefore everything I need," Roger said, chuckling. "But I'm afraid I don't have quite that much faith, considering this excursion."

"But you do have enough faith in Morgana to get you there and back?" the soldier asked.

"I'm afraid I have no other choice, however there are others who I will be relying on as well," Roger answered. "Do you know Morgana?"

"I know the name Cabezon. He was an Indian Chief and father of Cochise," the soldier said.

"You know him? I mean, you know Cochise's father?" Roger said, straightening up and looking squarely at the young soldier in his doorway.

"Let's just say that I know that Cochise's blood runs through Morgana, and she's well aware of it," the soldier replied.

"How is it you know all this? You seem kind of young," Roger quizzed.

"I know my history, Pastor. I just thought you ought to know too."

"Say, will you come with me to talk to Morgana?" Roger asked. "I'd like to verify what you just said."

"Sorry, I'm on duty, Pastor. I've got to get back to my post," the soldier said, and then stepped away from the doorway.

"No, wait a minute," Roger called out, striding toward the door. "I think I can find someone to relieve…" Roger stopped and peered across the compound. No one was there except a pair of soldiers walking past.

"Say, did either of you see a young soldier standing here just a moment ago?" Roger called out.

The two men stopped. "No," said one. "Were you looking for someone in particular?"

"Ah, no, just a young soldier who told me he was on duty and disappeared," Roger responded. "So, you didn't see anyone?"

"Sorry, Pastor, I didn't see anyone. Did you see someone?" the one soldier said, turning to his companion. The other man just shook his head.

"Sorry," he called out, and the two men continued on their way.

"Thank you," Roger called back as he stared at the two men.

He went back inside and sat down on his bunk. He began to ponder what the soldier in the doorway had said and wondered about the significance of it.

The following morning, Lieutenant Gateway assembled the volunteers selected to recover the silver and took roll call.

"All present and accounted for, Captain," Gateway said. Sitting atop his mount, he saluted the post commander and turned to Davis. "Sergeant, move 'em out."

"Yes, sir," Davis said. "Detachment, ho."

The wagon began to roll while mounted soldiers moved into position surrounding the wagon. Roger pulled up alongside Gateway with Morgana riding at his side.

Chapter 8
Charlie Bluefeather

U.S. Marshal Nik Brinkman sat in a chair on the barracks front porch watching the soldiers of Fort Concho loading barrels of water onto a buckboard. His interest was the fact that the buckboard would also be his transportation to Phantom Hill where Post on the Clear Fork of the Brazos was located. Despite the post's sobriquet, the silty water of the Brazos' fork was not clear and its access too difficult to sustain the fort.

The fort was also no longer used as a military post and served only as a stopping station for the Wells Fargo Stage Line. Since the fort's original mission was to protect the stagecoaches from attack, the Army continued shipping water and patrolling the area.

"Marshal Brinkman," Colonel Mackenzie said, as he approached where Nik was sitting. "Are you going to press charges against that boy?"

"I'm on an important assignment, Colonel," Nik replied. "I really don't have the time to process him. Although he did attempt to perpetrate a crime, he failed to steal anything or hurt anyone."

"I can tell you that the boy is telling the truth," Mackenzie said. "We're aware of what happened to his parents. We have spent quite some time searching for his mother, without much luck."

"What I'm thinking is, I'll keep him here as my office boy. There isn't much mischief he can get into, and at least he'll have three squares and a roof over his head."

"That's mighty generous of you, Colonel," Nik said, rising to his feet to shake Mackenzie's hand. "And should you ever find his mother, it would be wonderful if you could unite the two."

"That's a consideration, too, but the odds are against it, I'm afraid," the colonel said. "She's been missing for quite a while."

"Hopefully being here will be good for him," Nik said. "Who knows, maybe he'll make a good soldier when he comes of age."

"The boy notwithstanding, when I spoke with Geoff Stevens, he did not have a favorable opinion of Lieutenant Butler," McKenzie said.

"Nor do I, Colonel," Nik replied. "I don't think Geoff or I are anxious to continue this journey with him riding along."

"No problem, Marshal," Mackenzie replied. "I'll hold him over here for a few weeks and send him on to Fort Bliss after you men have long gone."

"If you could do that, I'd be mighty grateful to you. I know he doesn't care a lick for me, either," Nik said, smiling.

"I understand, Marshal, glad to do it," Mackenzie said, with a laugh.

After a nourishing meal and a good night's sleep, Nik rose early to join the small detachment assigned to take the buckboard and water up to Phantom Hill. There were two buckboards, both loaded with barrels of water. Fort Concho was located close to the good water of the Concho River and helped to keep the stage stop at Phantom Hill supplied with the precious liquid.

Nik placed his gear under the driver's seat and took his place next to the driver. Texas Ranger Geoff Stevens and Chili Buck rode on the second wagon driven by Corporal Cameron Brady.

"Brinkman, Nik Brinkman, U.S. Marshal," Nik said, looking at the driver.

"Yes, sir, Mr. Brinkman," the driver said. "I have you on my passengers list. Coosman's my name, Sid Coosman. I drive for Wells Fargo."

"If it's okay that I call you Sid, it'd be fine with me if you called me Nik," Nik said. Coosman gave a slight smile and nodded in the affirmative.

"It must be comforting to have a detachment of soldiers riding with you on these trips," Nik said.

"Not a problem heading north," Coosman said, "but coming back can be a problem. It's on our way back that the most valuable cargo is transported."

"So, I've been told," Nik responded. "Do you run into a lot of trouble on this route?"

"It has happened, even when we're carrying water. It's mostly renegade Indians in that case, though," Coosman remarked. "They're pretty much just raising hell, though. They really don't need the water or even try to take it. They just try to sabotage the shipment and maybe pick off a soldier or two."

"And when you come back?" Nik speculated.

"It's not frequent, but that's happened too," the driver continued. "We don't always carry gold or anything else valuable, and this is too far out of the way for bandits to wait around for us to come by. The times it has happened we had gold. It has always puzzled me how they know. Wells Fargo is careful about keeping special shipments secret."

"Bribery," Nik said.

"Pardon?" Coosman remarked.

"Bribery," Nik added. "Outlaws know who to bribe to tell them when such shipments are on the way. It can sometimes turn out to be some of the most loyal employees, but then they turn out otherwise."

"I suppose you're right, Marshall," the driver said. "Money can be hard to come by out here. A bribe's as good a way to make a buck as any, I imagine."

"Yeah, but people can get killed that way, Sid, and it's not always the bad guys who end up that way."

"There's been more than one driver who's spilled blood along this trail, or even on Curly's run, for that matter," Coosman remarked, referring to the stage line from San Antonio to Fort Concho.

The buckboard procession stopped at a familiar location to spend the night. It was used as a halfway station established shortly after Fort Concho began supplying Phantom Hill with water. A campfire was started, but the fare was beef jerky, rice cooked over the fire, flatbread, and coffee. The need for a chuck wagon on the trip was abandoned because of the short duration of the journey.

"So, where are you two headed?" Coosman asked Nik and Ranger Stevens between bites.

"El Paso," Nik answered.

"What's in El Paso that they need a U.S. marshal and Texas rangers?"

"I'm on a diplomatic mission," Nik said, measuring his words. "I think Geoff, here, is to add more security."

"We Texas rangers are starting to focus on the trouble in west Texas," Stevens added. "I'm going to try to recruit some new rangers in El Paso to run patrols along the Rio Grande. Chili, here, has been hired to assist me for as long as I need him."

"I'm happy to hear that the Rangers are beefing up security in that area," Coosman continued, "but what's happening in El Paso that they need a diplomat?"

"I'm meeting with some dignitaries from Mexico," Nik said, keeping his explanation short, so as not to offer any more information than necessary.

"It must be interesting work," Coosman remarked. "I did not know U.S. marshals was used for that sort of thing."

"We're trying to establish better border security with the help of Mexico in assisting the rangers," Nik responded, stretching his imagination while glancing over at Stevens. The ranger offered a slight smile and kept on eating. "So, how long have you been driving for Wells Fargo, Sid?" Nik asked, changing the subject.

"I've been doing it for over a year now," Coosman answered. "Shortly after Fort Concho was established to replace Fort Chadbourne."

"How often do you have to make this trip?" Nik asked. "How much water do they need in Phantom Hill?"

"It used to be more when Phantom Hill was known as the Post on the Clear Fork of the Brazos," Coosman said, "but now it's just a stopping station for what used to be the Butterfield Overland Stage before Wells Fargo bought it. There's only a caretaker at the station now and he doesn't use any more water than he has to. Wells Fargo worked out a deal with the Army to supply it."

"Seems like quite an undertaking to keep all of this going," Nik replied.

"It's on its way out, though," Coosman commented. "They're laying tracks for a railroad to make the run that the stage does now.

Shouldn't be too long before that iron horse comes chuggin' through there. I spect my job will end when that happens."

"What will you do then?" Stevens asked.

"I guess I'll see if Wells Fargo needs any more drivers, or maybe go to work for the railroad," Coosman said. "They're building railroads all over Texas now."

"The times, they are changing," Nik commented.

Following the meal, the soldiers set up sentry duty for the night while the rest of the party settled down for the evening. It was a peaceful night until just before dawn.

A zzzzz-thock broke the morning's silence. The sound came from a flaming arrow that planted itself into one of the water barrels. A few shots could be heard coming from just outside the camp, along with shouts of a raiding party.

"Indians!" one of the soldiers running into the camp cried out. "Take cover!"

Nik jumped up to grab his pistol and rifle from the back of the wagon. He could see the flaming arrow stuck in the water barrel but decided against exposing himself by trying to pull it out. The shouting was now growing louder.

"Roll under the wagon," Coosman called out. "They're attacking from the east and using the sun to blind us."

Nik did as the driver suggested, and could see Stevens, Buck, and the corporal doing the same under their wagon. Nik hid behind one of the wagon wheels and peered into a sun-bleached landscape. As Coosman had described, the sun made it near impossible to see the marauders. Another arrow hit the wagon just above Nik's position. He poked his rifle between the spokes of the wagon wheel and began firing.

Nik could hear horses' hooves pounding the ground as they drew near. He continued to fire blindly until the sounds of battle passed and quickly faded into the distance. As the echo of rifle fire faded, the raid ended.

"What's the damage?" a corporal called out.

"Lost a couple of horses," came one of the answers. "None of the barrels were destroyed though," came another.

Nik moved out from under the wagon and looked around. The soldiers were racing back and forth trying to restore order and soon had things back to normal.

"What was that?" Nik asked the corporal.

"Indian raid to try and steal our horses," the corporal answered. "As far as our cargo is concerned, it's all pretty much intact."

"Just raisin' hell," Coosman said, pulling up alongside Nik. "Probably Comanche and Kiowa just stirring up trouble."

"Was anybody hurt?" Nik inquired of the corporal.

"No, sir," the corporal responded. "Just one man burnt his hand trying to put out one of them arrows."

Fortunately, there were enough horses to continue pulling the wagons and it didn't take long until the detachment was again on its way to Phantom Hill.

The water wagons moved with a little more caution after the loss of the horses. However, there were no further incidents as the team reached the fort at Phantom Hill with all cargo and personnel accounted for.

"When does the stagecoach arrive?" Nik asked the station caretaker the next morning.

"Should arrive around mid-morning, barring any mishaps along the way," the caretaker answered while tending to the teams of horses. "I don't expect no trouble, though. Things have been pretty quiet lately."

"How about from here to El Paso?" Nik continued.

"There could be trouble. But seems to me, thanks to you and the Ranger, you should be okay," the caretaker said.

Nik, Ranger Stevens, and Chili enjoyed a good breakfast and several cups of coffee while waiting for the stagecoach to arrive.

"You're not sure what awaits you in Mexico, are you Nik?" Stevens said, sipping his cup of java."

"I have never done anything like this, other than joining the Army," Nik answered. "I come from a foreign country and realize things are different in other parts of the world. But I have no idea what to expect on this expedition."

"Who is going with you?" Chili asked.

"I have been authorized to take along some soldiers, although they will be acting as civilians. My brother is stationed at Fort McRae in the New Mexico Territory and is doing the recruiting for me." Nik explained. "They are to meet me in El Paso."

"So, is your brother going along?" Stevens asked.

"I hope so, Geoff," Nik said, setting his coffee down on the table. "I told him in a letter that I was not going to take him along, but my fiancée suggested that I do. So, I'll have to try and talk him into it."

"Is he a marshal, too?" Chili asked.

"Ahh, no…," Nik began. "He's a traveling minister in the New Mexico Territory."

"A minister?" Stevens remarked. "Is he used to this sort of thing?"

"No more than I am, but he's had a lot of experience with the Apache, Mexican citizens living in the area where he preaches, and the U.S. Army. He used to be a marshal, so I could most certainly use him on this trip."

"For moral support, if nothing else, right?" Chili said, setting his coffee carefully down as he chuckled.

"He could prove to be the complete package, but I cannot force him to go. So, it'll be up to him." Nik concluded, just as the sounds of the stagecoach arriving interrupted their conversation.

"I guess our ride is here," Stevens said, pushing his chair back from the table and getting to his feet.

The three men placed a dollar down for their meal and exited the station to greet the stage.

"Ned Borchers," Nik called out, as the first passenger swung open the stage door and stepped down. Nik grabbed his former Chief Marshal by the hand and slapped him on the shoulder with the other.

"Nik, you are a sight to see," Borchers said, embracing his former deputy. "How has Galveston been treating you?"

"I would say fine, but as you can see, they're already sending me away." Nik said, laughing.

"I understand they are sending you on a wild goose chase,"

Borchers said, returning the laugh. "However, if anyone can do this, you are the one."

"I hope so, Ned. I'm really venturing into unknown territory, where I'm concerned."

"Because of that, I've got a little surprise for you," Ned said, turning back toward the stage. "Charlie, come out here."

A familiar figure emerged, as Nik's eyes widened.

"Charlie, Charlie Bluefeather!" Nik called out. "What are you doing here?… Ned?"

"I knew you could use some help, Nik, so I recruited the best I could find for you."

Nik rushed up to give Charlie a hug and nearly knocked the Wichita Indian's hat from his head. Charlie Bluefeather was Nik's companion and camp cook while Nik was working as a deputy marshal out of the Wichita, Kansas office, covering the Oklahoma and Texas territories adjacent to the Red River.

"Ned, I can't believe you did this," Nik said. "But then, you always did the right thing at the right time."

Nik introduced Ned and Charlie to Rangers Geoff Stevens and Chili Buck. They took the time to have another cup of coffee and a brief chat before the stage left on its final leg to El Paso.

"So, Charlie, what have you been up to?" Nik asked.

"I work now with Deputy Marshal Warneke," Charlie said. "He is coming along nicely."

"That's because of you and Ned, Charlie," Nik said. "No one was better at federal law than Ned and there's no one better than you to teach raw recruits about life on the trail. I have to admit, I've missed you, Charlie."

"I do not know Mexico," Bluefeather said. "I hope my service will be of value to you."

"Just having you around will be service enough," Nik assured. "Ned, are you going to be able to get along without Charlie?"

"Wouldn't have brought him along if I thought otherwise," Ned said, grinning. "Willie has made tremendous progress and is running the office right now. We picked up a replacement when you transferred to Galveston, who is doing well under Warneke."

"I have some news about Judge Kensington," Nik said. "It appears he was behind the silver-shipment heist that we're going to be looking for."

"How do you know that?" Ned asked.

"A pirate he hired to help in the theft identified the judge as the mastermind behind the plot," Nik began.

Nik gave Ned the details of the event, describing how the hot-air balloon carrying the silver was blown off course and believed to be somewhere in the Sierra Nevada Range of Mexico.

"That was a pretty elaborate plan," Ned said. "Do you think you'll run into Kensington and his men who might also be looking for the lost silver?"

"Anything is possible at this point," Nik replied. "We're basically going on pure speculation. Fortunately, I think Roger has recruited someone native to Mexico to help out."

"Is Roger joining you?" Ned asked.

"I told him I wasn't going to include him, but I've changed my mind on that," Nik said. "Now I just hope I can change his mind on it."

"You guys make a good team. I hope you're successful," Ned added.

After a fresh team of horses was harnessed to the stagecoach, Nik, Charlie, and Rangers Stevens and Buck got on board for the trip to El Paso. Sid Coosman, Corporal Brady, and their escort also departed to return to Fort Concho. Neither the coach nor the wagons carried anything valuable, so no trouble was anticipated other than another possible Indian attack.

Chapter 9
Roger Renews
Acquaintances

Roger Brinkman and his band of volunteers left Fort McRae early in the morning. Peter Zimmerman was driving the chow wagon with Kelly Laumpagh riding on the seat next to him. Lieutenant Gateway led the procession, with Roger to his right and Sergeant Beau Davis directly behind him. Morgana Cabezon rode behind Roger on a Paint she called Tarak, the Apache word for Star. She told Roger she gave her horse that name because of a white patch on its face that resembled a five-point star.

Riding on either side of the wagon and near the rear were Indian Scout Nantan and Private Carter Townsend. Townsend had ambitions to become the army's first black officer.

The detachment rode south along the Sierra del Caballo Range near Palamos, where Paul and Sally Zimmerman, Peter's parents, lived. Peter asked that they not stop as he did not want to have to say goodbye to his parents a second time, when he enlisted in the army.

After reaching the southern end of the mountain range, they turned southwest across the Jornada del Muerto Desert heading for Fort Selden, where they would spend the night.

"We'll stay at Fort Selden and then leave in the morning for Fort Bliss," Gateway said, without looking at anyone in particular. "It's a cool day, so it shouldn't be too uncomfortable crossing the Jornada del Muerto sands."

"The desert is quite beautiful this time of year," Morgana said, "but not so beautiful when the summer winds blow through."

"The desert is also a relatively safe place to travel," Davis remarked. "Not many places to hide out here, but one can never be too careful."

"Wise advice, Sergeant," Gateway said. "I swear that the Mescalero can hide behind a grain of sand if necessary."

"They become the sand, Lieutenant," Morgana said. "It is your eyes that deceive you."

"I can't argue with that," Gateway responded. "Don't get too engrossed in the desert flowers because I'm certain the Apache can resemble those, too." Gateway added, casting a smile Roger's way.

"The Army has done a pretty fair job of keeping the peace in these parts, Lieutenant," Roger said. "My missionary circuit is near here and I've yet to have any trouble."

"Most Apache have moved west into Arizona or south into Mexico," Gateway replied. "There are several Army posts in this area, and the Buffalo Soldiers have done a marvelous job of keeping the peace."

After a brief stop for a quick meal, the volunteers rode into Fort Selden. They were greeted by Captain Doyle Turpin and shown their accommodations. Morgana requested an area outside the billets. Her preference was to sleep outdoors. Turpin suggested sleeping on the Terreplein, a raised platform running along the inside of the fortress wall.

"If you're not afraid of heights, I can inform the guards not to disturb you up there," Turpin said.

"That would suit me fine, Captain. Thank you for making special arrangements on my behalf."

"I understand you folks are headed into Mexico?" Turpin asked.

"We're going in search of silver," Roger said. "These soldiers are all volunteers and I could not be more grateful for their willingness to participate."

"I'm surprised Mexico is letting you do this," Turpin said. "Or are you doing it without their permission?"

"We have their permission," Roger said. "The silver was a shipment stolen and carried by balloon into Mexico. However, we believe the outlaws who did this were American, not Mexican."

"President Grant took care of the diplomatic arrangements."

"I could understand if it was a shipment of gold, but why silver?" the captain asked. "There must be a lot of silver in that shipment."

"There were two chests full of it, Captain, but the reason is because the U.S. Treasury is thinking of raising the value of sliver to match that of gold."

"Sounds complicated," the captain remarked.

"More complicated than I could explain to you," Roger said, laughing.

After breakfast, Lieutenant Gateway led the procession out of Fort Selden and followed the Rio Grande south. They passed near Las Cruces, occupying an area ceded to the United States by Mexico, following the Mexican-American War. Las Cruces received its name because of the three crosses erected north of the town.

The group stayed between the Rio Grande and the San Andreas Mountains that stretched south toward Fort Bliss, near El Paso del Norte, their destination.

At one point along the way, Lieutenant Gateway called out "Eyes left! Salute!" Everyone, except Roger and Morgana, saluted, although they both scanned the hills to their left.

After the gesture, Gateway said "That's Fort Fillmore, or at least it used to be," he explained. "It's abandoned now, but the cemetery contains several fallen soldiers, including Captain Henry Stanton, namesake of Fort Stanton. Even Captain George Pickett served at Fillmore."

"That's not General George Pickett, is it?" Roger asked.

"It is, Pastor," Gateway responded. "The same one who made the failed charge at Gettysburg during the war."

"How well I remember," Roger quietly uttered.

"You were in the war, Pastor?" Gateway asked.

"I was at Gettysburg, but never fired a shot, thank the Lord," Roger said. "And please, call me Roger."

"You'll have to tell me more sometime... Roger," Gateway replied. "I would never have thought that with you being a man of the cloth and all."

"There are some things in my past I'd rather forget," Roger confessed.

"However, everything I hold back is not a secret, just personal."

Gateway simply smiled and nodded his head and continued leading the volunteers along the river.

"We'll cross the river here," Gateway called out, turning his horse onto a trail that led into a wide but shallow stretch of the Rio Grande. Sergeant Davis rode back to the wagon to inform Peter and Private Laumpagh that he would lead their team across the waters.

"Why are we crossing the river," Roger asked. "Is it easier to travel on the west side?"

"It's safer, Roger," Gateway said. "Right now, if a raiding party would come at us from those mountains, we'd be trapped by the river. And the terrain on the west bank is about as good as it is over here."

"It is wise, Captain," Morgana offered. "Although most of the Apache have moved west into Arizona, there are still bands of renegades that could be hiding out in those hills."

Although the spring runoff had swollen the Rio Grande's waters, the crossing went without difficulty. It was not long after that the procession reached Fort Bliss as sundown approached. They were greeted by Post Commander Colonel Carl Jamison.

"I received word that you would be coming, but I was not told how many of you to expect," the colonel said. "I believe we can find a bunk for the soldiers, but the lady may want to stay in El Paso."

"She sleeps outdoors, Colonel," Roger said. "She's quite used to that."

"Is she Indian?" Jamison asked.

"She is mestizo-Apache," Roger replied.

"Apache," the colonel repeated. "I was going to say we do have a band of Comanche camping just outside the fort. I don't know if they would be comfortable accepting an Apache, though."

"Comanche? Gateway cut in. May I ask the reason for their presence?"

"They're being moved into Comanche Territory up north," Jamison answered. "They were a band camped along the Rio Grande, and we were given orders to relocate them into Indian Territory. A detachment headed by Captain Dunston is traveling with them."

"Captain Dan Dunston?" Roger asked.

"Yes," Jamison said, "do you know him?"

"I think so," Roger replied, "if those Comanche happened to be living on the river. Where were they camped, exactly?"

"They had occupied a village across the river from San Antonio del Bravo in Mexico," the colonel said. "They weren't happy about pulling up stakes, but Dunston was able to persuade the small tribe to relocate."

"Do you know who their chief is?" Roger continued.

"He goes by the name of Catfish," Jamison said. "I had not heard of a Comanche by that name before."

Roger was about to ask if Catfish also went by the name Pecos, but realized that may not be wise. "Is Captain Dunstan with them now?" he asked instead.

"I believe Dunston is somewhere here on the post," Jamison answered. "I would assume he has some soldiers on guard duty. However, that band of Indians is very cooperative, so I do not expect any trouble."

"I'll see if I can find Captain Dunston. I'd like to get his permission to visit with the Comanche and encourage them to continue on their journey," Roger said. "I appreciate your hospitality, Colonel."

"Dunston should be around here, somewhere," Jamison said. "Please, make yourselves at home."

Roger went in search of Dunston and found him and Sergeant Braxton talking in front of the colonel's office.

"Captain Dunston, Sergeant Braxton," Roger called out. "The colonel said I might find you here."

"Pastor Brinkman, is that you?" Dunston answered. "What are you doing here? I thought you were on your way to Galveston."

"I have been there and back," Roger said, extending a hand to both the captain and sergeant. "I'm supposed to meet my brother here this time."

"Was he the one you were going to baptize?" Dunston said, expressing surprise at Roger's sudden appearance.

"He's the only brother I have, Dan. It seems I may have to accompany him into Mexico this time."

"Mexico? What's in Mexico?" Dunston asked.

"I don't think the reason is meant to be common knowledge, but I think he's going to look for some stolen money," Roger said, lowering his voice.

"Does he have jurisdiction in Mexico?" Braxton asked.

"Not really," Roger stated. "But this is a special envoy. I've been told it was established and approved by the president himself."

"Amazing. That must be a hefty load of cash you'll be looking for to be going to that much trouble," Dunston added. "Are you expecting trouble?"

"I hope not, and speaking of trouble, can I visit with your Comanche chief? The colonel said you have a group of them camped outside the fort," Roger related.

"You mean Catfish?" Dunston asked. "Isn't he the one you sailed down the Rio Grande with last year?"

"That's the one," Roger replied. "I'd just like to say hello."

"Do you need someone to go with you?" Braxton asked.

"Just to let the sentry know you've cleared me to go into the Comanche Camp, Chuck," Roger said. "I know P… Catfish. We spent quite a bit of time together on the river."

"Fine, I'll be happy to do that, Pastor."

"Dan, good to see you again," Roger said, turning to Dunston. "Maybe we'll run into each other before we both depart."

"I'm leaving early in the morning," Dunston said. "We're anxious to get this band resettled in Comanche Territory. I'm not necessarily looking forward to it but those are the orders from headquarters."

"I'll tell Catfish to behave," Roger said with a smile. "May the Good Lord go with all of you."

"Thanks, Roger. We can use all the help we can get," Dunston said with a smile.

After passing through the gates to the fort, Roger and Braxton found a sentry and the sergeant gave orders to allow Roger entry into the camp. Roger thanked Braxton and proceeded on his own into the encampment. After inquiring as to the chief, a brave led him to Pecos, who was seated by a campfire.

"If it isn't the white shaman," Pecos said, greeting Roger. "I am happily surprised to see you. You made it safely to Galveston, I presume."

"And back, my friend," Roger said, sitting next to Pecos. "When I heard the army was moving you back into Comanche Territory, I was anxious to see you again." Roger looked around to see if anyone was nearby. "May I call you Pecos?"

"It is now best to stay with Catfish," Pecos said. "The name Pecos is known to the Army, although they think he is dead. I would like to leave it that way."

"I understand. I am sorry they are moving you and your band," Roger said. "Why are they doing that?"

"They are making an effort to move all Indians onto reservations," Pecos said. "We protested, but it did not matter. The captain said he was under orders to move us north. I told him we had moved south to help keep the peace, but he said the matter was out of his hands."

"So, Dunston does not know you as Pecos?" Roger asked.

"No, I do not let that name out to anyone in a uniform."

"Do you think you'll run into… your brother?" Roger asked.

"Quanah? I would hope not," Pecos said. "This migration is unfortunate, as I believe he is still marauding in this area."

"I will pray for you and your village," Roger said. "I wish I could do more."

"I fear it is our fate," Preacher man," Pecos said. "Why are you here?"

"It seems I and another detachment of soldiers are headed in the opposite direction – into Mexico," Roger said.

"Mexico is not a friendly place, right now," Pecos responded. "Why do you go there?"

"Like your name, that is something I am not at liberty to discuss," Roger said. "I just hope we both live long enough to see each other again."

"You have good medicine, white shaman. You will do fine, even in Mexico."

After wishing each other well, Roger departed the Comanche camp and returned to the confines of the fort.

***

After leaving Phantom Hill, the scenery offered Nik and his companions little in variety. The high desert stretched out in all directions dotted with different forms of vegetation, prickly pear cacti, and an occasional stand of trees bearing thin branches and very few leaves. But there were also patches of colorful flowers just coming into bloom.

"This is definitely not the scenic part of the trip, Nik," Stevens remarked.

"It reminds me a lot of the Llano Estacado," Nik said. "Charlie and I had to venture into areas like this looking for renegade Indians."

"So, you marshals are Indian fighters too?" Stevens said.

"With this part of the country being as unsettled as it is," Nik responded, "marshals are expected to do whatever the government asks them to do—like this expedition Charlie and I are on."

"Has the government given you a guide to take you into Mexico?" Stevens continued. "Someone who's familiar with the area where you will be going?"

"There wasn't anyone in Galveston I knew familiar with the circumstances that led to this expedition," Nik said. "I'm hoping my brother finds someone with some knowledge of the Sierra Madre Occidental and surrounding area."

"Why did you decide to rely on your brother to find someone?" Stevens asked. "Has the government really thought this thing through?"

"To be honest, Geoff, I think they were strictly going on what I knew about the silver shipment and the method by which it was stolen. As for Mexico's part, the U.S. State Department did little more than gain us diplomatic access to that country and give me an allowance to recruit a task force."

"Just how was this shipment stolen?" Chili inquired, taking an interest in the developing story.

Nik gave Chili and Stevens a description of the effort to ship the silver across Galveston Bay on a nondescript barge, which was rammed by a mock pirate ship, supposedly celebrating the history of Jean Lafitte, who had once occupied the island.

"Although the ship's captain thought he was supposed to abscond with the silver, it was carted away by a huge hot-air balloon," Nik explained. "That balloon, however, was carried by wind currents into Mexico and there are those who believe it came down somewhere in the Sierra Madre Mountains."

"Have you any idea where?" the captain continued to press.

"That's what we've been tasked to find out," Nik added, "and then to retrieve it."

"Marshal Borchers not tell Charlie these details," Bluefeather cut in. "Maybe afraid I would not agree to come."

Nik and the others laughed, "You might be onto something, Charlie," Nik said, "but I don't think Ned was all that familiar with the details either. All he really knew was that I had been selected to lead the detail."

Shortly after their conversation ended, the stage pulled into a stopping station.

"Another two days' ride," the driver called out, as he retrieved the luggage from on top of the stagecoach and tossed it down to Nik and the other passengers. "The only danger might be Guadalupe Canyon, but that's another four days' ride from here."

Four days, Nik thought, rubbing his backside. The marshal almost wished they would run into some trouble to break the monotony of the trip, but refrained from whispering any prayer that might make it happen.

As the trip continued, the passengers eventually ran out of things to talk about and either slept as best they could or simply stared out the coach window at what little scenery there was.

As the days went by, the driver called out they would soon be coming to Guadalupe Pass and to be prepared. All but Charlie made sure their rifles were loaded, and each pressed back in their seats so as not to present a target in the windows. However, the stage went through the pass without any trouble or delays and came to a stopping station in sight of Granite Peak.

"We'll push on through to El Paso tomorrow, stopping only long enough to get a fresh team of horses," the driver announced, as he again unloaded luggage from the top of the stage. "I don't expect any trouble from here on out."

It was now that Nik began to think about his arrival at Fort Bliss in El Paso and meeting Roger and the volunteers selected for the trip. He would brief them on what to expect, although he himself had little knowledge of what lay ahead.

Chapter 10
Into Mexico

Later that evening, the stagecoach Nik was riding on pulled into El Paso. Nik, Charlie Bluefeather, and the two rangers stepped out onto the main street of the west Texas town.

"Gentlemen, Charlie and I have to make our way over to Fort Bliss, where I think we'll be staying for the night," Nik said. "I want to say it's been a pleasure traveling with the two of you, and I hope our paths cross again soon."

"Marshal, I wish you and your expedition all the goodwill there is," Captain Geoff Stevens said. "Chili and I will be meeting at the sheriff's office tomorrow to get our orders. So, if we don't see you again for a while, good luck to you all."

The four men shook hands and Nik and Charlie headed for the livery stable while the rangers checked into the El Paso hotel. After securing two horses, Nik and Charlie took a short ride out to Fort Bliss. Upon entering the fort, they were directed to Roger Brinkman's billets.

"Well, who do we have here?" Roger called out when Nik entered the room. Roger made a quick trip across the room to embrace his brother.

"Roger, there's someone I would like you to meet—again," Nik said, breaking into a laugh. Then, Charlie walked through the door.

"Charlie? Charlie Bluefeather!" Roger said, his voice rising with each word, as he quickly grabbed the Wichita Indian into an embrace. "Am I glad to see you. I was worried about this trip, but I feel much better now."

"You look fit enough to travel without me, Roger Brinkman," Charlie said.

"Ned Borchers made the arrangements for Charlie to accompany us, Roger, but there's something I want to talk to you about."

"Before you say anything, brother, I have made up my mind to go along with you on this trip, so don't try and talk me out of it," Roger said in a serious tone.

Nik looked at Roger for a moment and then broke out with a big smile.

"You saved me the trouble of begging you to go along," Nik said, laughing. "Before I left, Esther insisted I have you go with us. I would hate to disappoint her."

"Whew," Roger sighed. "I thought I was going to have to arm wrestle you to get you to change your mind from what you wrote in your letter."

"I think the Good Lord is already showing his hand on this trip," Nik said. "When can I meet the others?"

"Why don't you two find a bunk to rest yourselves," Roger said, gesturing in the direction of the other beds in the room. "The others have split up for the night, so it will be easier to do introductions in the morning."

"Excellent advice, brother," Nik said. "After riding that stage the last few weeks, I'm not sure I could get used to a stationary bed."

The three men engaged in small talk as they prepared to rest for the night, and soon the trio was fast asleep.

The following day, Roger led Nik and Charlie to Colonel Jamison's office, where the other members of the expedition had already gathered. After introductions, Nik suggested they all break for breakfast and then reassemble in Roger's quarters.

"Gentlemen, and the lady," Nik said, tipping his hat in Morgana's direction. "I would like to learn more about each of you before discussing what lies ahead."

Lieutenant Gateway took the lead and gave a little background as to himself and Sergeant Beau Davis.

"Kelly Laumpagh and Carter Townsend are both Buffalo Soldiers stationed at Fort McRae in the New Mexico Territory," Roger stated. "Both are very capable men. Peter Zimmerman is a special guest, as I know his mother and father very well. I had planned on Peter and Kelly manning the chuck wagon, but I'm thinking Charlie should probably take the reins for that task."

"If I may speak, sir," Peter Zimmerman spoke up.

"Feel free, anytime, Peter. From this point on you are no longer soldiers," Roger answered.

"Sir, I'd like to stay with the chuck wagon, if I may," Peter said. "Maybe I could learn something from Mr. Bluefeather."

Charlie smiled, not being used to being referred to as "Mr. Bluefeather."

"I think we will all have to find our way around on this expedition," Nik replied, addressing the others, as well as Peter. "Although most of you are soldiers, you will be considered civilians on this trip. I've been running ideas through my head as to how we're going to approach the populace of Mexico and explain our presence there. I don't want the Mexican folks thinking they're being invaded. I also don't want it known that we're there to search for a lost shipment of silver."

"Because I had not met any of you before, I did not come up with a definitive answer as to our cover story and ask that if any of you have suggestions, I'd like to hear them."

"I think we should enter as a traveling evangelism show," Morgana said. "I believe that Pastor Brinkman and I could front that purpose and the others could fill in as traveling companions."

Nik looked over at Roger with a 'What do you think?' expression. Roger just shrugged.

Morgana Cabezon then gave a brief explanation as to her background, including her knowledge of Mexico. She said the Mexican populace are people of faith and would likely welcome having a revival, of sorts.

"It could just work," Roger said, looking at Nik. "I'm not sure about Morgana, but I've had plenty of experience with setting up my church for a day and then moving on to the next site."

"The sooner we settle this and get started, the better," Nik said. "Miss Cabezon, why don't you, Roger, and I spend a little time discussing this?"

"You other men can go into town and buy some civilian clothes for yourselves. I'll give you authorization to purchase what you need and settle up with the storekeepers afterward. Perhaps Miss Cabezon can give you some advice on the appropriate dress for Mexico and the Sierra Madre Mountains."

After offering her suggestions for proper attire, Morgana and the Brinkman brothers departed to discuss strategy.

Nik decided against Judge Conklin's suggestion of going in as a surveying party because of the instruments and expertise involved.

There was a briefing room next to Colonel Jamison's office where the three could meet. They sat down at a small table, and Nik opened the discussion.

"So, Morgana, let's hear more about your revival plan."

"The Roman Catholic Church has spent much time converting the souls of Mexico, so the people there are familiar with your religious history," Morgana began. "Although very few revival groups have ventured south of the border it's because of the language barrier. If Señor Brinkman can deliver the message to the people, I can translate into their native tongue."

"Have you been to one of these revivals before?" Roger asked Morgana.

"No, but I learned of them from my mother when I was younger."

"I attended one of these revivals while I was in the military," Nik said. "But I did not pay much attention as to how it operated. I just know it was in a big tent."

"A tent is not necessary in Mexico," Morgana replied. "We can use the wagon or even get up on a high place to speak. Our gatherings will not be that big, unless we enter a larger city."

"Anything's possible," Nik responded. "What our purpose is, though, is to find that lost silver shipment."

"The revival will give you cover, so the folks are not suspicious of us. Some of the other men can spend their time among the people asking for clues as to where you should look," Morgana suggested.

"She has a point there, Nik," Roger offered. "The men can ask about the red balloon. That is probably the best clue we have as to where that shipment came down."

"Do you not think others who saw this balloon may have followed it into the mountains?" Morgana asked.

"I'm afraid that is a distinct possibility," Nik answered. "There was an original destination for the silver, and those who were expecting it may be on that trail as well. That's why we have to get this show on the road as soon as we can."

"Do you have an itinerary worked out, Nik?" Roger asked.

"I have to procure river rafts to transport us down the Rio Grande to Boquillas del Carmen in Mexico," Nik began. "We'll work our way in a southwesterly direction following the Sierra Madre range. Hopefully, we will eventually find someone who saw the balloon and in what direction it was headed. That's when we'll head into the mountains, if indeed that's where it came down."

"That sounds like a plan," Roger said. "If you're heading into El Paso to set up passage down the river, Morgana and I will put the final touches on our traveling salvation show."

"We'll have a meeting in this room with everyone at oh eight-hundred hours tomorrow morning for a briefing," Nik concluded. "Then we're on our way."

After Nik and Roger returned to their billets, Nik penned a letter to Esther, and Roger wrote one to Pricilla to tell her he would be out of the country for a while.

At the meeting the next morning, Nik and Roger briefed the soldiers, now in civilian clothes, on what the plan was. Lieutenant Gateway and Sergeant Davis were to accompany Nik in trying to solicit information as to the balloon's landing. Nantan and Morgana would ride ahead to survey each stop and report back on what to expect pertaining to the prospects of a revival. Roger and Carter would prepare for each show while Peter and Kelly concentrated on keeping the task force fed.

It took three river rafts to contain the expedition force. After rolling the chuck wagon onto one of the rafts, the crew chocked the wheels and then secured it with ropes lashed to the gunwales. Two crewmen were stationed on the raft to steer it clear of trouble.

The horses were loaded on the second raft, having extra high gunwales to keep he animals from falling overboard. A cabin was filled with hay and feed, and a trough was strategically placed to keep the raft balanced.

The lead raft, skippered by Scott Bancroft, was loaded with most of the supplies. It also had a tarpaulin that rolled up on the back gunwale. When unfurled, the tarpaulin could be stretched over half the raft serving as sleeping quarters for the task force and a crew that worked in shifts day and night.

The rafts were all tethered to each other with ropes. There were also planks onboard for when it became necessary for members of the crew to transfer from one raft to another.

Due to the additional modifications and accommodations, the tri-craft flotilla did not set out until late afternoon.

"Do you think this setup is going to hold together long enough for us to reach Boquillas?" Roger quipped to Nik, as the two sat near the gunwale of the lead raft.

"If it doesn't, we either swim for it or salvage what we can and continue on land," Nik answered.

"We should be okay," Captain Bancroft said, drawing near after hearing the Brinkmans' conversation. "This is not the first time I and my crew have done this sort of thing. The biggest problem is usually that one of the passengers falls overboard. The horses seldom do."

"So, you think we can make this trip inside of three days?" Nik said, acknowledging Bancroft's presence.

"As long as there is no trouble along the way," the skipper added. "The spring runoff has the river moving rapidly, but not treacherously. The Rio Grande is a good river to run. My men know these waters well and have no problem navigating them, even at night."

Later that evening, when everyone but the pole men guiding the rafts had secured a place to sleep, Roger had trouble falling asleep. It was almost as if the great river had soaked up all the sounds of the night. As his ears strained to pick up a sound, any sound, his efforts kept him awake.

While he was trying to clear his mind and doze off, he felt the raft tip a bit followed by the faint splashing of water. He remained still until he was certain something was in the water near the raft. He quietly moved out from under the tarpaulin to investigate.

There was no moon, so he could not see very well. Even the torches near the front of the raft did not provide much light. As he peered over the side of the raft into the water, he could have sworn someone was swimming next to the raft. As he labored to make out who, or what, it was, a hand reached up and grabbed the side of the raft. In an instant, Morgana's face appeared above the water next to the raft.

"Morgana?" Roger said in a subdued voice. "Is that you?"

"What are you doing there?" Morgana said, between breaths. "I thought you were asleep. Hopefully the others are not with you."

"Ahh, no," Roger said, looking around.

The pole man on Morgana's side of the raft called out in a hushed voice, "Is everything all right back there?"

"No problem, sir," Roger said. "I was just getting some fresh air." The pole man went back to watching the river ahead.

"Will you please go back to sleep so I can get out," Morgana said, in a slightly exasperated voice.

"Since I can't sleep, I'll do better than that," Roger replied. "I'll grab a blanket and hold it up for you to wrap yourself in. It's going to be pretty cold when you get out."

"Only if you promise not to peek," Morgan said, still submerged except for her head and arm, extended to hold on to the raft.

"It's too dark to see," Roger said. "If I peek, you can have me kicked out of the ministry." Roger pulled a blanket out from under the tarpaulin and held it up.

Morgana nimbly climbed onto the raft and wrapped the blanket around herself.

"Kind of a crazy time to go swimming, isn't it?" Roger chided.

"For me, it's a perfect time to bathe," Morgana said. "I was not about to try doing it in broad daylight."

"You've got a point there," Roger said. "Are you okay now?"

"Yes, please go back to bed," Morgana said. "That is precisely what I plan to do."

Roger was a little surprised to see that Morgana did not seem phased by the cool evening air on her wet body. He obliged and returned to his sleeping spot while avoiding her silhouette outlined by the raft's torch lights as she moved out of sight to wherever she had made her bed.

That little interruption of his evening was just enough excitement to give Roger what he needed to rapidly fall asleep.

The trip was largely uneventful, other than an incident when one of the horses leaped over the gunwale for reasons unknown. The horse was rescued and pulled back onto the raft with the others.

"We are approaching Boquillas del Carmen," Captain Bancroft called out. There was a small pontoon dock on the Mexico side of the river coming into view. It was apparently built for citizens of Boquillas and rafters like Bancroft. The pole men pushed the rafts toward shore and into calmer waters. Once the crews had secured the rafts, the horses, wagon and passengers were assembled just outside of the Boquillas del Carmen village.

"I will enter the village and take Nantan with me to talk to the inhabitants," Morgana said to Nik. "It's quite small and perhaps we can try out our spiritual revival there."

"Let me go with you," Roger suggested. "It'll help me to prepare as well."

"If it's all the same to you, Roger, why don't you stay here and help the rest of us set up a game plan?" Nik responded. "I think the rest of the group isn't quite sure how they'll fit into this. Besides, I doubt you will understand what anybody says there."

"That's a good point," Roger acquiesced. "Morgana, I'll take Nik's advice and help get this traveling salvation show up and running."

Boquillas del Carmen was a small mining camp consisting of tents, a small mission, and about two hundred residents, all of whom were miners.

"Nantan, let's visit that mission first," Morgana suggested. "I am familiar with the Catholic faith."

The Boquillas mission was run by Franciscan Friar Jorge Diaz. He told Morgana he'd been running the mission for more than twenty years and was quite at home in Boquillas. But he feared the small mining village would disappear once the silver mines ran out.

Speaking in a mixture of indigenous native tongues blended with Spanish, Brother Diaz explained that many of the young men were closely tied to the mission. However, he said the miners were a mix of American and Mexican treasure seekers and paid little attention to religion.

"We put on a small nondenominational outreach program aimed at spiritual inspiration," Morgana said. "Perhaps through our efforts some of the miners would be drawn closer to the Church."

"You are mestizo, are you not?" Diaz asked. "Are you Catholic?"

"As a child, I was raised Catholic," Morgana said. "But after losing my father, my mother placed me with the Chihuahua Apache where I became a shaman."

"And you do this revival you speak of?" Diaz inquired.

"I am used as a translator," Morgana said, glancing over at Nantan. "I translate for a Señor Brinkman, who is an American preacher. His faith is much like yours."

"I will encourage the villagers to attend," Diaz said. "But know that a Señor Ortiz is the boss of most of the miners and is a hard taskmaster. I know he discourages his men from even attending the mission. He wants them to work all the time."

"Does he own the mine?" Morgana asked.

"The mine is owned by a Señor Bacca," Diaz replied. "I believe Señor Ortiz works for him."

"That wouldn't be Marteen Roberto Bacca, would it?" Morgana asked.

"Si, I think that is right, but we do not see much of him," Diaz responded.

Relieved to hear that, Morgana thanked the friar and she and Nantan departed the mission. They spoke with some of the villagers to get a better feel for the place and then went back to the site where the task force was setting up camp.

Chapter 11
The Boquillas Revival

Morgana Maria Cabezon and Apache Indian Scout Nantan returned to find the camp singing 'Jesus Loves Me,' led by Pastor Roger Brinkman.

The two riders stopped just short of the camp until the singing was done.

"Welcome back," Roger called, while standing up in the chuck wagon with the canvas rolled up over the bows. "We're just practicing a song to liven up the revival, that is, if we're having one. What did you find out?"

"That you're going to have to sing better than that," Morgana said, laughing.

"Oh-oh, trouble?" Roger remarked.

"Not really, I am just having a little fun at your expense," Morgana said. "Actually, we spoke with the Franciscan friar there, and he said the men in the camp may enjoy a revival."

"What kind of camp is it?" Nik asked.

"It's a silver mining camp owned by one of Mexico's most notorious outlaws, Marteen Roberto Bacca, but he is not there," Morgana continued. "A man named Ortiz runs the operation for Bacca."

"Remember, our mission here is not to save souls," Nik said. "I suggest that we canvass the camp to see if anyone remembers seeing a large red balloon flying overhead."

"Morgana," Roger said, directing his attention to the shaman. "Why don't we work out a plan to 'entertain' the miners while Nik and some of the men do the questioning?"

"I think Nantan and I can mimic the language many of the men speak," Morgana said. "If you can do the speaking, I will be happy to translate for the men."

"I think Peter, Kelly, and Carter can assist with the singing to get things started," Roger answered. "Then Nik can do the questioning along with Walt, Beau, and Nantan."

Nik took Gateway and Davis aside to instruct them on what to ask and a story to use as a cover for the questioning. Roger, Morgana, and the three civilian-attired soldiers from Fort McRae laid out a salvation show for the miners.

The next morning, Morgana and Nantan again returned to the camp to prepare for the arrival of Roger's revival show. Since this was a typical workday for the miners, not a lot of men were still in the camp. However, since the revival was only an excuse as to why Nik and his task force were even in Mexico, Morgana and Nantan were not overly concerned.

"Only those who do not feel well or have been injured mining are still in the camp," Brother Diaz from the mission said, answering Morgana's question. "But that does not mean you cannot hold your mass for those still in camp. I would like to attend."

Diaz offered to have his acolytes spread the word among those remaining in camp about the coming revival.

"We won't have too much of an audience today," Morgana announced to Roger on her return, "but that gives us an opportunity to rehearse for larger shows later on."

"If I can get one convert I would be happy, Morgana," Roger replied. "I'm just sorry Nik won't have a lot of folks to talk to about the balloon."

"So, let's pack up and head into their camp," Roger added.

Roger, Morgana, and Nantan led the rest of the group as they traveled into Boquillas del Carmen. After reaching the camp, they dismounted and began to mingle among miners who were well enough to come out of their tents to see what was going on. With Morgana translating at his side, Roger did his best to encourage as many men as he could to join in the revival. After Peter and Kelly drew up in the wagon, the men from the camp began to gather around it. The two men and Carter rolled the canvas back over the bows and Roger took his place center stage standing in the wagon.

"Morgana, Nantan, let the men know we are going to sing 'Jesus Loves Me,' and any of the men who know the song are welcome to join in," Roger called out, holding his Bible to his chest.

As Roger led Peter, Kelly, and Carter in song, they soon realized they were singing alone while Morgana did her best to translate and Nantan performed sign language. Oddly enough, the miners grew more enthusiastic as they sang along.

"I do not recall seeing such a thing," Brother Diaz said, in answer to Nik's question about the red balloon. The two men were standing at a distance from where the ceremony was taking place. Meanwhile, Gateway and Davis visited several tents asking the same question.

Roger had launched into his sermon, speaking slowly and pausing to let Morgana and Nantan translate to the men as best they could. Some of the men would smile and nod their heads excitedly when hearing or seeing something they understood.

"I just talked to a miner who came up from Monterrey to work in the mine," Gateway said, after meeting up with Nik. "He did not see the balloon but said he overheard some people talking about just such a thing while he was in Monterrey."

"I would like to meet this man…" Nik started to say when a loud blast was heard coming from somewhere west of the camp. "What was that?"

Those who were gathered around the revival wagon got to their feet and started running in the direction of the explosion.

"I fear there has been an accident at the mine," Brother Diaz said as men hobbled past, some on crutches and some holding onto one another. "This is not an unusual thing."

"What's going on?" Roger called out.

"Roger, there's apparently been an explosion at the mine," Nik called back. "Take the wagon and head in that direction. Just follow these men."

With the assistance of Brother Diaz showing the way, Nik's task force soon left the slow-moving injured minors behind in their effort to reach the mine, which took the better part of an hour. When they arrived, dust and the smell of gunpowder were still in the air. Miners were still stumbling out of the mineshaft covered in dirt, some bleeding, and all coughing.

"Can we help?" Nik said riding up to the men. Some shook their heads and pointed to their ears indicating they could not hear.

"What can you do?" a man, appearing unaffected by the blast and standing nearby, asked.

"First, tell me what happened. What's going on?" Nik responded.

"We had a little accident," the man said, matter-of-factly, "nothing new."

"Is anyone still inside?" Nik said, raising his voice.

"Could be," the man said, "too dangerous to go in there right now."

"This is Mr. Ortiz," Diaz said to Nik. "He runs the mine."

"Do you have a first-aid station?" Nik asked. "Surely, you have some medical supplies on hand for just such a thing."

"The best I can do is get them cleaned up and back to work," Ortiz said, scowling in Nik's direction. "You can help to do that if you wish."

"What's going on?" Roger asked as he pulled up next to Nik.

"Just a mine explosion," Nik replied sarcastically, "nothing to see here—apparently."

Puzzled by the inaction, Roger hurried over to where many of the miners caught in the blast were standing, sitting, lying down, and helping each other. Roger called for Peter to bring the wagon closer and pull out some of the medical supplies. Nik, exasperated by Ortiz's attitude, joined Roger in helping the wounded miners.

Roger glanced over to see Ortiz talking to Morgana and Nantan. Morgana quickly walked away and began assisting the wounded miners. Ortiz continued speaking to Nantan, but the scout just shook his head and followed Morgana.

Shortly thereafter, the other miners from the camp arrived shouting as they approached the mineshaft. Their excitement grew as they heard voices coming from the deep cavern. The ones previously injured but still able lit torches and slipped into the darkness. A few moments after they entered, another rumble could be heard, and they hurried back out.

"Aren't you going to help them?" Gateway, who was attending to one of the victims of the explosion, shouted to Ortiz.

"What would you have me do?" Ortiz responded. "My job is to mine silver and these men are paid to do it. If anything happens to me, the whole operation would be shut down."

With that, Ortiz mounted his horse and rode back toward the camp.

"Can you believe that guy?" Nik said to no one in particular.

"I wish he'd come to the revival. It might have done him some good," Roger quipped. "By the way, Morgana, what did he say to you?"

"He wanted to know who I was," Morgana answered. "He is a dangerous man, so I did not tell him."

"What did he say to you, Nantan?" Roger said, turning to the Apache scout.

"He asked about Morgana, and I refused to answer," Nantan said.

"You're a good man," Roger said.

"By the way," Nik cut in, "Gateway said he spoke to one of the miners who overheard something about a red balloon when he was in Monterrey. Unfortunately, Monterrey's quite a ways down south, so this revival is over."

"Let's get some of these injured folks onto the wagon and take them back to camp," Nik continued. "We'll patch them up as best we can and then head south in the morning."

Morgana and Nantan explained to the miners what Nik had ordered, and then began their long trek back to camp.

In camp, Gateway took Nik and Morgana to the tent where he last spoke with the man claiming to have overheard talk about a red balloon when he was in Monterrey, Mexico. The lieutenant introduced them to a man who was nursing a sore shoulder he suffered while mining. Nik took off his hat before speaking.

"Mr. Gateway, here, says you overhead some folks in Monterrey talking about seeing a red balloon," Nik began, with Morgana at his side. "Can you tell me about it?"

The man explained that he had been in Monterrey about a

month ago and overheard a discussion about the balloon. When Nik inquired as to when the balloon was to have passed over, the man said he had not paid enough attention to the conversation to find that out.

"Ask him something about the men talking about the balloon," Nik said to Morgana. "Find out if what they were discussing had excited the men in any way."

The man shook his head in the negative when hearing the question from Morgana.

"I'm afraid he's not going to be much more help," Morgana said. "I also asked if the men mentioned they were in Monterrey when the balloon was sighted, but he said he knew nothing about that."

"That means they could have been anywhere when they saw the thing," Roger added. "However, if we end up in Monterrey without any more information than what we've got now, we at least know someone there was talking about it."

"I was hoping we wouldn't have to go that far south," Nik replied, "but I can't just ignore that possibility."

Nik thanked the man, and the group made another round through the mining camp to help the injured men. After that, they headed back to their camp by the river. There they found Peter busy preparing the evening meal, with Charlie Bluefeather's supervision.

"Where's Kelly?" Nik asked. "I thought he would be helping you."

"No, I thought he was with you guys," Charlie answered. "The last I saw of him was after we transported those hurt miners back to their camp. I figured he was helping them."

"I'll head back to locate him," Gateway said. "He may have gotten involved with something and got left behind."

Later, as the rest of the task force was eating Peter's prepared dinner, Gateway came riding up with Kelly riding on the back of Gateway's mount.

"I found him, Nik, but he's not in very good shape."

Nik got up to see what the problem was, fearing Kelly might have sustained an injury as well. When Kelly slid off the back of Gateway's horse, Nik could see he was drunk.

"Kelly, what the…" Nik sputtered. "How did you get …? Man, you're drunk."

"I'm sorry, Mr. Nik," Kelly said, maintaining his balance with some difficulty. "I wasss helpin' one of them hurt miners who pull… pulled out a bottle of wishkey to ease his pain and he offered me some. I said no," Kelly backed up one step to maintain his balance, "but he insisted. I am sorry."

"You're a volunteer, so there's nothing I can do to discipline you, but I'm not happy about this," Nik said with disappointment.

"If you wish, I can put this in a report to his commanding officer when we return to Fort McRae," Gateway offered.

"Thanks, Walter, but that's not going to help now," Nik answered.

"I'll look after him," Peter said, joining the conversation. "I knew he had a problem, but he's been a lot of help to me up until now."

"That's not a bad assignment for you," Roger chimed in. "It'll teach you what that stuff can do to a man."

"Come on, Kelly," Peter said to his inebriated friend. "Let's get you down to the river and sober you up."

"Carter, why don't you and I help get things cleaned up for Pete, so we can be ready to go in the morning," Charlie said to the young soldier.

"Good idea, Charlie," Nik said. "We need to get this show back on the road. We'll head for another mining camp in La Cuesta and continue our inquiry about that balloon."

Kelly was sober by morning and helped Peter and Charlie put together a small breakfast of bacon and biscuits, and soon the task force was loaded up and headed for the Sierra Madre mountains.

Chapter 12
Navigating the Sierra Madre Occidental

"I don't know what came over me," Kelly Laumpagh said, as he rode alongside Peter Zimmerman. "I volunteered for this trip thinking it would be a good way to avoid temptation, but I failed miserably."

"Yeah, Kelly, you did, but thank your lucky stars that Marshal Nik Brinkman is as nice as his brother when it comes to dealing with people," Peter responded.

"I do, Pete, but now knowing I failed, I'm afraid I might do it again and Marshal Brinkman might not be so kind a second time," Kelly said.

"You're just going to have to do a better job of looking after yourself," Peter replied.

"That's what I wish I could do, Pete," Kelly said, "but I think I'm going to need your help to stay out of trouble."

"Why, what can I do?" Peter asked.

"Just keep an eye on me," Kelly added. "Stay next to me so's I don't make that mistake again."

"Why don't you do this," Peter responded. "Why don't you stay next to me? That way you bear part of the responsibility for what you want. I'll watch out for you as long as you're close by, but I'm not going to have to track you down every time you wander off, like you did back in Boquillas."

"Fair enough, Pete," Kelly said. "I think I can do that."

"Just think of me as a shot of whiskey and that way you'll be tempted to stay close to me," Peter replied with a laugh.

Meanwhile, Roger was busy trying to teach the others another song. He went through refrains of 'Give Me That Old Time Religion' and 'Rock of Ages,' to get a feel for what the others could perform best. The vote was close, but the group settled on '… Old Time Religion.'

"I believe La Cuesta to be a mining camp as well," Morgana said, between songs. "Singing will probably attract them as much as anything else. It's too bad no one here plays a musical instrument."

"I do," Kelly called out from the driver's seat of the chuck wagon.

"You do?" Roger asked. "What do you play? Maybe someone at the place where we're going will have what you need."

"Oh, I brought mine with me," Kelly answered. "It's a mouth harp or harmonica, as some folks call it."

"Do you think you can pick up on one of the tunes we've been trying to sing?" Roger asked.

"I can try, assuming you folks are singing it right," Kelly replied.

"It's best that I hum the tune for you," Roger said. "I think our harmonizing leaves a little something to be desired."

As the team rode along, Roger rode next to Kelly and the chuck wagon as he and Kelly worked on mastering the music.

When the task force drew near La Cuesta, located in the foothills of the Sierra Madre Occidental range, they found a mixed population. Morgana discovered she could effectively converse with many of the villagers. The town did have two adobe buildings, but most of the natives lived in crudely constructed huts.

"These people are mostly of Tlaxcaltec and Apache heritage. They speak broken Spanish and Chiricahua," Morgana announced when she and Nantan returned to the group. "They're open to a revival meeting and will understand most all of my translation."

"What topic do you recommend for a sermon?" Roger asked.

"They're mostly hunters, so offer some blessing for the animals they hunt," Morgana said. "There are small children, so a blessing for them would also be good."

"We'll open with 'What a Friend We Have in Jesus,'" Roger said.

"We're able to stumble through that one pretty good now, and Kelly has picked up the tune on his harmonica."

The revival group was well rehearsed as they approached the crude village where they were to set up their meeting. The locals were quick to come out to greet them. They built several campfires around the perimeter of an area where the locals gathered to sit. The wagon was placed in front of them with the canvas rolled back.

"Morgana," Roger called out. "Let the people know we're going to sing a song for the children. Ask them to have the children come forward, and I will bless them each before I begin speaking."

The native population was delighted at the ceremony and eagerly brought their children forward for blessing. They all recognized Roger's crucifix as being similar to the ones the Franciscan friars would display when visiting the camp.

Nantan and Charlie Bluefeather brought one of the villagers up to speak to Nik, who was standing just on the outside of one of the campfires.

"This man tells us he has heard of the red balloon," Charlie said, introducing the man. "He mixes his words, but between us, I believe we can get the information you are looking for."

The man explained that a village located higher in the mountains, called Ocampo, had seen a red flying object a few months ago. He said the inhabitants were also native, but less civilized than those in La Cuesta. The country there was very mountainous and difficult to navigate with a wagon.

"However, there is a pass," the man said to both Charlie and Morgana, who translated. "There is a pass beyond that ridge and canyon river," the man continued, pointing toward the distant ridge. If you follow that you will come to Ocampo."

Nik thanked the man and then turned to Morgana and Charlie.

"It sounds like we should visit Ocampo, but we'll have to make our way up that canyon," Nik said. "Let's enjoy the rest of the evening but keep our ears open for any new information anyone might have."

After the sermon, Kelly again used his harmonica to get most of the 'choir' on key, and they closed with 'Give Me That Old Time Religion.'

The next day, the travelers headed due south and camped for the night at the foot of the mountains behind which lay the canyon.

"I wish I had a better map of these mountains," Nik said to those sitting nearby eating a meal of pork, beans, and potatoes. "Depending on the difficulty of getting the wagon up those hills into that canyon, I would hope to reach Ocampo by tomorrow or the day after."

"Unfortunately, I think the natives there could present another challenge to this expedition," Morgana said. "Some of the tribes in these mountains are still quite savage."

"Do you think we'll run into hostility?" Roger asked, looking over at the mestizo shaman.

"I cannot say for sure, but when the European explorers came through, they drove many of these natives into the hills," Morgana answered. "Most of them became warrior-like to protect themselves."

"The man in La Cuesta spoke as if the Ocampo natives were friendly enough," Gateway offered.

"They probably are," Morgana countered, "but they are probably not the only tribe of people in these mountains."

"The Apache have had encounters with hostile natives in the past," Nantan added.

"I have been told that the hostile natives live in isolated areas and have very limited contact with outside populations," Gateway continued. "For that reason, they do not trust outsiders."

"I have to admit I was afraid we might run into indigenous hostility," Nik chimed in. "We have dealt with many problems in the United States but have virtually no experience of what life is like in Mexico."

"I am sorry that I cannot offer more help," Morgana said. "Although I was born here, most of my time was spent among the Chiricahua Apache."

"No one here is at fault where our situation is concerned," Roger cut in, "but we are in this together and have to rely on each other for our safety and hopeful success."

"We're not here to make trouble for the people of Mexico," Nik said. "I suggest we concentrate on our mission to find the silver and avoid confrontation as best we can."

"I think this stage of our journey is going to tell the tale of our success or the lack of it," Davis said. "As soldiers, we're trained to deal with hostility either by force or diplomacy. Being in Mexico, I would say our first directive would have to be diplomacy."

"Well put, Sergeant," Roger said. "We've done a reasonably good job so far."

"Let's hope it continues to work, Roger," Nik said. "I can't think of a better approach. At least we haven't presented much of a threat so far."

"Like you said, Nik," Gateway responded. "It's best if we just stay focused on our mission and deal with each situation, come what may."

"It's best we turn in now," Nik said. "We'll start our climb into these mountains tomorrow and begin dealing with the first real situation coming our way."

The trek to the foot of the mountains did not last long before the task force entered an area that seemed to carve its way around the ridge described by the man in La Cuesta.

"It may be shorter to go up over the ridge, but I'm not sure the wagon would make it," Nik said to everyone in general. "I suggest we follow that depression around the ridge and hope it will lead us into the canyon that the man in La Cuesta described, unless someone has a better idea."

"I have to agree," Lieutenant Gateway said. "I think to try to go over that ridge would mean having to either take the wagon apart and carry it piece by piece over that ridge or leave it behind."

"Marshal, I suggest a couple of us add our horses to the wagon and walk," Sergeant Davis said. "This could prove to be a pretty steep climb."

After a brief discussion, Nantan and Carter Townsend agreed to do the walking. Nik and Morgana would take the lead, while Gateway and Davis rode alongside the wagon driven by Peter Zimmerman and Kelly Laumpagh. Roger and Charlie would follow behind.

The group entered the trees but found a passage through them that indicated others had traveled that way. When they came to a clearing, Nik stopped the procession.

"Morgana and I are going to split up and ride on ahead to scout

out the best direction to take once we cross this clearing," Nik said. "Before you come looking for us, give us at least an hour since this is not familiar terrain. Once you cross this clearing, wait there until we return."

Nik and Morgana galloped to the far end of the clearing, with Nik turning southwest and Morgana continuing straight ahead. It did not take long before Nik returned to the clearing.

"Has Morgana returned yet?" Nik asked, as he rode up to the wagon.

"Not yet, Nik," Gateway answered. "How does it look?"

"The canyon the La Cuesta man spoke of is just beyond the trees. Travel looks pretty good for at least another five miles or more. It looks like it gets a bit steeper after that," Nik reported. "I'm going to go after Morgana and let her know we've found a passage through."

After a brief ride, Nik came upon Morgana standing on a ridge overlooking the canyon.

"Are you okay?" Nik asked, as he rode up.

"Sorry, Nik, but I had forgotten just how beautiful this country could be," Morgana answered. "I just had to stop and take it all in. Did you find a way?"

"It looks pretty good the way I went. It will take us into the canyon and down by that river. I think we can follow it quite a ways before heading into the higher mountains," Nik said. "I have to admit, the view from here is amazing."

Morgana then mounted her horse, and the two returned to the clearing where Nik led the group into the canyon they would follow most of the day. After they reached the point where the wagon would have to climb again, Nik suggested they make camp and start out refreshed in the morning.

With a few hours of daylight remaining, Kelly, Peter, Carter, and Bluefeather decided to try their hand at fishing the river. In spite of seeing some small fish in the stream, they were unable to catch anything substantial enough to make a meal.

"Many of these streams dry up later in the summer so fish are not plentiful here," Morgana said. "The native tribes tend to create their own fishing areas that help to supply them with food."

Although disappointed, Nik promised the fishermen he would still whip up a batch of hush puppies to add variety to their usual meal of salt pork and beans.

"Say, Marshal, these hush puppies are good," Kelly remarked during dinner. "A lot like my mama used to make."

"Where are you from, Kelly?" Nik asked.

"From the Creole country of Lou-siana," Kelly replied. "There was nothing my mama could not make taste good."

"She sounds a lot like Charlie," Nik said. "He has that same knack, but with more of a western flair."

"Do you miss that part of the country?" Carter asked.

"I miss my family, but I think they are all gone now," Kelly answered. "I have not been back there since joining the army. I've gotten used to life in the high desert, although army cookin' doesn't compare to Creole."

"I would have to say that army cooking doesn't compare to anything that I'm used to," Nik said, with a laugh.

"Go easy, Nik," Gateway said. "At least we get three squares a day. Not everyone can say that."

"I can agree with that, Lieutenant," Kelly said. "At home, sometimes, we were lucky to get one meal a day. Depended a lot on our success at huntin' and fishin'."

"That worries me out here," Charlie said, looking around at the terrain surrounding them. "I am not familiar with what one hunts out here, and I now know the fishing is terrible."

"Morgana, Nantan, what is your take on edible game hunting in Mexico?" Nik said, addressing the only two familiar with the Central American country.

"The fishing and hunting was better in the Chiricahua area north-west of here," Nantan said.

"That part of Mexico and America has been fiercely defended by Chief Cochise," Morgana said. "The Apache there have learned how to live off the land, but his people have to fight with both the Americans and the Mexicans to maintain it."

"Did you know Cochise?" Roger asked, having heard that from

Carlos and the vision of a soldier he had. However, he realized Morgana had never mentioned it to him.

"I do," Morgana said. "He is a great chieftain among the Apache people."

"Listen, folks, it's great that we're getting to know each other, but let's remember our mission here," Nik cut in. "We're searching for a stolen silver shipment believed to be in these mountains. I'm hoping we learn about its possible whereabouts when we reach Ocampo. In the meantime, keep an eye out for anything that might resemble a red balloon."

After their supper, everyone went to bed except Nik and Roger, who stayed up chatting over the campfire.

"Do you really think we're going to find anything?" Roger asked.

"Roger, like me you have seen those chests and the balloon. My only hope is that I can gain enough information to satisfy the efforts of this task force. If we go back empty-handed, I at least want to give a good account of our attempt to recover that silver."

"I'll definitely pray on it," Roger replied.

"Thanks, Roger, and if Morgana is a shaman as she claims, see if she has had any visions concerning our goal."

"I'll do that, Nik. Did I mention to you that she may be the grand-daughter of Cochise?" Roger related to his brother.

"Is that important?" Nik asked.

"I don't know, but I have experienced powerful medicine from an Indian shaman before," Roger said. "There may be more to her than she has shown us so far."

"Right now, I'll take all the help I can get," Nik concluded, as the brothers laid out their bedrolls in anticipation of the morning's next adventure.

Chapter 13
The Friendly Natives of Ocampo

Marshal Nik Brinkman, Mestizo Shaman Morgana Maria Cabezon, and Mescalero Apache Army Scout Nantan rose early to search for a passage through the mountains to Ocampo. They came upon a footpath leading up the slope into the mountains but taking a wagon along the trail would be difficult—at best.

"We'll have to try and get the wagon as far up this mountain as we can," Nik said to Morgana and Nantan. "If we can't reach Ocampo with it, we'll have to find a safe spot to keep it."

"I'm afraid we are going to have to do much of our searching for the silver on horseback or on foot," Morgana replied. "We may have to use the wagon as a base to operate from."

"That's not a bad idea," Nik said as the trio reached the top of a treeless knoll, giving them a panoramic view of where the trail would lead them.

"If we can get the wagon down into that canyon below us, I believe there is a stream of water down there where we could leave the wagon," Nantan suggested.

"What makes you think there's water down there?" Nik asked.

"I can hear it," Nantan replied, "but it is hard to distinguish the sound of running water from the wind that is blowing through the trees."

"I think Nantan is right," Morgana offered. "There are sounds of running water if you listen closely."

"I'll take your word for it," Nik said, turning his horse back to return to where the others were breaking camp. "I'm too used to hearing the roar of the ocean to pick up on a stream of water."

"Let's head back and get this procession started."

When the three pathfinders returned to camp, they found that the remaining crew had already eaten and were preparing for the coming trip up the mountain. Nik, Morgana, and Nantan filled their plates and Nik, between bites, began discussing the next leg of their journey.

"It's doubtful we will be able to get our wagon all the way to Ocampo in one day," Nik began. "After our initial climb, we'll have to descend into a canyon a few miles from here. If we can get the wagon safely down that slope, Morgana and Nantan said there is a stream at the bottom where we may be able to set up a base camp. We can use that to coordinate our search for the silver. From there, we'll send a small party ahead to Ocampo and hopefully find someone who saw that giant balloon."

"Do we know that everyone up here is friendly?" Charlie asked as he climbed onto the driver's seat of the wagon.

"We don't know that," Nik responded. "I'm open to other suggestions on how to do this."

"Once we set up camp, Davis and I can establish the perimeter and determine if there might be any threats to contend with," Lieutenant Gateway offered to Nik. "Leave Kelly, Carter, and Peter behind just in case we have to defend ourselves from a possible attack."

"Solid idea, Walter," Nik said, as the task force began climbing up the trail. "We'll determine who goes on to Ocampo and who stays in camp once we find a place to settle."

The going was slow and required that the riders cut some of the foliage to allow passage of the wagon. It took the better part of the morning to reach the knoll where Nik, Morgana, and Nantan had discussed strategy earlier.

"The trail running down into this canyon gets a little steep in some areas," Nik said. "I want to check the brakes on that wagon and see if we can come up with an emergency brake system in case this thing tries to run away from us."

"I suggest most of us dismount and place some of the supplies inside the wagons onto our horses," Roger said. "I think it would help if we moved two horses from the team and tethered them to the back of the wagon to create drag. It might help if we keep two large rocks or logs handy to chock the wheels to help prevent a runaway."

"I'll take the reins of the wagon on this one," Nik said. "I don't want anyone else in the wagon if this rig takes off on us."

The precautions taken to make the trip into the canyon paid off, as the group reached the bottom of the canyon safely and with the wagon intact. The task force stopped for some nourishment and to survey the narrow path ahead to determine where it would take them next.

"Do we know for sure if this trail takes us to Ocampo?" Roger asked.

"Why don't you and Morgana continue to ride ahead and see where it goes?" Nik suggested. "I have to believe it leads to Ocampo, otherwise why would they have made it? It does look like it's been well traveled by those, whether on foot or horseback."

Roger and Morgana urged their horses and rode on ahead as quickly as the terrain would allow.

"I do not believe many horses have traveled this path," Nantan said, inspecting the trail more closely, "but some animals have used it."

"What kind of animals?" Carter asked.

"Not sure," Nantan replied. "I am not familiar with all the animals in these mountains."

"I can tell you that bears and big cats are found in these mountains," Nik cut in. "I read up a little on it before leaving Galveston. However, there are also deer and quail up here, which are good to eat."

"If they haven't already been eatin'," Carter quipped.

"We have plenty of firepower to deal with any 'dangerous' animals," Gateway said, smiling. "And you've been taught how to shoot, Carter."

As Roger and Morgana continued to explore the trail, they found a suitable place to set up the wagon as a base camp. It was an area where they would have to cross the stream to continue on the trail they hoped would lead to Ocampo. The two then rode back to meet the rest of the task force.

"The trail crosses the stream less than two miles ahead. There's a nice clearing at that spot, if we can get the wagon there it would be a good place to set up camp," Roger reported. "However, the climb gets pretty steep on the other side of the creek."

To get the wagon through to the site required widening the trail, but by late afternoon the group rolled into the spot Roger and Morgana had suggested as a base camp. On the east side of it rose a cliff wall about one hundred feet from the creek. That presented easy access to water, and the stone wall provided a natural defense on one entire side of the campsite.

"Walter, you and Beau can begin securing this area tomorrow," Nik told the lieutenant. "Roger, Morgana, Nantan, and I will follow that trail across the creek that hopefully leads to Ocampo. I can't say how long we'll be gone but will ask that you hold down the fort until we get back."

"I think we can fortify this site against any hostility that might be in the area," Gateway said, turning to survey the small meadow. "We've got the firepower to do that. But, more importantly, we should be able to turn it into a comfortable place to stay."

"It is peaceful here," Roger said. "As the days get hotter, these surrounding trees and nearby running water should keep things comfortable."

The following day, after a good breakfast, the four riders crossed the stream on their horses and headed up into the timber on the other side. They disappeared quickly into the trees and were completely out of earshot within minutes.

"Okay, gentlemen, let's get started on this place," Gateway said. "Charlie, why don't you and Kelly set up the kitchen, while Pete and Carter dig us a latrine well away from here. Beau and I will ride the perimeter to get a better idea of what's out there."

Davis took Peter and Carter downstream and located a desirable place to construct an undesirable, but necessary, facility for the crew. With the site being well away from the stream, the sergeant instructed the two young men to also create access to a spot where one could wash up before heading back to camp. After giving his charges the details on how to construct a latrine, the two soldiers were given the tools to complete the job.

"I'll be riding farther downstream and will spend the day exploring the area before returning to camp," Davis said. "Lieutenant Gateway will be riding upstream, and when we're done. We'll meet you back at the wagon."

The two men looked at each other knowing most of the day's work would be on their backs, but they accepted their task without complaint.

∗∗∗

The following day, it did not take Nik and his companions long before the trail they were following turned south, and the climb more gradual. As they cleared a stand of pines, they could see a small figure in the distance running in their direction.

"Hold up, it looks like we may be getting some company," Nik said, pulling back on his reins.

"We may be nearing Ocampo," Morgana said. "Whoever it is appears to be a runner or messenger, likely Raramuri."

"Likely what?" Roger asked.

"The Raramuri, a tribe that lives northwest of here," Morgana explained. "They are excellent runners and are often used as messengers."

"I'm wondering what kind of message he has for us," Nik said, pulling his pistol from its holster.

"Do not shoot him," Morgana cautioned.

"I have no intention of shooting him," Nik replied. "I just want to make sure he stops long enough to tell us if we're on the right trail to Ocampo."

"Let Nantan and me approach him," Morgana said, giving her horse a slight kick. "Nantan and I may be able to speak his language."

As they rode off, Roger was gazing at the vastness of the Sierra Madre range. "You know, brother, I don't know how in the world we're going to be able to find that silver in these mountains," he said.

"I've given that some thought, Roger, and I don't think we're going to. What I do believe is that someone has already found it and our job is going to be finding whoever that was."

"So, you think the idea that we might stumble across that silver isn't the plan," Roger remarked.

"Are you familiar with the term 'needle in a haystack?'" Nik said, gazing at the surrounding landscape. "At first, I thought someone might steer us to it. But now, I believe that someone was way ahead of us in trying to locate that shipment. Perhaps even Judge Kensington, for that matter."

"Considering all that he went through to steal that shipment, I would say you could be onto something," Roger said as the two men approached where Morgana and Nantan were speaking with the local native.

"We're only about an hour's ride from Ocampo," Morgana said, turning toward the two approaching riders. "This man is a commerce trader between Ocampo and Chihuahua."

"Just what is he trading?" Roger asked.

"Information," Morgana answered. "He negotiates what is desired between the two villages and then sets up a caravan to complete the trades. It's how he gets paid."

"Clever," Nik replied. "Did you ask him about a big red balloon flying overhead?"

"I did," Morgana said, "and it appears we're not the first ones who have asked him that."

Nik and Roger just looked at each other and nodded.

"Tell him that if he's following this trail he may run into our camp," Nik said. "If he does, have him let them know that we're on the right path to Ocampo."

"I'm afraid he does not stay on this path," Morgana said. "Chihuahua is west of here."

"Thank him anyway and let's get on our way," Nik said.

As the four riders approached Ocampo, they were surprised to see it was a quaint town with a few stores. They discovered it started as a small trading post with most of the goods being transported between Ocampo and southeast to Monclova. The residents of the village were a mix of mestizo, Spaniards, and Apache, with an encampment of Tepehuan natives to the west of town. The four horsemen stopped in what appeared to be the town square, dismounted, and tethered their mounts to one of the four hitching rails that fronted a small succulent garden.

"Ocampo will work in our favor," Morgana said. "There are many who speak my native language and the native tongue of Nantan's."

"What about that encampment on the far side of town?" Nik asked.

"I have to think someone in this town speaks their language," Roger said, smiling. "Who knows, someone might even speak English."

"Why don't we take Nantan and ride over there and find out what they know, Roger?" Nik said. "I have a feeling we have a lot to learn."

"What do you think, Nantan?" Roger said, turning to the Apache scout.

"I will go if you think it will help," Nantan responded. "If they have been influenced by the Spanish Church, they may speak English, as you say, Pastor Brinkman."

"That is a good point, Nantan. The Catholic Church has had a great influence on the natives of this country."

"What have we got to lose, brother?" Roger said, turning to Nik.

The three men entered what appeared to be a neighborhood separate from the rest of Ocampo. There were log and stick homes where some women were outside cooking over open fires. As the three men rode through the adjoining village, men began to emerge from the wooden huts.

"Does anyone here speak English?" Nik called out, standing up in his stirrups.

An elderly man approached the men. "I speak your language," he said.

Nik, Roger, and Nantan immediately got off their horses and removed their hats as a gesture of cordiality.

"We have come from America," Nik said, attempting to assimilate the man's manner of speaking. "We are in search of…" Nik turned to Nantan. "Do you think he would understand if I said, 'big red balloon?'"

"Say it and I will relate it with sign," Nantan replied.

Nik turned back to the village elder. "We are in search of a big red balloon … in the sky."

The elderly man watched as Nantan signaled Nik's words with his hands.

"I understand," the man said.

"Did you see it?" Nik asked.

"We know of this balloon you speak of," the man said. "It was a time ago."

"Where did you see it?" Roger quickly asked.

The man turned and waved his hand across the southwestern sky.

"This could be a breakthrough," Nik said. "The balloon apparently passed over this area a little south of here."

"How high was it?" Nik asked, turning to the old man.

The man did not speak but looked to Nantan to translate.

"He does not understand what you mean, Marshal," Nantan said.

"Without knowing the balloon's altitude, we can't know how far from here it may have come down," Nik lamented.

Nantan turned to the man from the village. "Do you know where?" he asked, accompanying his speech with sign.

The man nodded his head in the affirmative but with a strange expression on his face.

"Ask if he could take us there," Nik said to Nantan.

The Indian scout did as Nik asked, then paused. "He said he would but not without a favor."

"What favor?" Roger interjected.

"He wants us to kill something," Nantan said. "He wants us to hunt down a killer cat."

"A killer cat?" Nik interjected. "Can you get more information?"

After a lengthy discussion consisting of language exchanges and the use of signing, Nantan related what he had learned.

"It is a jungle cat that has become a man-killer," Nantan said. "It started when some men from the village went in search of the red balloon. After the men separated, the cat attacked one of the men. After a search to find him, they only found his remains."

"So, this cat actually ate this man?" Roger inquired.

"Apparently so," Nantan said, "but that's not all. It seems the cat has now snuck into the village and made off with small children too."

"This does sound serious," Nik said. "Why hasn't someone from Ocampo gone after this… cat?"

"Townspeople have little concern for the Tepehuan people," Nantan answered. "The Tepehuan do not have the weapons needed to kill the cat."

"What do you think, Nik?" Roger asked, turning to his brother.

"I don't see that we have much choice," Nik returned. "We need to find that balloon and, if these people know where it is, we're going to have to invade that cat's territory anyway."

"Why don't we send Nantan and Morgana back to the camp to make sure everything is okay there?" Roger said. "You and I can make arrangements with the Tepehuan to both find that balloon and that cat."

"That's a good idea," Nik replied, "but if we find that silver, we're going to need some help bringing it out. If Nantan and Morgana find our base camp is secure, they can return with Gateway and Davis and wait here until we return from finding that silver. Then we'll have what we came here for."

"Do you think Bluefeather and his crew will be okay on their own?" Roger asked.

"I have no doubts about Charlie," Nik said. "And the other three are soldiers. If the camp is secure, they should have no problem maintaining it until we get back."

After riding back into Ocampo, the three men found Morgana and related their plan. Following the departure of Nantan and the shaman, Nik and Roger returned to the Tepehuan village to lay out a plan to destroy the cat and recover the silver.

Chapter 14
Big Cats, Balloon Scraps

Before leaving Ocampo and returning to the task force's base camp, Morgana introduced Nik and Roger to Mateo Valencio, who could translate Tepehuan into English. After offering Mateo compensation for his services, he agreed to be part of their journey to find the red balloon. He hesitated when Roger mentioned going after the killer cat the Tepehuan villagers mentioned. Roger convinced Valencio he would be in no danger by trimming small limbs from a nearby tree with his Winchester, at Valencio's request.

"Do you think our Winchesters will be enough to kill that cat, whatever it is?" Nik asked.

"Not knowing what we would be up against on this trip, I brought along my .45-70," Roger answered. "Between the two of us, we should be able to stop this thing if we can get a clear shot. I'm thinking it can't be anything like the cats you hunted in Africa."

"I still don't like interrupting our hunt for the silver just to convince our guide it's safe enough to take us to that balloon," Nik lamented. "However, the Tepehuans may just help save us from a long and fruitless search."

Along with Valencio, the Brinkmans returned to the Tepehuan village to learn more about what lay ahead in their search for the silver. Most of their discussions were with an apparent tribal chieftain called Pawhetah, who indicated the Tepehuan natives had led another group of men to the site where the downed balloon was found.

"You took someone else to the site?" Nik asked Pawhetah, directing his question through Mateo.

After listening carefully, Valencio said "It was Marteen Roberto Bacca, a very notorious outlaw in Mexico. Apparently, Marteen and some of his men forced the villagers to guide him to the spot where the balloon went down."

"Ask them what they found," Nik asked. "Did they take anything?"

After consulting Pawhetah, Mateo said "They do not know. During the trip, they lost one of their men to the great cat. They tried to rescue him, and when they returned, Marteen and his men had departed."

"Great, this means we may be on a wild goose chase," Nik said.

"Not necessarily," Roger responded. "If we can kill that cat, we will have done a good service for these people. And, even if we don't find that silver, we can take back remnants of that balloon to prove we found it. That may not make your superiors happy, but at least it will prove we found the balloon and allow us to get back to our regular lives."

"I guess you're right, Roger. Looking on the bright side, if this Bacca character did gather up the silver, we won't have to lug it out of these mountains."

The tribesmen invited Roger and Nik to stay in the village that night to get an early start in the morning. From their discussions, Valencio estimated the excursion would take about three days. Through Valencio, Nik told the villagers more of their colleagues may arrive before their return. He instructed the Tepehuans to request that the visitors wait in Ocampo until Nik and Roger got back.

In the morning, Nik, Roger, and Mateo rode their horses while the villagers walked on foot. Pawhetah rode a burro, with a second one in tow carrying supplies. The first two miles of travel were easy enough, but they eventually came upon a deep canyon with a narrow trail cut into its wall on which the party would have to descend.

Before continuing, Pawhetah pointed out that the area on the opposite side of the canyon was where the downed balloon came to rest. As for the cat, no one could say where they might meet up with it.

"Since they really don't know where we can find this marauding cat," Nik said to Mateo, "ask Pawhetah if we can go to the balloon site first and then look for this killer animal."

After Mateo relayed Nik's message to Pawhetah, the villagers talked among themselves before answering Mateo.

"They are afraid that if they take you to the balloon first, you will abandon the hunt and not keep your word," Mateo said to Nik and Roger.

Nik looked over at Roger. "There is no telling how long we'll have to look for that cat," he said. "I need some assurance that they understand the balloon they speak of is what we came for. I can't waste the government's time looking for something we may never find."

Roger paused for a moment and then turned to Mateo. "Tell them I am a powerful shaman and I have given my word to kill the cat," he said. "If I fail to do so, my spirits will strike me dead."

"Wait, are you sure you want to tell them that?" Nik objected.

"Nik, it isn't worth arguing with them about this. If what they lead us to turns out not to be the balloon, I'll take the responsibility of going after that cat while you and the task force continue searching for the balloon that carried off that silver."

"That won't get you in trouble with Heaven, will it?" Nik asked.

"Nik, I'm already in trouble with Heaven," Roger replied, chuckling. "Ridding these villagers of that killer just might help get me off that hook."

Nik laughed and instructed Mateo to relay Roger's offer. After conferring with his fellow villagers, Pawhetah told Mateo Roger's offer was accepted.

The trip into the canyon prompted Nik and Roger to dismount and lead their horses on foot. Mateo remained mounted and seemed quite comfortable with his horse's ability to navigate the trail.

There was a swampy meadow at the bottom of the canyon but no flowing water. The villagers kept Nik, Roger, and Mateo on dry ground crossing the meadow before starting up the opposite side. The opposing side, fortunately, was more like a steep hill than a facing cliff.

After continuing to climb for nearly two hours, a loud growling roar was heard, causing several birds to fly from the tops of nearby trees. The villagers stopped immediately, as did Nik, Roger, and Mateo.

"Whatever that was," Roger said, "makes me think we may not have to go looking for that cat after all."

"I don't believe I've ever heard anything like that," Nik chimed in.

"Jaguar," Mateo said, almost to himself.

"Jaguar. I've heard of those," Roger said. "What do you know about them?"

"Very powerful cats," Mateo said. "They are rarely seen unless they intend to attack. Fortunately, they rarely do that, but for unknown reasons, one has been raiding the Tepehuan village. To my understanding, it has not been seen in Ocampo."

"I guess we've got our work cut out for us, Nik," Roger said.

"I wish we had more experience hunting these things," Nik replied. "If this one is a man-killer, my guess is we will see it before this journey is concluded."

As evening descended on the travelers, they made camp and the villagers built a large fire and attended it.

"The cats do not like fire and the villagers will take turns keeping that fire going as long as they think that jaguar is on the prowl," Mateo said. "You can sleep easy but keep your rifles handy."

"Sleep easy?" Nik replied. "Roger, did you hear the sound of that thing?"

"I've been told they are in the lower part of the New Mexico Territory," Roger said, turning to Nik with a slight smile. "And I can't say that I'm sorry that I have never seen one."

"I've got an uneasy feeling that our luck is going to change on this trip," Nik said, half to himself.

***

Morgana and Nantan arrived at the base camp to discover Lieutenant Gateway and Sergeant Davis had created a living space more accommodating than anything they'd seen in Ocampo.

"Very efficient," Morgana said, as she dismounted. "I have to admit that your military expertise would be useful in some of the Apache villages I have visited."

"The Army has learned a great deal about nomadic life from the Indian," Gateway responded. "We combine what we learned with what we know and that way we avoid trial-and-error bivouacs."

"Have you had any trouble or unwanted visitors?" Morgana asked.

"We found a trail that leads to the top of the cliff behind the mess wagon," Davis said. "From that vantage point, we can visualize the perimeter above the surrounding trees. One sentry is all that's needed and, so far, there has been nothing to see."

"That's good news because Nik and Roger are going to need our help," Morgana said.

"I take it they're still in Ocampo?" Gateway asked.

"They are, and Nik sent us back to get help," Morgana continued. "They believe they are on the trail of that red balloon. If they recover that silver, they're going to need help bringing it out."

"I think, with Charlie's help, Pete, Kelly, and Carter could hold down the fort here," Gateway said, looking to Davis for confirmation. "That way the sergeant and I could go back with you."

"We haven't encountered any real threats on this entire trip," Davis offered. "These men are soldiers and have plenty of supplies. Just how long would we be gone?"

"I think four or five days would do it," Morgana said. "There are some Tepehuan villagers near Ocampo who apparently know where that balloon is. If Nik and Roger confirm that, then all that's needed is to carry out that silver shipment. Although I don't know how difficult the terrain is where it's located."

"Should we take extra horses?" Davis asked.

"That would be a good idea," Nantan remarked. "Finding the silver may be the easy part, bringing it out, another matter."

The campers then prepared for the four to depart in the morning. Gateway spoke with Bluefeather, while Davis gave Peter, Kelly, and Carter final instructions concerning camp security.

***

There was a heavy mist hanging over the treetops when Nik and Roger woke up the next morning. The Tepehuan natives had kept the fire going all night but seemed anxious about something. They dined on flatbread and dried meat that neither Nik nor Roger recognized, but the flavor was good.

"What are we eating here, Mateo?" Roger asked.

"I don't know for sure," the translator responded, "but if the natives eat it, you can be assured it is okay. It's probably best that you don't ask what it is."

"I think Charlie would like to have this recipe," Nik joked.

"My guess is, he could even improve on it," Roger replied. "Although I have to admit, it is quite tasty."

"Kind of like the first time you tried rattlesnake, right, Roger?" Nik said, with a chuckle.

"It's all just a matter of keeping an open mind," Roger countered.

After breakfast, the Tepehuan hesitated to move forward.

"What's the holdup?" Nik asked, speaking through Mateo.

After a brief conference with the natives, Mateo answered. "They do not want to lead. They fear the big cat may be lurking about."

"If they don't lead, how are we going to know where we're going?" Nik said.

After another conference with Mateo, it was agreed that the Tepehuan men would take turns leading, but only with Nik and Roger riding on either side of them.

"I guess that will work," Nik said. "Are you okay with that, Roger?"

"It's not an effective way to hunt, but since we do not know the terrain, I don't think we have much choice," Roger answered.

After extinguishing the fire, Pawhetah rode his burro forward and motioned for Nik and Roger to bring their mounts to his flanks. Both men had their rifles in one hand resting across their saddles.

The climb before them seemed interminable, but the group's progress was steady and soon they entered a clearing and stopped to discuss certain details about the landscape and the best direction in which to go. What the villagers feared was a small canyon they had to pass through before coming upon the site where the red balloon came down to rest.

"Since there's only one way through that canyon, Roger and I can lead," Nik assured the native leader. "Once on the other side, we'll bring you up with us. I'm hoping we can reach that site with enough daylight to find that silver before dark."

"Even if we find it, it may be too much for us to haul back," Roger said.

"My fear is those chests broke open and that silver was scattered," Nik replied. "If that's the case, we'll need everyone to try and recover it."

"You do need a more positive attitude, brother," Roger chided. "I was just beginning to enjoy this trip."

"I just have an ill feeling about all this, that's all," Nik said. "But I'm glad you're enjoying it, and I hope your attitude is the one that plays out."

After coming to the canyon that had the Tepehuans suspicious, Nik took the lead. Roger rode behind the group as they slowly made their way through two towering cliffs with all eyes searching the rocky crags for any signs of a cat. Roger began singing one of the songs they had used at their revivals.

"What are you doing, Roger?" Nik shouted back over his shoulder.

"Noise just might frighten that cat away. I would not want to have to shoot with all of you in front of me," Roger called back.

"I have to admit, with the trouble you have carrying a tune it is frightening," Nik laughed as he spoke.

"It's beautiful music in the Lord's ears, no matter what you think," Roger remarked. "Besides, we can use all the help we can get."

Whether it was the song or the message, the group made it through the canyon without incident. After another short climb, they came up to an area where red material could be seen hanging from the trees.

"Glory hallelujah," Nik called out. "Eureka, we have found it."

After examining the red material, Nik was convinced it was the site where the balloon carrying the silver struck the ground. There were pieces of red material scattered over a large area.

"We have to find the basket," Nik said. "My guess is the two men had hauled the two chests of silver up into the basket to decrease drag."

"Even so, the basket should be somewhere farther down the slope," Roger said. "It would likely have hit the trees first."

"That's what I was afraid of," Nik said. "That would mean an impact at that height and speed could have broken open those chests and scattered the silver."

"That silver would have been in ingots, not coins, right?" Roger said. "Wasn't it on its way to the U.S. Treasury to be converted into money?"

"I regret I never saw the silver itself," Nik said. "But it was on its way to Washington. I would guess we are looking for bars about the size of your hand."

After studying the terrain to determine where the pilot's cabin would have come down relative to the balloon's remnants, Nik and Roger told the others to make camp while they worked their way down to where they believed the silver might be. Somewhat to their surprise, the natives refused to be left behind without the security of the two Brinkman brothers.

"They are really afraid of this jaguar," Mateo said. "I think the two of you had best get used to having them under your feet."

"I guess that was our part of the bargain, Nik," Roger said. "If we find that basket, you take half of them, and I'll take the other half to help us look for the silver."

"Let's hope that cat shows himself soon," Nik replied, "I'm not used to having this much company."

The group worked their way down the slope and finally came across material from the pilot's cabin. Following the trail of debris, they eventually came upon a tree where a large portion of the basket had lodged itself in the limbs.

"I don't see the ropes they used to pull those chests of silver out of the bay," Nik said, looking up at the basket in the tree. "I'm going to have to climb up there and see if I can find anything."

"Your boots are not built for tree climbing," Mateo said. "Please, let me climb up there instead. Just tell me what you're looking for."

"Anything that looks like a chest, or bars of silver," Nik said. "I have to know if that silver is anywhere around here. It may very well be that this Marteen character found it ahead of us."

"We'll scour the area just to make certain and then camp here for the night."

Meanwhile, Mateo climbed up to what was left of the pilot's cabin lodged in the tree.

"Nothing up here. There are some pieces of broken rope," Mateo called down. "Looks like maybe they were attached to something that broke off."

"Either the silver or they were attempting to snag something and slow them down," Roger mused out loud.

"Let's gather up some of this balloon material to take back with us, anyway," Nik added. "When we break camp in the morning, we'll head back in the direction where this debris seems to be scattered."

The Tepehuan natives helped gather the red material, and then the group found a nearly level area to camp. The natives again began to build a large fire when another chilling scream-like roar was heard, similar to the evening before.

"I do believe that animal has been stalking us," Roger said. "It may be keeping its distance just waiting for one of us to get separated from the others."

"I've always enjoyed hunting," Nik said. "This brings back distant memories of hunting in Africa. You could never tell if you were hunting or being hunted. Not knowing is what cost my father his life."

"You don't suppose that creature could be after our food, do you?" Roger quipped.

"No, it's concentrating on those eating that food," Nik countered. "You might want to say a few prayers tonight and request a safe journey back."

Chapter 15
Be Careful What You Promise

The Tepehuan natives kept the fire burning throughout the night through a genuine fear that the jaguar was stalking them. Roger and Nik stayed up a bit later to discuss strategy. "Mateo, talk to Pawhetah and see if there isn't another way out of here by going around that canyon we passed through on the way up," Nik asked. "I have a fairly good idea in what direction that balloon was traveling, judging by how the debris was scattered."

"What about our promise to hunt down that man-eater that has these natives so afraid?" Roger queried.

"We don't know that it's in that canyon," Nik answered. "There were no signs of it when we passed through it two days ago. Angling more to the southeast with this group may prove better hunting."

"Pawhetah said there is another way to go but it will take us longer. And, some of the natives object to it," Mateo added.

"Why, are they anxious to get back?" Roger asked.

"No, the other way back was where their companion was killed when they were last up here," Mateo answered.

"There you have it, Roger," Nik said, smiling. "I may be able to find some silver and you may be able to get a shot at that cat."

"How are we going to convince the reluctant Tepehuans to take us that way?" Roger asked, speaking to Nik.

"We've got the guns, and we can't kill that cat for them if we can't find it," Nik answered.

"That makes good sense," Roger quipped. "Mateo, tell Pawhetah that the new way is the way we are going to go and they're welcome to go with us. Reluctant or not, I've got a feeling they'll go along with our plan."

The Tepehuan group did grumble but soon agreed to take the expedition in the direction Nik requested. With the matter settled, the men retired for the night with the natives volunteering to keep the fire going.

In the morning, the air was heavy with humidity. The treetop cloud cover had moved into the canyon below them. The Tepehuan natives were busy talking among themselves, discussing the best way to return to satisfy both Nik and themselves.

The breakfast was again simple fare that was edible despite the fact Nik and Roger were not used to it. They had not suffered any ill effects from it, but both agreed their digestive systems had trouble adjusting.

The Brinkmans and Mateo Valencio saddled their horses, and the Tepehuans loaded supplies onto the pack burro. They would again ride with Nik in the lead, and Mateo directly behind riding alongside Pawhetah on his burro. Roger followed directly behind the procession with his rifle across his saddle.

"Let's take it slow because I want to scour the ground in case any of that silver was left behind. However, my guess is that outlaw Marteen got it all," Nik said.

"Which means you can't go after him because you do not have jurisdiction in Mexico, right?" Roger said.

"That is true, but I would like to be sure he has it before asking the Mexican government to extradite him and return the silver," Nik countered, as the men lined up in single file.

The Tepehuan leader offered directions to Mateo, who passed them on to Nik. Meanwhile, Nik kept his eyes trained on the ground, hoping for a possible flash of light reflecting off a bar of silver.

The new route leading off the mountain was not as difficult as the climb up, but it was the longer way to go. While Nik was leaning over and peering at a slight glint that caught his eye, his horse suddenly reared up and twisted, throwing Nik to the ground.

Nik's horse broke into a gallop back up the slope, as Roger reached for its reins. Mateo's horse also balked and began to back up.

Unhurt, Nik started to struggle to his feet when he was knocked to the ground by a large cat that managed to rake its claws across Nik's back. Hearing the unmistakable snarl made by the cat as it turned to attack Nik again, Roger immediately stopped his mount from pursuing Nik's horse and jumped to the ground.

Nik managed to pull his pistol and shot at the attacking animal to slow it down. Roger recovered in time to bring down the cat with his first shot. When it tried to rise again, he finished it with a second shot.

The Tepehuan men had scattered but stopped when they heard the shots. Mateo was able to get his horse under control and dismounted. He and Roger approached the large cat lying less than a foot from where Nik sat trying to regain his composure.

"Thank God you're such a good shot with that thing," Nik gasped, realizing what had just happened.

"Thank God you're still alive," Roger said, approaching his brother. He poked the cat with his rifle, but it did not move.

"It is a jaguar," Mateo said, peering down at the carcass.

"I'll help Nik," Roger said. "Mateo, why don't you go after our horses?"

"Let me take a look at you," Roger said, helping Nik to sit up.

Nik let out a groan. "It's my back. I think it got me there."

"I'll say it did," Roger replied, seeing that the back of his shirt was shredded. "Someone find that pack burro and get something to cover Nik's back with," Roger called out.

"Can you get up?"

"Yeah, I think so, with a little bit of help," Nik said, as he reached out to grab Roger's forearm to help pull himself to his feet. Roger led Nik over to a large rock for Nik to sit on. The natives slowly began to return, talking excitedly and pointing at the dead jaguar. However, they refused to approach it.

The Tepehuan leader took a piece of pottery out of the pack burro's pannier and handed it to Roger.

"What is this?" Roger asked, trying to communicate with the Tepehuan without Mateo's help.

Pawhetah gestured applying its contents to Nik's wounds. Roger smelled it and quickly threw his head back.

"Whew, this smells terrible. What is it?" Roger demanded rhetorically. Again, Pawhetah used his hands to mimic smearing the gel on Nik's back.

"Here, you do it," Roger said, handing the pottery back to the leader.

Pawhetah did as asked and dressed Nik's wounds with the foul-smelling salve. Nik let out a groan as the native applied the balm, but it soon began to take effect.

"I have to admit, that stuff feels a whole lot better than it smells," Nik said, with a slight smile.

"A kick in the head would feel better than that stuff smells," Roger replied.

"I'm afraid you've had it too soft, brother," Nik said, chuckling. "You're not used to roughing it."

"Me?" Roger responded. "You're the one that lives in Galveston. I ride circuit in the New Mexico Territory."

While they were wrapping a cloth around Nik's torso, two small jaguar kittens emerged from the brush and attempted to wake the fallen adult jaguar. The Tepehuan natives again began pointing and talking excitedly.

"Oh, oh," Roger replied, "that jaguar was a mother, apparently."

Pawhetah began gesturing to Roger to shoot the kittens.

"I don't want to shoot them," Roger said. "They're too small to hurt anyone." Mateo rode up with two horses in tow just as Roger was speaking. He dismounted and approached where the men were gathered around Nik.

"I see where the madre has company," Mateo said. "It is best to shoot those kittens. They cannot survive."

"I can't do that. Killing their mother was bad enough," Roger protested.

"He's right, Roger," Nik said, looking up at his brother. "If she's been feeding them human flesh, they will grow up to be man-killers also."

"Then you shoot them," Roger said.

"I can't hold my rifle steady with my back torn up like this," Nik replied. "It needs to be a clean kill, and no one is better at that than you."

"Damn," Roger said under his breath, and stood looking down at the ground. After a brief pause, he retrieved his rifle and destroyed the two small jaguars. He then turned away and walked a few paces into the forest whispering to himself.

Once Nik was feeling strong enough to mount his horse, he rose to his feet and turned to Mateo.

"Tell Pawhetah that we can go back through that canyon now," Nik said. "I think we're done here, and I doubt we're going to find any silver."

The men changed course but still entered the canyon with caution. Once on the other side, the Tepehuan natives were satisfied that the Brinkmans had fulfilled their promise.

Chapter 16
Tracking Down the Silver

Nik Brinkman rode easy in the saddle, belying the jaguar's slash wounds on his back. He smiled frequently and often chuckled to himself.

"How are you feeling," Roger asked, riding alongside his brother.

"I know this will sound strange, but I have to admit I feel as good as I ever have," Nik replied with a smile. "I don't know what was in the salve Pawhetah smeared on me, but I have no pain to speak of."

"Mateo, do you know what was in the ointment that Pawhetah used to cover Nik's wounds?" Roger called back to the translator, who was riding alongside the Tepehuan leader.

"All I know is they use it for just about everything," Mateo answered. "I'm not sure it cures, but I know it does relieve pain."

Roger assumed the salve used on his brother's back likely contained a euphoric compound like that found in peyote. "I think you may be high on something, maybe peyote," Roger relayed to Nik. "I know the Mescalero Apache have used it before. I just hope it helps to heal your wounds."

"I don't feel like I'm drunk or anything," Nik said, turning to look at Roger. "How do I look?"

"Your eyes seem a little strange, but other than that you look okay," Roger replied. "Just keep me informed as to how you're doing because the side effects are not all good."

"I will," Nik said. "But for now, I never really noticed how beautiful this country is, don't you think?"

"It is," Roger remarked. "But then I've never seen it the way you're seeing it now."

Nik gave out a loud laugh at Roger's comment and continued to ride easy.

As the group entered the steep slope into the canyon that would lead to the narrow trail up the wall on the far side, Roger noticed that Nik had slumped in his saddle.

"Nik, are you okay?" Roger asked, looking at his brother with concern.

"I don't know," Nik replied. "I feel kind of sick to my stomach."

"Mateo," Roger called out, "tell the Tepehuan we are going to stop here to rest."

Roger slipped out of his saddle and helped Nik to do the same.

"Are you in pain?" Roger asked.

"A little," Nik said in a weak voice. After taking a few steps, the marshal doubled over and vomited.

Pawhetah said something that caught Roger's attention, although he did not understand what had been said. Roger helped Nik to lie down next to a tree.

"The chief said the medicine made him sick," Mateo said. "It will wear off before long."

"I'm going to take a look at that wound," Roger said, kneeling beside his brother. "Sit up for me, if you would, Nik. I need to take your shirt off and check your bandage."

After slowly unwrapping the cloth from around Nik's body, Roger noted that the bleeding had stopped.

"Nik, Pawhetah said the salve he put on your wounds is what caused you to throw up. It looks like it did help to stem the bleeding and hopefully will speed up the healing. Are you okay with it if I apply some more?"

"Yeah, go ahead," Nik answered.

Roger asked Mateo to have Pawhetah put some more of his medicine on Nik's wounds but to ask him to apply a lighter coat. Pawhetah obliged, and Roger rewrapped the wound, only reversing it to avoid placing the bloody part back onto the slash marks.

After resting for an hour, Nik said he was ready to travel again. Some of the euphoria returned, helping Nik to feel stronger, even if he wasn't.

They reached the canyon wall that would take them up the ridge and eventually to Ocampo. Roger decided on a different strategy.

"Pawhetah, let Nik ride on the pack burro. We can put the pannier onto his horse," Roger said, directing his speech to Mateo. "The burro is more surefooted than his horse."

"Nik, are you okay riding the burro?"

"Sounds like fun," Nik said, smiling.

"Do you think you're strong enough to hold on?"

"I don't know," Nik answered, maintaining his smile.

Roger took a piece of rope from the pannier and tied Nik's arms around the neck of the burro.

"This isn't the most comfortable way to ride, but I'll feel a lot better about your safety," Roger said. "At least, until we reach the top of the ridge."

Pawhetah took the lead with Nik right behind and Roger following them. The Tepehuan natives traversed the rocky trail on foot, and Mateo brought up the rear riding his horse.

Nik began to hum softly to his burro but rode securely until the procession reached the top of the ridge.

"Mateo, do they have a doctor in Ocampo?" Roger asked.

"No, the nearest doctor is in Monclova," Mateo answered. "It is a three or four-day ride."

"Nik's in no condition to make that trip as of yet," Roger stated. "Is there a hotel or inn where we can at least have him rest and regain his strength to make that trip?"

"There is, Señor," Mateo answered. "It is not fancy, but it is clean. You can take your brother there."

"That should work just fine," Roger said. "Tell Pawhetah we are going to borrow his burro to go into Ocampo and find a place where Nik can rest."

Once the group returned to The Tepehuan village, the expedition natives began telling the villagers that the marauding jaguar had been killed. They kept pointing to Roger and excitedly explaining what had happened. When the native women heard what had happened to Nik, they immediately came to assist him.

"Ah, no," Roger protested. "I need to get him to Ocampo for rest."

The women continued to ignore Roger's wishes and untied the rope that had Nik tethered to the burro. After helping him off the animal they escorted him to one of their dwellings and took him inside.

"What are they doing?" Roger asked, turning to Mateo.

"They insist they know how to treat him," Mateo answered. "Pawhetah told me the same thing. These village women know how to care for wounds like your brother has."

"Mateo, do me a favor and stay with Nik," Roger requested. "I am going to go into town and see if I can't find some help that I recognize."

"Si, Señor," Mateo replied. "I will stay with your brother."

Roger quickly mounted his horse and rode into Ocampo to look for the cantina that Mateo had described to him. Much to his pleasant surprise, when he found it, Morgana was there with Nantan, Lieutenant Gateway, and Sergeant Davis.

"What a welcome sight you guys are," Roger said. "Nik has been mauled by a jungle cat and is in the Tepehuan village where some native women said they were going to look after him. I protested, but they ignored me."

"Take me to where they have Nik," Morgana said. "I am familiar with the kind of injury your brother has suffered."

"Great," Roger exclaimed. "I need someone to give me a better idea of how to care for him, at least until we get him to Monclova."

"Why Monclova?" Morgana asked.

"Mateo said there is a doctor there. I think if Nik can get back his strength he can make that trip."

"Please, just take me to him," Morgana insisted.

Morgana and the others followed Roger into the camp. After reaching the dwelling where Roger saw the Tepehuan women take his brother, he stopped and dismounted. Morgana and Roger entered, while Gateway, Davis, and Nantan stood by the doorway. Morgana knelt by the native women caring for Nik and was soon talking with them. She examined Nik, said a few words to the native women, and turned to Roger.

"Let us step outside for a moment," Morgana said.

After exiting the hut-like dwelling, Morgana said, "I think Nik is exactly where he needs to be. These women know what they are doing. I will stay with them, and I believe we will have Nik back on his feet in a day or two."

"Are you sure?" Roger asked. "I doubt there is a doctor among them, or even a trained nurse."

"Roger, these people have lived with these animals for centuries, and they know what they're doing," Morgana said. "I would guess you did not even know what a jaguar was until one attacked Nik."

"Well, not exactly," Roger said. "But I've seen mountain lions. Other than the spots, they seem similar."

"Did you shoot it?"

"Yeah, but it wasn't a gratifying experience," Roger started. "I had to shoot her two cubs, too."

"That was likely best," Morgana advised. "They probably would have grown up liking human flesh, like their mother."

"If you're sure about Nik..." Roger began.

"Trust me on this, white shaman. This is not a new experience for me. You and the others go on into Ocampo and get a room in the cantina," Morgana suggested. "Nantan will stay here with me. I'm not sure how friendly they would be toward Nantan there."

"Just keep an eye on Nik," Roger said. "I'll be back in the morning to see how he is doing."

Roger, Gateway, and Davis returned to the cantina and secured a room. It contained three cots to sleep on and access to an outhouse in the back. There was also a small eating area with one meal included with the price of the room.

For dinner, even though the proprietor and his wife did not speak English, it was not difficult for the three men to order. There was only one dish on the menu and fortunately for each, it was quite tasty.

That evening, Roger excused himself and went for a walk. He had spotted a small mission not far from the cantina and decided to go there and pray. The front door was open, so he went in and sat in one of the mission's pews.

He reached into his jacket and unbuttoned a special pocket he had sewn into the garment. He pulled out the white stone his sister had given him when he went away to college. He rolled it between his fingers and began to pray. As he was praying, the mission friar approached and said something in Spanish.

"I'm sorry, I don't speak your language," Roger said, looking up at the rather robust man clothed in a brown robe that hung down to the tops of his sandaled feet. A slightly ornamental woven cord girded his waist.

"I speak some English," the friar said. "I am Brother Bernardo. May I help you?"

"I am just here to pray, Brother Bernardo. I am content just being here."

"Are you Catholic? Do you need to be absolved?" Bernardo continued.

"I am not, Brother, but if you want to say a little prayer on my behalf, I would appreciate that."

"What are you praying about?" asked Bernardo.

"My brother," Roger said. "He was injured by a wild animal, and I'm praying that he heals and regains his strength."

"What is your brother's name?" Bernardo asked.

"Nik, Nik Brinkman," Roger answered.

The friar bowed and walked up to the altar in the front of the mission, kneeled, bowed his head, and began to pray.

"Thank you, Lord," Roger said quietly to himself. "I can use all the help I can get."

Roger continued his prayers until he heard the friar stand up and turn toward him. Brother Bernardo bowed slightly and then made his way over to a door located next to the altar and disappeared through it.

Roger sat staring at the elaborate adornments behind the altar and assumed they must have been placed there by the Spaniards, perhaps centuries earlier. He then whispered the Lord's Prayer, put his sister's stone back in his pocket, and made his exit from the mission.

The next morning, he and his soldier companions returned to the Tepehuan village to check on Nik. When they entered the village, they were surrounded by a large crowd smiling and speaking their language.

Roger dismounted to see what the occasion was, and several children showed him the small paws of the young jaguars he had to destroy. It was not something he wanted to see.

"They're celebrating to let you know they appreciate what you've done," Morgana said, making her way through the crowd. "You liberated them from a great fear."

"Somehow, I don't feel like being celebrated," Roger replied, looking up at the shaman. "At least not like this."

"There is more cause for celebration," Morgana added. "Your brother is doing much better and should be able to travel in a day or two."

"Now that is worth celebrating," Roger responded with a smile. "May I see him?"

"Of course, he's asking for you."

Gateway and Davis also dismounted and the four made their way over to the dwelling where Nik was taken. When they walked inside, Nik was sitting up and smiling.

The Tepehuan women who had been looking after Nik came forward taking Roger's hand, bowing, and saying something he did not understand.

"You're a hero, Roger," Nik called out. "Mine too, as well as these ladies and Morgana for the help they've given me."

"He's not still high, is he?" Roger asked Morgana.

"No, and I think we interrupted the peyote soon enough that he won't be wanting more anytime soon." Morgana answered.

Roger then went over to where Nik was seated. "So, if I'm a hero, what does that make you, the jaguar's trophy?"

"Not anymore," Nik said, laughing. "If I didn't know better, I would say my back is practically healed."

"That will take more time," Morgana said. "You are healing well but those gashes were deep. It's best you continue to rest for a day or two."

They decided to transport Nik to the cantina and let him convalesce there. Before leaving, Pawhetah asked them to remain for a village celebration as the guests of honor. Nik seemed to enjoy it, but Roger could not help but feel uneasy about seeing the paws of those jaguar cubs.

Chapter 17
Back to Camp

After being transferred from the Tepehuan village to a room in the Ocampo cantina, Nik was up and around by the second day. Although his wounds were still tender, he wasn't feeling any additional pain. Nik was anxious to get back to camp but Roger and Morgana convinced him to rest an extra day. They said if he was feeling strong enough in the morning, they would consider riding back to their campsite.

"Are you sure those guys are okay back at camp?" Nik asked, speaking to no one in particular.

"When we left, we had encountered no problems and Bluefeather and the others had things pretty well under control," Lieutenant Gateway answered.

"I have plenty of confidence in Charlie, and even Townsend, but Laumpagh's a bit of a loose cannon," Nik said. "You didn't leave any booze in the camp for him to get into, did you?"

"I think Ocampo is the closest place where one could buy it," Sergeant Davis said. "Otherwise, it would have to be a traveler passing through willing to sell him some whiskey."

"I hadn't thought of that," Gateway responded, "but no travelers passed by while we were there."

"I really would like to start back first thing in the morning," Nik said, "I'm starting to feel uneasy."

"You're taking on more responsibility than you have to, Nik," Roger said. "Kelly's drinking problem seems to be when he's bored, and I would think Charlie would have kept him busy enough in our absence. If Kelly did get into some liquor, the others would probably have thrown him in the creek to sober him up."

While the group was engaged in conversation, Morgana took the time to inspect the wounds across Nik's back.

"These gashes look like they're healing pretty well," she said. "But if they break open, they could get infected. If you try to ride tomorrow, take it easy."

"I don't plan to race any of you down that hill," Nik said. "I just want to get back and break camp so we can head for Monclova and find that silver."

"You will visit the doctor there, first," Morgana said. "You may be able to ride but you're in no shape to tangle with Marteen Bacca and his men."

"I don't plan to tangle with him," Nik said. "I'll make him an offer for the silver. If he refuses, I'll simply report back what happened to the shipment. The government can deal with Mexico after that."

It was agreed that the six would leave for camp in the morning to prepare for their trip to Monclova.

Morgana had been boiling some herbs she'd found, creating a solution she used to clean Nik's wounds. What she applied to his back did not affect Nik's sobriety but did seem to hasten the healing process. The next morning, Nik was up early and ready to return to camp.

The trip back down to the camp from Ocampo proceeded without mishap and the six travelers reached the camp in mid-afternoon. They were surprised to find no one was there.

"I'm surprised they would all take off," Gateway said, as he stood up in his stirrups. "I wonder if they're hunting."

Roger and Beau Davis looked inside the wagon to see if anyone was resting in there but found no one.

"Our weapons are missing," Davis called out.

Nantan climbed up to the top of the ridge at the back of the camp to see if there was a sentry on duty and found no trace of anyone having recently been there. Davis joined Gateway to make a quick survey of the perimeter around the camp and found no sign of the four men they had left behind after joining Morgana and Nantan on their return to Ocampo.

"They had been waiting for us for quite a while," Roger commented. "They may have gotten bored and started exploring the area."

"That would have been careless for Private Townsend to do that," Gateway said, after discovering parts of the missing rifles. "The guns have been smashed against the rocks of the cliff."

"Our ammunition has been thrown in the creek," Nik announced, as he searched for clues along the bank of the water.

"None of this makes sense," Gateway offered. "Three of those men were soldiers."

"There are signs that other men were here," Nantan said, returning from the ridge, "some barefooted."

"It appears as if there was an encounter with intruders," Nik interjected.

"It looks as if our men left with whoever it was that came into the camp," Nantan said.

"It appears that a band of native warriors may have taken our companions with them," Morgana advised, surveying the evidence. "For whatever reason, they only took the men and the horses, and not our supplies."

"Can we follow those tracks?" Nik asked, directing his question to Nantan and Morgana.

"The tracks are many," Nantan answered. "We can follow them if they didn't enter the creek."

"If they are on the march, Charlie will leave clues behind," Nik assured. "Besides, it looks like we'll be following a pretty large group."

"Unfortunately, we have only the weapons we took with us," Roger commented. "We don't know what this group may be armed with."

"Smashing our rifles and destroying our ammunition tells me their weapons are rather primitive," Gateway said. "I have to believe it's a rogue band of Indians or natives."

"Let's get some rest and start out following these tracks in the morning," Nik said. "We'll gather our supplies and leave the wagon here."

***

Bluefeather, Carter Townsend, Peter, and Kelly had grown restless waiting for the Ocampo group to return and began looking for ways to entertain themselves. It was not long before they stopped going up onto the ridge to keep watch or patrol the perimeter.

Kelly had hidden a bottle of whiskey in his supplies and smuggled it out to the latrine while the others were busy. He would occasionally excuse himself to use the facility and would enjoy a few swigs of liquor before returning to the camp.

Bluefeather suspected what the apprentice cook was doing but thought better of confronting him. Kelly's drinking habits were not causing any harm and his drinking did keep him quiet, most of the time.

The day after Gateway and Davis departed, Kelly visited the latrine only to find a band of painted natives waiting for him. Their skin was almost as black as his, but their hair was straight and cropped just above the shoulders. They gagged the soldier and tied his hands together. The marauders then quietly approached those remaining in camp.

Unawares, Bluefeather was back at the camp instructing his young charges on the Wichita method of cooking wild game. Before the three men knew it, the natives were upon them, threatening them with spears and clubs. Soon, all four of the men were in captivity. The captors removed the firearms from the wagon and destroyed them, along with throwing all the cartridges into the creek.

The captors tied the hands of their prisoners in front of them to allow them to scramble up hills where their hands were needed. The natives sprang easily up the hills, resembling deer running through the forest.

"It appears they know what our weapons can do, but they do not know how to use them," Carter said, as the band of raiders prodded the four men along. "That may be to our advantage when we try to escape."

"When we try to escape?" Peter asked. "How do you propose we do that?"

"It is our duty to do that," Carter replied. "But let's not say too much. Some of these people may understand English."

"What do you think they're going to do to us, Charlie?" Peter asked, turning to Bluefeather as the captives were hurried along.

"We can only wait and see," Charlie said in a lowered voice. "I'm not sure what they want from us, maybe to teach them how to ride the horses."

The natives were loosely dressed in fabric, with some wearing colorful robes over their shoulders. Their weapons were crudely fashioned with decorations attached. The unknown warriors were strong and short in stature. Some had their hair tied in buns and others wore decorative headbands.

"They wanted only us and our horses. They left everything else behind," Peter continued. "Why would they do that?"

"I know the American Indian," Charlie offered. "I do not know much about the people of this land."

One of the native guards walking nearby protested the conversation between Charlie and Peter, so both men fell silent.

At the end of the second day, the four men were led into a small village of crudely constructed huts, made largely from palmetto fronds. Many members of the tribe came out to welcome the warriors and their captives. They spoke a language that none of the four members of Nik's task force had ever heard before.

The four men were led into the middle of the village where the men, women, and children of the tribe gathered around to view them. The villagers were excited, but the strange language they spoke gave the captives no clue as to what was in store for them.

The warriors used gestures and threats to get the four men to sit down in the middle of the circle of humanity that stood around them. The crowd of natives then parted slightly as an elaborately dressed native wearing a large headpiece walked through to inspect the prisoners. He smiled broadly as he shouted at the warriors what appeared to be orders.

Eventually, the crowd grew quiet and began building what seemed to be a wooden wall around the men. After they finished, the wall of sticks and debris was set on fire. The four seated captives pushed themselves back and closer together, forming a quadrangle with their shoulders pressing against each other.

As the crowd around them began to chant, Kelly slowly moved his hand toward his shirt pocket. Suddenly the natives stopped chanting and began shouting what sounded like threats. The warriors thrust their spears into the air as they shouted. Almost as if hypnotized, Kelly reached into his pocket and pulled out his harmonica.

Two of the warriors facing Laumpagh stepped forward just as Kelly put the mouth harp to his lips and began playing.

"What are you doing?" Townsend asked in a near whisper.

Suddenly, the entire village quieted down and began turning to look at each other. Before long, smiles began to cross their faces. The apparent chief who wore the headdress began to give orders again. Soon, women came forward to pour water on the ring of fire.

"Whatever he's doing, don't stop him," Peter said, speaking nervously.

Once the fire died down, several warriors jumped the embers and pulled Peter, Carter, and Bluefeather to their feet. Another stood by Kelly, as the private continued to play. The chieftain shouted a couple more phrases and three warriors took Peter, Carter, and Bluefeather over the embers, through the crowd, and into the night.

Kelly, who stopped playing when the warrior closest to him grabbed his arm, was led over to where the chief was standing. Kelly still appearing in a daze, the chieftain was smiling broadly as Kelly approached.

The three men in the custody of the three warriors were eventually brought to a hut and led inside. They were ordered to sit down. The warriors went outside, two remained by the doorway and the third went back to where the crowd had gathered.

"What do you suppose is going on?" Peter said, loud enough for his companions to hear.

"It seems these people like Kelly's music," Bluefeather responded. "I am just glad he was sober enough to play. These people seem to respond to it."

"That's good for us, isn't it?" Carter said, directing his speech to Bluefeather.

"Time will tell. Time will tell," Charlie answered.

Charmed by the music, the villagers took Kelly to the chief's dwelling, a much larger and elaborately decorated dwelling than the other huts in the village. Going inside, the chief stepped onto a platform and sat down on a large, throne-like chair. He gave some more orders and the warriors guarding Kelly gestured for him to continue playing.

Whether out of fear, panic, or hope, Laumpagh remained in the hut and played late into the night.

Awakened the next morning by loud chanting, Charlie, Carter, and Peter sat up wondering what the shouting was all about. While seated, three women entered carrying bowls of what looked like soup. The women encouraged the men to drink the liquid from the bowls.

Charlie hesitated after taking a small taste.

"Pretend to drink but do not swallow," Charlie said to his companions, with an odd grin on his face. "Let the women know that you like it and maybe they will leave."

Carter and Peter did as Charlie instructed, nodding their heads with smiles on their faces. Charlie mimicked their moves but indicated the women should leave and then they would finish the broth. The women looked at one another, spoke their language, and turned and left.

"It is something to dull your mind," Charlie said in an audible whisper. "Pour it out behind you and try to cooperate as best you can."

The two young soldiers complied and quickly threw dirt over the spilled liquid. The women re-entered a short time later to retrieve the bowls. They smiled and talked among themselves, presumably satisfied that the three men had finished drinking the potion.

The shouting and chanting grew quiet outside as the three prisoners sat wondering what to expect. Suddenly, two warriors burst into the hut and loosely looped a single rope around their necks, with the warriors holding each end. They motioned for the three to rise to their feet and follow the lead warrior out from the hut.

After their eyes adjusted to the bright sunlight, they saw two parallel rows of natives that led up to a stone stair step. The chieftain they remembered from the night before was sitting on a large chair off to the side of the stairs. Kelly was standing next to him.

The two warriors led the men up the stairs and turned them around to face the crowd. The chieftain, in his oversized, decorated headdress, got up to speak to the crowd. As he spoke, he would occasionally turn and gesture toward the three men roped together standing behind him. At certain intervals, the people in the crowd would shout and raise their hands, or those with spears would thrust them into the air.

When the chieftain stopped addressing the crowd, Kelly pulled out his harmonica and began to play, much to the delight of the chieftain and the crowd. Suddenly, Kelly stopped playing.

He approached the man in the elaborate headdress and began talking and gesturing. The chieftain's smile began to fade as the two men struggled to understand one another. After a brief pause, the chieftain turned and spoke to the crowd and a hush fell over the gathering. He then ordered the two warriors holding the rope binding the three men to lead them back to their hut.

Once inside, the three men were freed from the rope and the warriors departed, with two guards remaining at the door. Charlie and the two soldiers turned to one another in confusion.

"What just happened?" Peter exclaimed.

"Some kind of ceremony," Charlie answered, "and not in our favor I do not think."

"What do you suppose they are planning to do?" Townsend asked.

"I fear we will find out soon enough," Charlie said. "Just know that the drink they brought us was to dull our minds. It's best if we stay alert."

Later that day, a meal was brought in for the three of them. After tasting it, Charlie encouraged his two young companions to eat the meal. Toward evening, Kelly was allowed inside their hut.

"Are you guys doing okay?" Kelly asked.

"As well as can be expected," Carter responded. "What's going on Kelly?"

"I fear they want to sacrifice you to their gods," Kelly said, with a worried look on his face. "That platform they had you stand on this morning is an altar. There was a stone platform behind you that is bloodstained."

"How did you figure this out?" Charlie asked.

"I feared it from the beginning, but picked up on it as that chieftain fellow began to speak to the crowd," Kelly answered. "That's why I began playing my mouth harp. It seems to calm them."

"It does seem to have that effect," Peter interjected. "Do you really think they intend to kill us?"

"I cannot speak their language, but I know in history the natives in this part of the world used to do that to please their gods," Kelly said. "I was able to buy some time using my hasty sign language, convincing him today would be a bad day for a sacrifice and that tomorrow would be better."

"So, they plan to sacrifice us on that altar tomorrow?" Carter said in a voice that caused Kelly to raise his fingers to his lips to quiet him.

"I have brought you a knife," Kelly said, producing a dagger-like instrument carved from stone. "I plan to stir up a celebration tonight. Cut your way out of here and run. They won't be able to hear you with all the noise they make."

"Are you coming with us?" Charlie asked, taking the knife.

"I can't. They are watching me like a hawk. I was fortunate to have convinced the chief to let me see you," Kelly said. "I had best be getting back before they become suspicious."

Kelly quickly exited the hut, spoke briefly to the warrior guards, and was gone.

"How are we going to do this?" Carter asked Charlie.

"We'll have to cut our way out, but I fear we may have to kill those two guards if we are discovered," Charlie responded. "Otherwise, I do not think we shall get far."

Chapter 18
Escape

Charlie Bluefeather, Peter, Zimmerman, and Carter Townsend sat in stunned silence after Kelly Laumpagh left their hut to return to the chieftain's.

"What do we do now, Charlie?" Peter said in a shaky whisper. "Are we going to kill those guards?"

"I have to give this some concentrated thought," Charlie said. "I must ask you to remain silent while I consider our situation."

Bluefeather sat with his legs pulled up, knees out, and ankles crossed. He began rocking gently to and fro and humming quietly to himself. Peter and Carter looked at one another, unfamiliar with the trance Charlie was putting himself into. However, they complied and said not a word.

The two young men were too frightened to sleep and too afraid to talk while their Indian companion was in deep meditation. Soon, Charlie sat perfectly still, eyes closed, and he stopped humming.

To Peter and Carter, it seemed like hours before Bluefeather addressed them again.

"There is a way we can escape, but we must be careful and as quiet as possible," Charlie began. "We will sit back-to-back and I will face the rear of the hut. I will cut open an area for us to escape through, but we must be ready to do it when the natives are occupied with their ceremony. Once outside, it is important that you follow me as silently as you are able if we are to make our escape."

"Do not answer me, just nod your head if you understand," Charlie concluded.

Both soldiers nodded without whispering a word. The three men positioned themselves as Bluefeather had instructed and he put the knife under his shirt.

"If the guards come in, as best you can, try to tell them I am asleep," Charlie whispered.

Although there was a lot of activity in the village, the three men knew they would have to wait until they heard Kelly playing his harmonica to know that the natives had started their ceremony. After a short time, the three women who had earlier brought them the bowls of broth again entered with their bowls in hand. Peter and Carter took the bowls but indicated to the women that Charlie was sleeping. The women seemed pleased, apparently assuming their intoxicating broth had done its work. They departed the hut and Charlie turned and nodded approvingly at the two young men.

"If the guards come in to check on us, try to mimic what I am doing," Charlie advised.

"What if they try to wake us?" Carter asked.

"Leave that to me," Charlie said. "Just be ready to follow my actions."

Carter and Peter looked at one another trying not to imagine what Charlie's action might be.

As the day wore on, the three men could hear the soft beating of what sounded like drums, followed by chanting. Meanwhile, Charlie worked on cutting a hole through the palmetto leaves forming the back wall of the hut.

The drumming was growing louder but still no harmonica music could be heard. It was also evident that most of the tribe was gathering at the far end of the village, near where Kelly described the sacrificial altar. Although evening shadows were spreading toward the mountains west of the village, it was still early afternoon. Suddenly, the sound of Kelly's harmonica could be heard.

Charlie quickly raised his hand to keep his companions from getting too anxious. "Wait until the chanting gets louder," he said in a low voice. "Then we must move quickly and head directly for the wooded area behind us. Try to keep the hut between you and the village as you run."

Charlie then carefully pulled one side of the palmetto leaves back and signaled for the two young men to exit.

The chanting was getting louder, which worried the escapees that others would soon enter the hut to retrieve them for the ceremony. Once they reached the woods, Charlie signaled for the two young soldiers to follow him, quickly and silently.

Time was on their side, as Bluefeather led Carter and Peter in a semicircular route around the village.

"Charlie, I think our camp is this way," Carter said in a hoarse whisper while indicating a westerly direction to go. But Charlie waved his hand to keep him silent and to continue following him.

It was not long before they were scrambling up the steep slope of the eastern hills, now in shadows. The forest was dense and covered with undergrowth, making travel difficult. The sounds from the village that were fading from behind them suddenly increased in volume.

"They know we escaped," Charlie said. "Keep climbing as fast as you can."

The thought that the villagers would soon be coming after them inspired the three men to quicken their pace, as their lungs burned and their hearts pounded. After reaching the top of a ridge, they made a brief stop.

"Charlie," Carter said, while struggling to catch his breath. "We… we're going the wrong way."

"No," Charlie corrected, "we are going away from where they think we have gone." Bluefeather paused as he tried to catch his breath. "They… at first… believe we would run for camp and attempt to pick up our trail. We are upwind so they also will not pick up our scent. They will eventually catch on to the direction we've gone, so we must hurry. They can move swiftly through this forest, much faster than we can."

"So, what do we do?" Peter asked.

"They will expect us to try to circle back toward camp," Charlie continued. "We split up. I will go north. You go south. I am hoping they will assume we all went north, and I will lead them away from you. When you think you have gone past the village, turn toward the setting sun and try to make your way back to camp. Your path should be clear then."

"But what about you, Charlie?" Peter asked. "If they catch you, you'll be fighting them alone."

"No use to fight," Bluefeather answered. "I have been in trouble like this before. I can move better alone, and you should have enough head start to elude them. Now go! Hurry!"

Bluefeather quickly disappeared into the forest. Carter and Peter stood looking after him for a moment and then heard shouts coming from below. With great haste, they both ran in the direction Charlie suggested.

✷✷✷

"It looks as if they followed the stream but avoided walking in it," Nantan announced, as the six remaining members of the task force searched for signs of where the missing members may have passed by. "They appear to be moving swiftly, although I think the captors may be slowed down because our men would be unfamiliar with this terrain."

"And probably too far out of shape to keep up with whoever has taken them," Nik said. "Nantan, continue in the lead, and let's move as fast as we can and stay on horseback for as long as we are able."

When nightfall came upon the six pursuers, they were forced to stop for the night.

"We can't risk starting a fire," Lieutenant Gateway advised. "If they see our fire, there's no telling what they might do."

"You mean like kill the captives?" Roger asked.

"Or come back and attack us," Sergeant Davis cut in. "We do not know how many of them there are, but these tracks say there are far more of them than us."

"Whatever we have to eat, we're going to have to eat it cold," Nik said. "I agree starting a fire would be a bad idea. I just hope there are no jaguars around."

"By the way, Nik, how are you holding up?" Roger asked.

"Not as well as I thought," Nik said. "I think, whatever they were putting on me, it made me feel better than I actually was."

"Yes, you'd best get as much rest as you can, Nik," Morgana advised. "We don't know how far this trail is going to take us."

"We can fan out and set up a secure perimeter with you in the middle," Gateway told Nik. "I'm guessing we won't be disturbed tonight, but they might be back in the morning. We're less of a target if we're spread out."

"And we have firearms," Davis interjected. "Judging from the way they destroyed those weapons in our wagon, they would have been useless to them."

"Good point, Beau," Gateway said. "I think we'll be okay until we come upon them, or they surprise us."

Although distant sounds did echo off the canyon walls, none posed a threat to the six in pursuit. Unfortunately, those distant echoes also did not offer any indication of where their lost companions might be.

In the morning, Nik was feeling stronger and the team of seekers set out again to find the four missing men.

"It appears they turned east," Nantan said, dismounting to examine the tracks.

"I was afraid of that," Roger remarked. "We're going to have to start climbing."

"Nantan, ride ahead and see if you can find an easier route to the top of that ridge," Nik suggested. "It looks as if those tracks go straight up, but I don't think they could have taken our horses that way."

"I think Gateway, Davis, and I should go with him," Morgana proposed. "We can spread out and increase our chances of finding a different route sooner. We don't know what kind of danger our men might be in, so we need to move fast."

"Whoever finds a better way to go, fire off a shot and we can all converge at that point," Nik said.

It took little more than fifteen minutes before a shot was fired. Still, trying to determine in which direction the shot came was made difficult by the repeated echoes bouncing through the canyon.

"I think the sound of the original shot came in a direction south of here," Roger said. "I suggest we head that way. Hopefully, everyone will end up in the same place."

It took about thirty minutes for all six members to find Nantan, who had fired the shot.

"I think your idea was a good one, Morgana," Nik said, once the group had come together, "but we failed to consider the echo a gunshot makes in this canyon. We may have to come up with a better idea if we do this again."

"Sorry, Nik," Morgana said. "Maybe it's best if we just follow Nantan and make our way the best we can."

After climbing for another two hours, the group reached the top of a ridge but the trail disappeared altogether.

"What now?" Roger said to no one in particular. "We really have no idea where we're going."

"We will have to fan out again," Nik said. "Echo or no echo, let's form a line spreading out north and south and move steadily up this mountainside. If anyone finds tracks or a trail, shoot off another round. It will take more time but it's the only way I can think of to try and find our companions."

All agreed. Nantan, Gateway, and Davis turned north and Nik, Roger, and Morgana went south.

By mid-afternoon, the team reached the top of a second ridge, when a rifle shot rang out.

Roger halted in his tracks, recognizing that what he heard originally came from the right of his position. Morgana had taken the route farthest south, so Roger decided to wait until Nik or one of the others reached his spot. It wasn't long before he could see Nik riding through the timber just below him.

"Nik," Roger called out. "I'm up here."

Nik turned his horse and started up to where Roger was waiting.

"Roger, did you shoot?" Nik asked as he approached his brother.

"No, the shot came from the south of me," Roger said. "I think it must have been Morgana."

"Let's ride slowly in that direction and see if any of the others catch up to us," Nik suggested.

Sergeant Davis was the first to reach them, riding through the trees about fifty yards above them. He soon joined the brothers and within minutes they had reached Morgana.

"I hope you're the one who fired off a shot," Nik said.

"I am, Nik," Morgana replied. "I would like you to look at this,"

Morgana offered, holding out a small piece of torn cloth.

After examining it, Nik said, "I'm almost positive that Charlie left this behind. I'm not sure how he managed it, but then Charlie always surprises me with what he can do under duress."

"He took a big chance," Roger said, "but for the sake of the others, I'm glad he is with them."

Then the four riders heard what sounded like a shout.

"Did you hear something?" Morgana said. "It sounded like someone's voice."

From out of the trees, Carter and Peter rushed toward the surprised foursome, who had their guns pointed in the direction of the two soldiers.

"Peter, Carter… how?" Roger started, quickly swinging out of his saddle. Instantly, the others dismounted and were hugging the two tired, but happy, young men.

"What happened to you guys?" Nik said, gushing with excitement. "And where's Charlie and Kelly?"

"We don't know about Charlie," Carter began. "But we don't think Kelly is coming back."

As Carter spoke, Lieutenant Gateway and Nantan arrived on the scene.

Between excited greetings, Peter and Carter explained what had happened to them.

"So, Charlie went off on his own?" Nik asked, rhetorically. "I have to admit, that sounds like him. He sent you guys in the direction those natives would figure you would not have gone."

"Do you know who these people were?" Morgana asked.

"Just very primitive," Carter responded. "Maybe even into human sacrifice. All I know is there's a lot of them."

The two soldiers explained how Kelly's harmonica playing had fascinated the people of the village and it was Kelly that brought them the knife with which to escape.

"Kelly stayed behind?" Gateway mused. "Do you think he was planning to escape later?"

"We don't know," Peter said. "He was very popular among the people of that village."

"Kelly had a difficult time as a soldier," Davis said. "He might have seen this act as one of redemption."

"He's certainly a hero to us," Carter said.

"Charlie too," Peter added.

"Well, we're not giving up on either one," Nik said. "But if we don't find them out here, I don't think we're in a position to do battle with any entire tribe of people in a foreign country."

The reunited group made camp that night using the same sentry technique from the night before. The next morning, they spread out and moved back in the direction they believed Bluefeather would have gone.

Chapter 19
End of Search

The group spread out in single file, only stretching east to west and moving in a northerly direction, using the information Carter and Peter had given them. The two young soldiers doubled up on horseback, Carter riding with Nik and Peter with Roger.

"I don't know what I would have done if you and Carter had not shown up," Roger said, speaking over his shoulder to Peter. "I don't know how I would explain that to your parents."

"I'm sorry if I've caused you any problems," Peter responded, "but as a soldier, my folks have to be prepared that something bad might happen to me."

"Yes, but not on my watch," Roger replied. "This is a voluntary mission and not the responsibility of the U.S. Army."

"I realize I haven't been away from home all that long and Fort McRae is not far from our home," Peter said. "I have to grow up sometime."

"I'm afraid everybody had a stake in this, except maybe Morgana and Nantan," Roger said. "I think Nik is sick about Bluefeather and what may have happened to him. I'm fortunate you are safe, and I think Lieutenant Gateway feels you, Carter, and Kelly are his responsibility."

"I guess we could have been more careful in camp," Peter said. "But things had been quiet for days and those natives just caught us off guard."

***

"Mr. Nik, sir," Carter said from his position riding behind the marshal. "You're starting to bleed through your shirt. Are you okay?"

"I won't be okay until we find Charlie," Nik responded, as he was beginning to list in his saddle.

"Maybe we ought to stop and let you get some rest," Carter suggested. "I'll take the horse and get some help."

"I'll be okay," Nik mumbled.

It wasn't long before Nik slumped over and nearly fell from his horse. Luckily, Carter was able to keep him from falling and reached around Nik to grab the reins. Carter stopped the horse and slid off the back of the mount. He then helped Nik, who nearly fell out of his saddle. After finding a safe place to lie Nik down, Carter mounted up and went in search of Roger.

"Mr. Roger," Carter said, riding up to where Roger and Peter were riding.

"What's up, Carter? Where's Nik?"

"His back is bleeding bad and he nearly fell from his horse," Carter said. "I helped him lie down in a good spot and came to fetch you."

"Take me to him," Roger said, and the three men headed back to where Nik was left to rest.

After reaching his brother, Roger dismounted and began to tend to him.

"Carter, you and Peter find Morgana. She was searching about one hundred yards from where Peter and I were," Roger said. "I think she's got something that can help."

"And be careful, I don't want the two of you getting lost," he added.

"No, sir," Carter replied, as he and Peter rode off. A half-hour later, they returned with Morgana. She dismounted to examine Nik's wounds. Roger had laid him prostrate and was trying to remove his brother's shirt.

"Let me do that," Morgana said, pulling a jar from her saddlebags.

"Do we have anything we can put over those wounds?" she asked.

Roger rifled through his saddlebag and pulled out a shirt. "We can fashion this into a bandage of sorts," he said.

"Don't make a fuss over me," Nik mumbled, although it was obvious he didn't have much strength.

"This ointment will help him to feel better, but we're going to have to stay here for the night, at least," Morgana said. "Nik's in no condition to travel right now."

"I think we need to get him back to camp," Roger said. "We need to get him to a doctor."

"We can do that when he is able to ride. It will take at least a day to reach camp," Morgana said. "If you want to continue searching for Charlie, I can take Nik and these two back to camp and wait for you there."

"I don't think Nik's going to want to give up on Charlie," Roger said. "Losing Bluefeather is bad enough. I don't want to lose Nik as well."

"Nik is strong. He will be okay if he gets some rest," Morgana said. "But if those natives are still chasing Charlie, and they know where the camp is, we may be in for a fight after all."

"I'm going to fire off a shot," Roger said. "Hopefully that will bring the others back and we can camp here. Let's hope those natives are afraid of gunfire."

Doubling up on two horses, Morgana, Peter, and Carter left to take Nik back to camp, Roger fired off a shot with his rifle. Sergeant Davis was the first to show, followed by Gateway. Roger explained to the men Nik's predicament and prepared to fire off another shot, just as they saw Nantan coming through the forest.

"Bluefeather has been here," Nantan said, as he rode up to the others. "There are marks not far from here."

"Mount up, boys," Roger said. "Nantan, lead the way to where these marks are."

It took the riders almost an hour to reach a tree that had been clearly marked with a knife.

"This is the second one I found," Nantan said. "The other was farther up the ridge."

"Then Charlie must have been heading back toward camp," Roger said, "how fortunate that Kelly was able to get a knife to him."

"There were signs of many men following Charlie above the ridge. As you can see, he marked the trees so those following him would not see the mark," Nantan said. "The many footprints continue but no sign of Charlie's."

"I don't understand," Gateway remarked. "What happened to Charlie's markings?"

"It is likely he tried to lead them away from the camp being afraid we would have returned," Nantan said. "It looks like they continued toward the camp so they must have lost Bluefeather's trail."

"So, you think Charlie escaped and the natives expected to catch him back at the camp?" Davis surmised.

"If that's the case, Morgana and the others may be in danger," Roger said. "They should reach camp sometime tomorrow. We'd better hurry."

"What about Bluefeather?" Nantan asked.

"He either eluded them or they caught up to him," Roger said, grimacing at the thought. "We'll have a better chance of finding him if we're all together and that means reaching the camp before the others do."

Wasting no time, the men decided to continue riding through the night in hopes of reaching the camp before the others arrived. It meant not knowing which direction Charlie or the natives might have gone. They loaded their weapons on the chance they would run into the pursuing natives.

By daybreak, they stopped to see if they were on the trail of the natives but saw no sign of them. They scanned nearby trees and found none of Charlie's marks, spurring them on to reach camp before Morgana's group did.

By mid-morning, the four men rode into camp, only to find no one there.

"We either made it ahead of Morgana, Nik, and the boys," Roger said, "or they ran into trouble along the way."

"Do we know in what direction they would be coming?" Gateway asked. "We could ride out and hopefully meet up with them."

"Our horses are near exhaustion," Davis said. "If we go out now, we may have to come back on foot."

"He's right," Roger said to Gateway. "We might want to fortify this place in case those natives show up."

"I will go up on the ridge and keep watch," Nantan said. "Meanwhile, eat and regain your strength."

Nantan dismounted and took care of his horse. After watering the animal, he grabbed his rifle and made his way up to the top of the ridge.

Shortly after Nantan's departure, Morgana, Nik, Carter, and Peter rode into camp. After a brief reunion, Nik was attended to and put into the wagon to rest. Peter and Carter set about preparing a meal to feed the hungry, but somewhat relieved, campers.

Roger offered to say a prayer for the safety of those who returned and a special request for the wellbeing of Kelly and Charlie. As he was closing, asking for the healing of his brother, Nantan and Charlie walked into the camp—a celebration broke out.

Charlie explained the different methods he used to throw the natives off his trail. He said he deliberately tried to steer them away from the camp but felt they would expect that and head in the camp's direction. He then said he made his way onto the ridge above the camp to see if the natives had gone there. It was on the ridge that Nantan found him hiding.

The sight of Charlie gave Nik a surge of energy and he embraced his old friend.

"I felt sure I had lost you," Nik said. "All I could think of was how I was going to explain that to Marshal Borchers back in Kansas."

"It would be as difficult as how I will have to explain to the marshal what happened to you if you do not get better," Bluefeather replied.

After the joyous reunion, they set up a perimeter watch in case the natives arrived. They also made plans to get Nik to Monclova and a doctor the following day.

"We've lost some horses so we're either going to have to double up or two of us are going to have to walk," Gateway said. "First, we have to get this wagon across the creek."

"Some of the supplies in the wagon were destroyed by the natives," Bluefeather said. "Marshal Brinkman can ride in the wagon, plus we are down one man up front."

"Is there no chance we can rescue Kelly?" Roger asked.

"I sensed from him that, if he survived, he would be at home among the natives," Charlie said. "I do not think our world appeals to him now."

"I suggest if Carter and Morgana give up their horses, Peter and Carter can drive the team while Nik and Morgana ride in the wagon," Roger recommended. "That will leave enough horses for the rest of us."

"That sounds reasonable," Gateway added. "We can help the wagon through rough spots. It will slow us down somewhat but maybe we can pick up extra horses in Ocampo."

The team broke camp the next morning and made Nik as comfortable as possible to ride in the wagon. Roger took a white stone from his pocket.

"Here, brother, is a little something to ease your pain," Roger said, giving Nik the stone. "It's given me a lot of comfort when I needed it."

"Thanks, Roger," Nik replied, taking the stone from his brother. "I can feel it working already."

The supplies Morgana needed to assist Nik were loaded into the wagon as well. Gateway and Davis volunteered to push the wagon across the creek, while Roger and Nantan attached ropes to the harness and used the other horses to pull the wagon. The crossing proved easier than expected.

Once on the trail, they moved slowly, not wanting to overtax the animals. Fortunately, the return of Bluefeather proved to be good medicine for Nik, who rode easily in the wagon.

"Roger knew what he was doing when he asked you along on this expedition," Nik said to Morgana. "However, I don't think he did it so you would be here to look after me."

"Your strength is more help to you than I am," Morgana said. "You and your brother have strong medicine within you. Is it the God you worship that does that for you?"

"Probably not in my case," Nik answered with a laugh. "Roger's the one who carries us spiritually. And he's a pretty tough customer when he needs to be."

"You are brothers. How is it that you two are so different?" Morgana posed.

Nik gave the mestizo shaman and brief explanation of Roger's father rescuing him from slavery and making him a part of the family. He did not mention the murder of the family and went on to tell Morgana about the two of them serving in the war and as deputy marshals.

"The stone," Morgana said, looking at Nik's hand. "What is its power?"

Nik looked down at the stone and tears welled up in his eyes as he lifted his head. "It… it's a gift our sister gave Roger when he first went away to school," he said. "It's a power I cannot describe. I can only feel it."

Morgana could tell talking about the stone was difficult, so she cautioned Nik to relax and get some rest. Nik squeezed the stone in his hand, closed his eyes, and let the rocking of the wagon quiet his mind.

The task force, minus one, stopped for the night about 10 miles out of Ocampo. Charlie and Peter put together a meal out of almost nothing to help get the group into Ocampo in the morning, where they would replenish their supplies.

By this time, Nik was feeling much stronger and climbed out of the wagon to gather around the campfire with the others.

"You seem better," Sergeant Davis said, looking up at Nik.

"All of you have done such a wonderful job, I could not feel any other way," Nik replied. "To think that Charlie and I are the only ones I added to this bunch, I have to give all the credit to Roger."

"I can only take credit for Morgana, and I had help doing that," Roger said. "These other folks stepped forward on their own."

After making the best of what little food they had, they all retired for the night. Nik approached Roger before getting back into the wagon.

"Here, brother," Nik said, handing the white stone back to Roger. "I'm feeling much better now, and this talisman is much safer in your hands than mine."

"I had a hunch it would do you some good," Roger confided, and returned the stone to the special pocket in his jacket. "Let me know if you need it again."

Nik smiled, put his hand on Roger's shoulder, and climbed back into the wagon.

The following morning, the remaining members of the task force enjoyed a cup of coffee without breakfast, deciding instead to wait until they reached Ocampo to eat.

They entered Ocampo almost unnoticed the second time. They stopped to replenish their supplies and bought two strong horses to harness to the wagon. Nik felt his strength returning but the others insisted he stay in the wagon until they reached Monclova, where they were told there was a doctor.

The route to Monclova took them down out of the Sierra Madre Occidental range and the road was well-traveled. At the rate they were traveling, they estimated it would take three days to reach Monclova. Besides having Nik seen by a doctor, they were also hoping they were on the trail of the lost silver shipment.

The first night out of Ocampo, Charlie Bluefeather prepared a stew of salt pork, potatoes, and beans, along with biscuits bathed in honey. After eating their fill, Nik asked Morgana what she knew about Marteen Roberto Bacca.

"He is a ruthless man who killed my mother in an attempt to kidnap me," Morgana said, nonchalantly poking a stick into the fire and showing no emotion in her voice. "Fortunately, my grandfather tracked him down and rescued me. Marteen escaped along with many of his men."

"Was he going to hold you for ransom?" Nik asked. "Was your family wealthy?"

"No, he wanted me for his own pleasure. That is why I fled to the New Mexico Territory after my rescue," Morgana said.

"Are you nervous about running into him again?" Nik continued. "My goal is to meet this man."

"I doubt he remembers me," Morgana said. "I was much younger then. I would like to learn more about him, but I do not seek revenge for my mother's death."

"If he has that silver, as we suspect, it doesn't sound like he would be anxious to return it," Roger said to both Nik and Morgana.

"He might return it for a price, but I would imagine his price would be more than the silver is worth," Morgana said. "For you, Nik, he would probably try using it as a ransom against your government."

"It's not worth that much," Nik said. "I would just be happy to know he has it. I can report that to my superiors and let them handle the matter however they wish."

"Is silver worth more than gold in your country?" Morgana asked.

"Not yet," Nik answered, "but there are those putting pressure on the federal government to make the price of it equal to gold."

"That sounds crazy," Gateway chimed in. "Wouldn't bringing silver up to the value of gold have a negative effect on the value of gold?"

"You make a good point, Walt," Roger interjected. "Nik, has this re-evaluation of silver been thought through?"

"I wish I could tell you, Roger. That's why I'm not willing to pick a fight with this Bacca character. If I can just tell Judge Conklin who has it, the feds can do whatever they think is necessary to settle the matter."

"It almost sounds as if this is nothing more than a wild goose chase," Davis said. "I know we're not getting rich off of this expedition, but this is beginning to sound like they're spending more money on this silver than it's worth."

"I hope this doesn't mean you guys are giving up on me," Nik said.

"Not at all, Nik," Gateway said. "This won't be the first dead-end assignment Beau and I have been on while serving in the U.S. Army."

Gateway's remark brought a laugh from the group, all except Morgana.

"What actually, was your motivation for doing this, Morgana?" Roger asked. "You will be compensated, but will it be worth the risk?"

"I have my reasons," Morgana said. "I wasn't really accomplishing much living in that cave on Carlos Santana's land. My roots are here in Mexico."

The conversation soon died down and the task force turned in for the night. All went to sleep wondering what to expect in Monclova.

Chapter 20
Marteen Roberto Bacca

After reaching the outskirts of Monclova, the task force set up camp. Nik then told his group of volunteers what he had planned.

"Tomorrow, Roger and I will go into the town and inquire as to the whereabouts of Marteen Bacca. I will then arrange to meet up with him."

"I am not sure that Bacca speaks English," Morgana said. "You will need to include me as an interpreter if he does not."

"Are you sure you want to do that?" Nik asked.

"I may have to do this alone. It's my responsibility to conclude this expedition, whatever the outcome," Nik said. "If this Bacca person is as bad as I have heard you say, Morgana, I would rather you didn't take the chance on having him recognize you."

"Like I said, I do not think he would remember me. I was not yet sixteen when he attempted to kidnap me and that was years ago," Morgana replied.

"What if he does recognize you and challenges you?" Roger asked.

Morgana just shrugged her shoulders.

"I could try to find an interpreter in Monclova," Nik responded.

"You don't know that you could trust someone else to translate for you," Morgana insisted. "It could be someone instructed by Bacca to give you false information."

"Well, if it puts you at ease, I'm just looking for confirmation that he has the silver," Nik explained. I will then make an offer to take it off his hands, that's all."

"If he is the outlaw we suspect, do you really think he is going to let you take that silver off of his hands?" Gateway said.

"No," Nik replied. "But I do have to present my case and bring closure to this treasure hunt."

"What are you going to tell him your interest is in the silver?" Roger asked. "You're not going to tell him you're a lawman, are you?"

"No, just someone representing the United States' interest in the silver," Nik said. "I can't do more than that. However, I would ask that you gather as much information as you can about Bacca and the size of his outfit."

All agreed and discussed preparations for their return to the States.

"I'll be glad when this is over," Nik said to Roger. "I've been unable to let Esther know what's been going on since we left Fort Bliss."

"If you don't mind, I'm going to go into town tonight," Roger said. "I have something I need to do."

"Don't get into trouble," Nik cautioned. "We don't know how friendly this town is. They may all be in cahoots with Bacca."

"No, I just need to find a quiet place to get my thoughts straight," Roger said. "I don't even plan to take my gun with me."

"Okay, but be careful," Nik replied.

Monclova was a growing town in Coahuila, Mexico. It had once been the capital of the state but that was eventually conferred to the settlement of Saltillo farther south. It was late afternoon, and the sun was slowly descending behind the Sierra Madre Mountain range.

Roger drew very little attention as he rode into the town. Locals were completing the last-minute details of their day and Roger assumed most were on their way home. He rode until he came to a mission. He dismounted, tied his horse to a nearby hitching rail, and went inside. It was empty and reminded him of the mission he visited in Ocampo, except larger.

He stood for a time in the alcove entryway and allowed the solitude and peacefulness of the old edifice to put his mind at ease. He then walked slowly down the aisle between pews and stopped just short of approaching the altar. He sat down, removed his hat, and began to pray.

"Would you like me to pray with you?" came the soft sound of a voice. Roger looked around and discovered that a friar was sitting at the far end of his pew.

"I'm sorry, I did not see you there," Roger apologized. "I hope I'm not disturbing anything."

"Not at all," the friar said, turning his hooded head toward Roger, but the shadows of his cowl made it difficult to see the man's face. "I would consider it an honor to pray with you. What is it that troubles you?"

"It's a little complicated," Roger said. "I appreciate your help, but I do not want to bore you with the details."

"Are you here to see Señor Marteen Roberto Bacca?" the friar asked. "If you are, it is good to pray."

"Is he that bad?" Roger asked, startled by the friar's mention of Bacca's name.

"You would not know it to talk to him. He visits our mission frequently and most of the townspeople admire him," the friar said. "But most either do not know him well or those who do ignore what they know."

"I have heard he is not a nice man, and my brother plans to meet with him to discuss business," Roger said, almost without thinking. "I'm just trying to get some guidance as to how to keep my brother safe."

"Depending on the business your brother wants to discuss, he should be in no danger," the friar continued. "But, if the business discussed threatens Señor Bacca, treachery could follow."

"What do you mean by that?" Roger asked.

"Señor Bacca is not one to let a business opportunity pass him by if he can profit from it," the friar said. "But he does not always let on how he intends to profit."

"I can't say as I like the sound of that," Roger replied. "What else do you know about him?"

"Are you okay, Señor?"

Roger felt a hand on his shoulder and turned immediately. There next to the pew where he was sitting was another frocked friar. His head cover was pulled back revealing an older man with short white hair. He wore a wooden crucifix around his neck and kindness was etched on his face.

"I'm sorry," Roger said. "I was just relaying some information to the other friar."

"What other friar?" the man asked.

"Oh, that…" Roger turned and saw that the one he had been speaking had vanished. He paused and added, "Ah, I guess I was praying out loud and you must have overheard me."

"Please continue on," the man said. "I am Father Benedict and I am here to serve you if there's anything you need. I'm afraid I'm quite alone here."

"I was just finishing up, Father," Roger said, standing up and extending his hand in salutation. "I really must be going."

Roger moved into the aisle and began walking toward the door. He turned suddenly to see the friar looking after him. "There is one thing," he said. "Could you maybe say a little prayer for my brother?"

"What is your brother's name?" the monsignor asked. "And what would you like me to pray about?"

"His name is Nik Brinkman. He's going to be involved in a difficult, ah… business deal tomorrow and I would like it if things went well."

"What kind of business?"

"He's seeking to have something returned to him that we believe a man named Bacca has," Roger said. "I cannot tell you what, but I can assure you that it is nothing nefarious."

"I see," said Father Benedict. "I will pray, but Señor Bacca is not in the habit of returning the things he has taken."

"I'll let my brother know," Roger said. "Thank you, Padre," Roger added as he departed the mission.

The next morning, Roger told Nik what he had learned, without mentioning the disappearing friar.

"It sounds like this Bacca hombre will be interested in what I have to say, but what you're saying is that he may try to do something after I leave?" Nik responded.

"That's how it sounded to me, Nik. From what I gather that is how he does business. He extracts the information he needs and then plots how he can steal, or murder, his way to benefit himself."

"Any idea how big of an outfit he has?" Nik asked. "I don't suppose we would be in a fair fight if it came down to that."

"It sounds like Monclova marches to his drum," Roger replied. "I get the impression he runs this town and most of the area. As you know, he owns that mine we visited in Boquillas del Carmen."

"That means he could be a big enough wheeler-dealer to listen to what I have to say since I represent the United States Government," Nik commented. "I may not be able to strike up a deal, but from what you tell me I will bear in mind that he might be up to no good."

"Since we can't be sure about this, how about I stay in the background to make sure you and Morgana come out okay?" Roger suggested.

"That's not a bad idea," Nik said in agreement. "Maybe stay behind me far enough so they won't see you with me. If anything bad happens, hightail it back here and get everybody out as fast as you can."

"Okay, but we're making a stop at the doctor's office before you meet up with Marteen," Roger advised. "I want to make sure you're healed up enough to take care of yourself if the situation demands it."

"Anything to get you people off my back about this," Nik said. "I feel fine now."

"Morgana's done an excellent job but she's a spirit doctor, not a trained physician," Roger said.

"If the doc in town gives me a clean bill of health, you might have to eat those words," Nik said, smiling.

"I'd be happy to," Roger remarked. "Are you ready to go?"

The two brothers rode into Monclova with Morgana and located the local doctor's office. After a brief inspection of Nik's wounds, the doctor stitched up the deeper gashes but was satisfied most were healing satisfactorily. He gave Nik some salve to apply to the wounds, along with some gauze with instructions to bind them loosely to allow air to get in.

"By the way, Doc," Nik said. "I have something to discuss with Marteen Roberto Bacca, can you tell me where to find him?"

"Bacca?" the doc responded. "You can find him in the large hacienda at the end of this street. What do you need with him?"

"Just some unfinished business," Nik answered. "Nothing too serious. By the way, you speak excellent English. Are you from the States?"

"This is my home, but I studied medicine in your country at Bellevue Hospital during the Civil War," the doctor replied. "I was in New York with my father, who was doing business there."

"Then you came back here after the war?" Roger inquired.

"Yes, after the war my people needed me more than Bellevue did," the doctor said. "Oh, and you'll need to go through the local sheriff to present yourselves to Señor Bacca. He is the frontman for Marteen."

The Brinkman brothers thanked the doctor and departed for the sheriff's office, along with Morgana. The office was easy enough to find and the three tied up their horses to the hitching rail in front of it.

"Just a minute," Nik said, reaching inside his saddlebag. "I may need this," he said, pulling out his letter from Judge Conklin authorizing Nik's entry into Mexico. The three then went inside.

"Does anyone here speak English?" Nik asked an apparent deputy sitting behind a small desk. He was young and had dark hair and a complexion to match. He looked up at Nik and just shook his head, no. As they contemplated what to do next, an older gentleman entered the office from the back room.

"May I assist you?" he said in English, with a thick accent. He was heavy set and wore a large mustache similar to Nik's. He was dressed in light cotton pants and a cotton shirt, with a badge on the shirt's breast pocket.

"Yes," Nik responded. "I would like to meet Marteen Roberto Bacca. Can you help me?"

"Who are you?" the man asked.

"I represent the United States Government. The two with me are assistants of mine," Nik began. "I think Señor Bacca may be able to help me recover what my government has lost."

The man eyed Nik and his companions for a moment and said, "You do not look like representatives from the United States Government."

"We ran into trouble getting here and have not had time to refresh ourselves," Nik replied. "I apologize for our appearance, but I have papers that explain who I am and what I'm doing here."

"I will see what I can do," the man responded. He turned and said something in Spanish to the young man at the desk who got up, donned a sombrero, and left the office.

"My deputy will soon return with Señor Bacca's answer," he said. "You may have a seat and wait here for the deputy's return. Now if you'll excuse me…"

"Just one thing," Roger interjected, stopping the man from leaving. "Who is this Señor Marteen Roberto Bacca?"

"You come here from the United States to see Señor Bacca and you do not know who he is?" the man asked.

"We did not know that Señor Bacca would be part of our mission," Nik quickly answered. "It was by chance that his name was given to us, and we think he could be a big help to us."

"I see. Well, to answer your question, Señor, Marteen Roberto Bacca is the head of Monclova and a very important person in Coahuila," the apparent lawman answered. "I am Señor Gonzalez, the sheriff."

"Señor Bacca is not always easy to see, especially if you were not expected."

It did not take long before the deputy returned and relayed his message to the older man wearing the badge. He informed the sheriff that Bacca would be open to a meeting with the visitors but requested more information.

"May I see your papers?" Gonzalez asked.

Nik reached into his shirt and pulled out the letter from Judge Conklin. He handed it to Sheriff Gonzalez.

After reading over it, Gonzalez replied, "I will see to it that Señor Bacca sees this."

"He won't be able to see it unless I'm holding it," Nik cautioned. "I cannot allow that to get out of my sight. What did Bacca have to say?"

"He wanted more information on who you were but agreed to see you," Gonzalez said. "I will pass this information on to him and if you want to return in the morning. I will let you know if there are any problems."

"I would appreciate it, Sheriff," Nik said. "Tell him I will present this letter when we meet. Thank you for your time and effort."

Nik, Morgana, and Roger left the sheriff's office and mounted up.

"I am going back to that doctor's office and see what he knows about Bacca," Nik said. "Why don't you two see if you can get some additional information on him?"

"I think I'll pay another visit to that mission I stopped at last night," Roger said. "I think that monsignor knows him. I think Bacca's even attended mass there."

"I might just hang around and see if I can get some information from that deputy," Morgana said. "I'll have to wait until the sheriff is away."

"Great," Nik said, "we'll meet back at the camp later and discuss what we've learned."

Later that evening, Charlie Bluefeather surprised the returning trio with a full meal of tamales, rice, and beans purchased by Gateway and Davis in Monclova. Afterward, the task force sat around the campfire discussing their next move.

"I did not find out too much from the doctor, other than he has had to treat several of Bacca's men," Nik said. "Most of the problems have been gunshot wounds or other injuries."

"The deputy was reluctant to tell me much, other than the fact that the entire sheriff's department is a part of Bacca's army," Morgana offered. "He said very little about Bacca's operation, other than he runs the town like its mayor and Coahuila like the governor. The deputy said Bacca had plans to become the next president of Mexico."

"Father Benedict wasn't willing to tell me much more than what I found out last night," Roger added. "He said Bacca has allies throughout Coahuila and mentioned his aspirations to become the president of Mexico. I asked how an outlaw like him could rule like a governor and hope to be elected as president. The monsignor said his chances were enhanced by the fact his opponent wasn't much better."

"Who is his opponent?" Nik asked.

"Some general, a man by the name of Diaz, I believe," Roger said.

"Diaz, I know that name," Nik replied. "We believe he was tied in with Kensington in masterminding the silver heist. After the shipment was stolen, Judge Conklin said the U.S. Navy came across a ship with Diaz on board. When Diaz heard the news about the balloon being blown off course, the general left in haste."

"So, we're now getting involved with this outlaw Bacca, who we believe has the silver, and this general who wants that silver as well?" Gateway surmised. "And they both have their eye on Mexico's presidency. I hate to say it, but we might be getting ourselves into the middle of a civil war."

"This does sound a little dicey," Roger said. "I wouldn't push Bacca too hard on this issue, Nik. We don't have the men or the ordnance to do battle."

"Nor do we have the authority," Nik answered, taking a sip of coffee and stroking the moisture from his mustache. That's why I only intend to determine if he has it if he's willing to give it up, and at what price. Then, my job is done."

"What about Kelly," Carter asked. "Are we just gonna leave him behind?"

"I do not think we have much choice, Carter," Charlie said. "I think it is best he be remembered as the one who rescued us, maybe at the cost of his own life."

"So, you think those natives killed him?" Peter interjected.

"We don't know. They liked his music and maybe he is still playing his mouth harp for them," Charlie offered.

"We'll see to it Kelly gets full credit for his brave sacrifice," Gateway said, "regardless of whether he's still alive or not."

"It just seems sad," Carter added.

"What would be even sadder, son," Nik said, "is if we were to lose someone else while looking for him. I cannot authorize that. I'm just happy you, Charlie, and Peter are still with us."

"Amen," Roger said. "Amen, and I think we'd best get some sleep. It could turn into a big day tomorrow."

Chapter 21
A Meeting with Bacca

Nik Brinkman, Roger, and Morgana made final arrangements to meet with Marteen Roberto Bacca. Meanwhile, Lieutenant Gateway and Sergeant Davis prepared the camp for a hasty retreat should that become necessary.

After riding into town, Morgana stopped to pick up a sombrero to help hide her face when meeting with the notorious outlaw who tried to kidnap her as a child.

"With that thing on, you could probably pass as one of Bacca's men," Roger quipped.

"That's the idea," Morgana replied, "I don't want to take the chance someone would recognize me."

They rode on to the sheriff's office for final details on approaching Marteen Roberto Bacca. Gonzalez was not on duty but the deputy in the office instructed the three to follow the main road through Monclova. He said it would lead to a large cast-iron gate manned by guards. They were to inform the guards that their visit was authorized by the sheriff.

"I'll hang back," Roger said, as the three mounted up to head over to their meeting. "I'll keep a lookout for anything suspicious and help out if necessary."

"I don't expect any trouble," Nik advised, "but if something breaks, it might be best if you rode back to camp to alert the others."

"Marteen Bacca is no fool," Morgana interjected. "It would not be wise for him to harm a United States dignitary, especially if he wants to become Mexico's president."

"Good point," Roger responded. "I'll still keep an eye out just in case."

After reaching the outskirts of Monclova, Bacca's mansion came into full view of the three riders. It had all the appearances of a well-guarded fortress and intimidating to any would-be visitor.

"I'll stop here," Roger said, "and make myself inconspicuous. I'll stay out of this unless I sense something is wrong."

"I think Morgana is right," Nik said. "It would not be wise for this man to have the United States on his bad side."

Roger rode into a grove of trees, while Nik and Morgana approached the front gate.

"We're here on official business," Nik said, stopping his steed just short of the two main guards. "We have been authorized by Sheriff Gonzalez to meet with Señor Bacca."

The main guard said something in Spanish and turned to signal the second guard to open the gate. The first guard again said something in his native language.

"He's asking about Roger," Morgana relayed to Nik. "They must have seen him and are wondering who he was."

"Tell him the man was someone we met in town who offered to show us here," Nik replied.

After Morgana gave the guard Nik's message, both guards stepped aside and ushered the two riders inside. The lane leading up to the main door of the palatial estate was lavish and well-maintained. There were high stone walls on either side where other guards could be stationed, hidden behind them. There were two militarily attired guards at the front door, one of whom spoke English.

Nik and Morgana dismounted, and the second guard took their horses while the English-speaking guard tended the door for them. They entered a large cascading room that was not overly decorated. After crossing the tile floor, the guard opened two double doors and announced the arrival of Nik and Morgana, without revealing their names.

Another man in a uniform came up to greet them and had the English-speaking guard remain at the door. The second man spoke broken English, led the two before a large mahogany desk, and had them sit down. There was no one seated behind the desk. After a short wait, a middle-aged man entered wearing a rather gaudy military uniform and sat down in the large leather chair behind the desk.

"I am Señor Marteen Roberto Bacca," the man said, introducing himself. "I speak some English but have not yet mastered it."

Morgana replied in Spanish, introducing Nik and identifying herself as "Manuel." An agreement was made that Morgana would verify the conversation for Nik and Bacca's guard would do the same for him.

"What is your business?" Bacca asked. "And why does your translator not remove his hat?"

"I have been asked by my government to locate a shipment of silver that was lost over Texas when a balloon carrying the cargo was blown off course into Mexico," Nik began. "Manuel has a scalp disorder, and the hat contains medicine for it."

"I see," Bacca responded, staring at Morgana. He then looked at Nik. "And how does that… silver… involve me?"

"We believe you and your men may have found it."

"Why do you believe this?" Bacca asked.

Nik explained how they learned of Bacca's involvement through the Tepehuan Tribe in Ocampo, which led them to the site of the destroyed balloon.

"They must be mistaken," Bacca said, turning in his chair and leaning over, his arm now resting on his desk.

"There was no way we could verify that," Nik said. "Our only option was to come here and ask you."

"And what if I… my men had found this silver, what would you expect me to do?"

"Return it," Nik said.

"If I had this treasure of which you speak, why would I go to the trouble of… having my men retrieve it and then just give it back? What would be my reward?" Bacca asked, smiling.

"If you had it, Señor Bacca, what would it take for my government to get it back?"

"What is it worth to you? Or your government, as you say?" Bacca inquired, leaning back in his chair.

"I do not know the answer to that, Señor Bacca," Nik replied. "We did not know that we would have to negotiate to get it back. My mission was authorized by your government and no request for compensation was made."

"My government is very stupid at times," Bacca responded, with a menacing smile. "Maybe they have it already and have been reluctant to return it."

"That I would not know," Nik said. "At this point, all I do know is what I've been told. If the Tepehuan lied to me, then I am the fool."

"That you would be," Bacca replied, stifling a chuckle. "But I will tell you what I'll do. I will ask around about this... this silver of yours. If I should discover where it is, how do I get in touch with you?"

Nik and Morgana looked at each other wondering if revealing their location was wise. Nik then answered, "You can reach us through the sheriff's office. Just leave word with him."

"Then we are done here," Bacca said, rising from behind his desk. "Manuel, I am sorry about your head. You seem to have a kind face under that hat."

Morgana nodded but did not comment.

"My men will escort you out."

After riding out of the gate, Nik and Morgana traveled back toward Monclova. Once they were out of sight, Roger rejoined them.

"What did you learn?" Roger asked.

"Not as much as I would have liked," Nik said. "I could not confirm that Bacca had the silver, but he did speak like a man expecting a reward for it."

"That's at least something," Roger added. "Did he offer you anything else to go on?"

"Only that he would 'ask around' and get back to me. I don't know what that meant, except that I was unable to bring this expedition to a close," Nik answered. "I'm afraid we're going to have to stay in touch with Sheriff Gonzalez because I told Bacca he would be our contact."

The trio returned to their camp to plan their next strategy.

"So, you didn't find out if Bacca had that silver shipment?" Gateway asked. "What now?"

"As far as we know, according to the Tepehuan natives, he does have it," Nik said. "We know there was no trace of the silver where the balloon came down."

"What about the Tepehuan tribe?" Davis suggested. "Maybe they have it."

"I can assure you they do not," Morgana said. "They have no need of silver, as it only causes trouble for them."

"I have to agree with Morgana," Roger said. "If they tried using it for money, scoundrels like Bacca would find out and raid them for it."

"So, are we done here?" Gateway asked.

"I'm not sure but I also can't ask you to stay," Nik replied. "Technically, you volunteers have fulfilled your obligation. We found where the silver should have been and who we think has it. I cannot ask more of you because this seems to be coming down to a standoff between Bacca and me."

"Well, you know I'm not going anywhere," Roger said, offering his brother a sly smile. "I'm not leaving you here to tangle with Bacca alone."

"I am not ready yet to leave," Morgana added. "I am not sure how much more help I can be, but I'm prepared to see this thing through."

"Where you are, I am," Charlie Bluefeather said.

"I think Davis and I are in this for the long hall as well," Gateway chimed in. "And I don't think it's a good idea for Carter and Pete to try and get back to Fort McRae on their own."

"We wouldn't go anyway," Carter said. "It's been a little scary at times but a great adventure as well."

"That goes for me too, Marshal Brinkman," Peter joined in to make the vote unanimous.

"Great," Nik said, smiling broadly. "I'll tell you what. Why don't I treat you all to a dinner in town? We passed a good-looking cantina on our way to see Bacca."

The vote on the second count was also unanimous.

The next morning, as the Mexico sun cast its light on the Sierra

Madre mountains and quickly worked its way down to Monclova, Charlie Bluefeather, Carter and Peter were busy cooking breakfast. The rest of the task force sat around the morning campfire enjoying their first cup of coffee.

"I don't know of any way to hasten this process," Nik said to all sitting with him. "I feel helpless in this situation because I have no authority in this country."

"I suggest we speak to as many people as we can and see if someone in Monclova knows about Marteen Roberto Bacca retrieving that lost silver," Roger said. "If we can find enough witnesses to confirm it, then perhaps we can use it as proof that he has it."

"Obviously, we do not have any leverage here," Lieutenant Gateway commented. "The sheriff is part of Bacca's cadre and would be of no help. I doubt the Mexican government would be of help, considering it's located quite a distance from here."

"I think I'll give Bacca a day or two to get back to me and then…"

Nik's sentence was cut short as Sheriff Gonzalez and a deputy entered their camp and rode up to them.

"Señor Brinkman," the local sheriff said, addressing Nik. "Señor Marteen Roberto Bacca sends you an invitation to visit his hacienda this afternoon."

"What's the occasion?" Nik asked.

"He was not specific but said it would be helpful in the pursuit of your cause."

"Do I have to come alone?" Nik asked.

"Oh no," Gonzalez replied. "Bring your interpreter. There will be some influential men there you may question concerning what you seek. It would be easier for you to communicate if you have your interpreter with you."

"As for the others?" Nik inquired.

"They are prominent citizens of Mexico, but Señor Bacca did not specifically say who they were," the sheriff said. "I think it would show an attitude of trust if just the two of you came."

"Tell him we'll be there," Nik said. "And thank him for going to all this trouble."

"Si, Señor, I will do that," Gonzalez said, as he turned his horse around and rode off with the deputy at his side.

"Now, what do you suppose that was all about?" Roger remarked.

"I don't know but it might put Morgana in a difficult position," Nik said, glancing over at the Apache shaman. "I don't know how polite it would be to rub shoulders with 'influential people' with that sombrero on."

"I will cut my hair," Morgana said, without hesitation. "I do not want to miss this."

"I will ride into Monclova and buy some clothes that will help me pass as a man," she concluded.

"I appreciate you volunteering to do this Morgana," Nik said. "I will be more comfortable having an interpreter I can trust."

Morgana solicited Charlie's help in cutting her hair and assisting her in becoming a 'man' or at least resembling one.

"Are you sure you want to do this?" Charlie asked. "It's possible your power could lie in your hair."

"I have my reasons, Charlie," Morgana answered. "For now, I'm going to have to rely on my own power in dealing with Bacca."

After cutting Morgana's hair and giving it a more masculine look, Charlie prepared a mixture of dirt and charcoal from the campfire to rub into her skin. The darkened skin made her look more native to Mexico and masked her clear complexion.

After finding suitable clothing in town to wear, Morgana was ready to accompany Nik to Marteen Roberto Bacca's silver-discovery gathering.

"Are you two sure you're going to be okay?" Roger remarked as the two mounted their horses to depart.

"You'll know when we get back," Nik replied.

"You mean, if you get back," Roger commented.

"In which case, brother, you'll have to find a way to bring us back," Nik said, smiling, as he and Morgana rode off in the direction of Monclova.

Needing time to think, Roger informed the others that he was going to take a walk down by the river. With multiple thoughts going through his head, he saw what looked like one of the locals sitting on the bank fishing. The position of the person's sombrero gave the impression the fisherman might be asleep.

"Catching anything?" Roger asked as he approached.

"Just some of your thoughts," the fisherman answered.

"Excuse me?" Roger replied, stopping in his tracks.

"I know what's troubling you, Roger Brinkman," the person answered while seemingly peering out onto the river.

"How do you know me?" Roger inquired. "Have we met before?"

"Let's just say I'm someone who has taken an interest in your journey here," the stranger said. "You know that Marteen Roberto Bacca is a bad man and yet you let your brother and Morgana ride off to meet with him. Does that trouble you?"

"Ahh, wait a minute, are you..." Roger began.

"Let's just say I have some insight into what you're up against and leave it at that," the stranger said from beneath the sombrero that shadowed his face.

"I have to admit that I am troubled about that visit," Roger said hesitantly.

"Do you think that Nik is the only one interested in that silver shipment?" said the fisherman.

"No, there is Judge Kensington and a general by the name of Diaz," Roger replied. "They would be interested but I'm not certain what role they would play if it's discovered that Señor Bacca has it. We have not heard that anyone other than Bacca was looking for it."

"Mexico's army moves slowly, much slower than Bacca's men," the stranger continued. "What do you think General Diaz will do if he's convinced that Señor Bacca has that silver?"

"So, you're saying that if Diaz was too slow to recover the silver and now believes Bacca has it," Roger said, turning to look out over the river as he contemplated the stranger's remarks. "Then Kensington and Diaz are going to have to find a way to get that silver from him. That could complicate things."

Just as a fish jumped out of the water, Roger turned to look back at the stranger only to find there was no one there. Realizing he'd just experienced another of his visions, Roger hurried back to camp.

Chapter 22
Hostages

After returning to camp, Roger inquired of Lieutenant Gateway if he knew any more about General Porfirio Diaz. "Just what we learned about him at West Point," Gateway began. "He distinguished himself in Mexico's War of the Reform and became a general by the time he turned thirty."

"Sounds like an ambitious character," Roger remarked. "Why do you think he might be mixed up with this silver shipment?"

"He's been after the presidency for some time now," Gateway continued. "He earned the respect of the army during Mexico's war with France, but his attempts to overthrow Mexico's ruling class have been a failure. My guess would be that this silver shipment is tied into that effort in some way."

"So, he's got the army on his side and a government that isn't," Roger mused. "I'm hoping Nik gets this issue with Bacca cleared up soon and we can get out of here."

***

Nik and Morgana stopped at the sheriff's office before approaching Marteen Roberto Bacca's fortified mansion.

"Is Sheriff Gonzalez in?" Nik asked the deputy after entering the office.

"I believe he is at Señor Bacca's," the deputy replied in Spanish. "There is a big meeting going on there."

After Morgana's translation, Nik replied, "I believe we are to be at that meeting also. Unless you need to come with us to announce our arrival, we know how to find his place."

"If you are expected then you will not need my help," the deputy replied after hearing Morgana relay Nik's message. Morgana thanked the deputy and translated the answer to Nik. The two then mounted up and rode on to Bacca's estate. They were quickly ushered in by the guards and were again met by the same English-speaking guard they encountered on their first visit.

"Ah, Señor Brinkman, we have been expecting you," the guard said. "Please, follow me."

Instead of taking Nik and Morgana inside, the guard led them to a long corridor located on the side of the residence. They walked along, marveling at the size of the building before coming to a well-manicured garden that spread out behind the mansion. The guard then led them down a broad path leading to an ornate fountain where several well-dressed men were enjoying drinks and talking.

"Hola, Señor Brinkman," Marteen Roberto Bacca called out, approaching the two new arrivals. "I am pleased that you could make it."

"As you know," Nik replied, "I am anxious to learn what these men might know about the silver shipment we spoke of."

After a brief translation from Bacca's translator, the host responded with, "Of course, of course, but in good time. I would like to introduce you to these gentlemen who have come a long way to meet you and discuss your... your intentions."

The men turned out to be well-to-do landowners in Mexico and were supporting Bacca's run for office. They were cordial but did not take an immediate interest in what Nik had to say.

Eyeing Morgana as he spoke, Bacca explained that the men merely wanted to get to know Nik better. They examined Nik's letter and indicated how pleased they were to have a representative from the United States to grace the gathering.

After the introductions, Nik pulled Morgana aside and said in a low voice, "There is something about this meeting that bothers me. I'm afraid they're making more of my purpose here than simply trying to recover lost silver."

"I do believe they are of the same cloth that Marteen is made of," Morgana answered. "I believe they are trying to determine how to best use you to their advantage."

"Use me?" Nik responded, almost a little too loud, although he was somewhat assured the men did not understand English well enough to detect his suspicions. "How can I convince them that I do not have any kind of authority to assist them in their political endeavors or whatever they have in mind?"

"Perhaps if you again explain to them what you are after and nothing more, they will dismiss us," Morgana said.

"It's worth a try," Nik remarked.

After approaching Bacca and his companions, Nik asked for their attention.

"Gentlemen, I do believe you may have the wrong idea about me," Nik said in a loud voice while looking at Bacca's translator to do likewise. "Although I represent a party from the United States, I have no authority other than to try and recover a shipment of silver that was destined for my country's treasury."

The men began to ask questions, waiting for Morgana to translate for Nik. Morgana tried to speak softly to Nik so as not to reveal her gender. Anxious to hear what the men were saying, Nik asked her to repeat some of the questions, which caused her to raise her voice. Each time, she would cough to try and remove suspicion.

"Perhaps you underestimate yourself, Señor Brinkman," Bacca said, nodding to his interpreter to speak out. Smiling, he cordially approached the two guests and suddenly reached out and pulled the sombrero from Morgana's head. "Your hair seems much shorter than what I remembered when you were last here."

Bacca then pulled back a portion of Morgana's tunic to partially expose one of her breasts.

"Hold on a minute," Nik called out, stepping between Bacca and Morgana.

"No, you should hold on a minute," Bacca said, speaking with better English. "Why are you trying to deceive us by disguising your interpreter as a man?"

Bacca's other guests began to surround Nik and Morgana and no longer looked cordial.

"What are you up to, Señor Brinkman?" Bacca demanded. "Have you come here to spy on us?"

"Mor..." Nik hesitated, "Manuel was afraid you might not accept a woman here and she's my only interpreter."

"Why would we not accept a woman? If she is your interpreter then present her as such," Bacca said. "She certainly is not 'Manuel' so why the secret?"

"That's a personal thing," Nik said, looking over at Morgana, who was pulling her tunic around her neck. "It was meant for her to feel at ease and not to deceive you."

"Then what is her real name?" Bacca demanded.

Ahh... it's ah..." Nik tried desperately to come up with a Spanish name.

"Luana," Morgana blurted out.

"Luana? Luana, where have I heard that name?" Bacca said, searching his mind for a connection.

"That's my mother's name, the woman you murdered," Morgana said, glaring contemptuously at Bacca.

Suddenly, a light went on in Bacca's eyes. "Then, you are the shaman girl who escaped from us long ago," he said. "Now you return to us as a woman dressed like a man."

"Guards, seize them," Bacca called out, as several soldiers stepped in to take Nik and Morgana into custody. "Take them into the holding area below the hacienda. I will deal with them later."

Nik and Morgana were led to a small, obscure doorway at the back of the hacienda. The door led to a stairway that led down to a large room where six doors adorned two of the walls in the room. Each door had a small viewing port with a hinged cover. Sheriff Gonzalez was sitting at a small table located in one corner of the room.

"Sheriff Gonzalez, I might have known," Nik said, as the guards pushed him and Morgana forward. "You're not going to get away with this. The United States knows we are here."

Gonzalez just looked up from his desk and said nothing. The guards put Nik and Morgana into separate rooms behind two of the six doors.

***

As the evening shadows began to extend from the Sierra Madre Occidental, Roger grew nervous waiting for his brother and Morgana to return.

"I don't like this," he said. "How long does it take to ask someone if they have the silver or not?"

"It is beginning to get a little suspicious," Gateway remarked. "Perhaps it's time to visit the sheriff and see what's taking so long."

After riding into town, Roger entered the sheriff's office where the deputy was seated at his desk.

"Is Sheriff Gonzalez here?" Roger asked in a determined voice.

The Spanish-speaking deputy picked up on what Roger had asked and answered, "Marteen Roberto Bacca hacienda."

"What in the world is taking so long? What are they doing there?" Roger demanded.

The deputy only shrugged his shoulders. Roger couldn't tell if the deputy didn't know what was going on or didn't understand what Roger was asking.

"This is madness," Roger grumbled, realizing a conversation with the deputy was near impossible. He left the sheriff's office and rode off in the direction of Bacca's mansion. He was halted by the guards at the gate.

Roger dismounted and tried to communicate with the guards. While they were conversing, Bacca's interpreter came to the gate.

"I speak English," the well-dressed attendant said. "What is it you want?"

"I want to speak to Nik Brinkman," Roger said. "Is he here?"

"He is still in conference with Señor Bacca. It could take quite some time."

"Can I at least speak to him? Can't you interrupt their conversation for a few minutes so I can talk to my brother?"

"Your brother. Are you saying Señor Brinkman is your brother?" the interpreter asked.

"That's not important," Roger said, slightly regretting his revelation. "I have been waiting for him to return from this… meeting and was wondering why it is taking so long."

"Are you part of his treasure-seeking group?" asked the interpreter. "I can only tell you that Señor Brinkman will return to you when satisfied that he has the information he seeks. I am sorry, Señor, that is the best I can do for you."

"At least I know he is still here," Roger said and got back on his horse. He considered waiting until Morgana and Nik came back out but couldn't help thinking they may not come back out. He rode back to camp.

"The best we can do right now is wait," Roger said after Gateway inquired about the return of Nik and Morgana. "I am uneasy about this. Especially since Morgana went in there disguised as a man."

"Have some of Charlie's dinner and relax for a while," Gateway advised. "If those two are not back by morning, we'll know something is up."

Roger had no other option than to take the lieutenant's advice. That night, he sat by the campfire waiting for his brother and Morgana to come back. Eventually, he was satisfied they weren't coming back, at least not that night.

Roger awakened the next morning to the sound of hoofbeats. He arose to see the sheriff and his deputy approaching. He and the rest of the remaining task force stood silently until Sheriff Gonzalez reined his horse to a halt.

"I have good news," the sheriff called out. "Do not worry. Señor Brinkman and… his interpreter… are just fine."

"Then why haven't they returned?" Roger demanded.

"They have been detained, but I assure you that they are unharmed."

"Detained! What do you mean, detained?" Roger questioned.

"It seems Señor Brinkman and his interpreter were not honest with Señor Bacca," the sheriff said, looking accusingly at Roger. "I fear his interpreter was in disguise for some reason. Señor Bacca has detained them both to find out why."

"Maybe she didn't trust being the only woman at yesterday's meeting," Roger replied. "Why is that such a big deal?"

"Oh, you see, Señor Bacca is going to be Mexico's next presidente," Gonzalez said. "It is possible that Señor Brinkman is here as a spy from your country."

"A spy? Exactly what would he be spying on your future president for?"

"You forget," the sheriff noted. "It was not that long ago that our two countries were at war. Is it not possible that Señor Brinkman could be seeking information proposing another war?"

"That's ridiculous!" Roger said, raising his voice. "Look, I am his brother and a preacher of the Gospel. Do you think I would come down here with him in order to spy on your country?"

"You are Señor Brinkman's brother?" Gonzalez said. "I hope that does not complicate things even further. I can only say that, for now, your brother and his interpreter are safe. No harm will come to them if you and your fellow campers cooperate."

"Comprende, Señor Brinkman's brother… if that's who you truly are?"

The sheriff and his deputy then turned their mounts and rode off.

"This is not a good situation," Nantan remarked.

"Even worse than I thought," Roger added.

"So, what do we do now?" Gateway inquired.

"We come up with a plan and I think we best do it soon," Roger concluded.

***

"Is it possible we have overplayed our hand, Marteen?" said one of the men seated in front of Bacca's desk after returning from the garden.

"Yes, if this Señor Brinkman is indeed an official from the United

States as he claims, it would not be good for us to fall outside of favor with that country," said a second man.

"He seems honest enough to me," Bacca replied. "But I want to keep that shaman woman. She could be very helpful in plotting the future of my election."

"So, what is your intent?" said a third.

"I will wait to hear from Sheriff Gonzalez when he returns," Bacca answered. "Whatever he learns about the rest of Señor Brinkman's silver hunters, we may be able to use all of this to our advantage."

After Sheriff Gonzalez returned from the task force's camp, he was ushered into the meeting being held by Bacca.

"I spoke with a man at the camp who claimed to be Señor Brinkman's brother. Strange, since they are of opposite births," Gonzalez announced. "He also claims to be a Bible preacher like the Catholic priests. However, I feel there is no hostility, but they are concerned for Señor Brinkman and the shaman he uses as an interpreter."

"We have Señor Brinkman and the shaman in custody," Bacca pointed out as he assessed the situation. "And we have the silver that will help finance my campaign. They have no proof that I have it, only that the Tepehuan people have told them that I have it. We also have the lie they tried to perpetrate upon us yesterday as evidence of wrongdoing. I do believe we hold the best cards. We simply must decide how to play them."

"But how long can we hold them?" another of the men asked.

"As long as there is no opposition from anyone but his so-called brother," Bacca answered. "We do want to maintain good relations with America and that should please the voters."

"May I suggest you let me move Señor Brinkman to my jail," Sheriff Gonzalez offered. "That way we can help please his camp by letting them visit until we feel it wise to free him. The shaman you can keep here for interrogation purposes."

"We can do that," Bacca agreed. "If the situation gets heated, you can release him saying we have cleared his story with his authorities."

"Meanwhile, I would like to hear what the shaman has to say."

Chapter 23
The Journalist

Monclova Sheriff Miguel Gonzales entered the underground confinement of Marteen Roberto Bacca's hacienda. He approached the locked door where Nik Brinkman was imprisoned and nodded to the deputy to unlock it.

"You have been released to my custody," Gonzalez said to Nik, who was seated in one corner of his cell.

"Your custody?" Nik exclaimed. "What is the charge against me?"

"I have been ordered to hold you until we receive word from your American authorities confirming your claims," Gonzalez replied. "Bacca does not want you held privately and is turning you over to Mexico's authority."

"I suppose that is an improvement," Nik growled. "What about my companion in the other cell?"

"Since she has deceived Señor Bacca and has not the authority that you have presented, he has suggested not moving her at this time," the sheriff said. "She will not be harmed."

"I will hold you to that," Nik said. "However, I would like to be able to speak to her, if I may—in private."

Gonzalez thought for a minute and then remarked, "I will give you two minutes." The sheriff then instructed the deputy to open Morgana's cell and let Nik enter.

"Are you okay?" Nik immediately asked.

"I am fine," Morgana said, rising from her cot. "What is going on?"

"They are transferring me to the sheriff's office, but have decided not to release you, unfortunately," Nik answered. "I am not sure what they have planned for you, but I have told Gonzalez that if you are harmed in any way, he will have to answer to me and the United States."

"Bacca is superstitious and wants me to guide his campaign for president," Morgana answered.

"Can you do that?" Nik asked.

"No, but Bacca and his cartel do not know that," Morgana said. "I can play his game, however, and will do so until help comes my way."

"I will see to it that help comes your way, and soon," Nik replied.

Morgana's door swung open again and Nik was ordered to leave. Accompanied by a deputy, Gonzalez transferred Nik to the Monclova Jail. Afterward, Gonzalez and his deputy rode back to the task force's camp.

Roger rose to his feet as Gonzalez approached and walked toward the sheriff.

"I have good news, Señor Brinkman. Your brother has been moved to the confines of my jail, where you can visit him."

"Visit him? Why hasn't he been released?" Roger demanded. "On what charge are you holding him?"

"I am required to contact your authorities to verify you are all who you claim to be," Gonzalez said. "He will be released when and if that confirmation comes through."

"Get on it then," Roger said. "But wait up, I will go back with you and confirm that he is where you claim."

After reaching the Monclova Jail and being ushered into the cell room, Roger strode up to Nik's cell and grabbed the bars.

"Nik, are you okay?"

Nik rolled off his bunk and strode up to where Roger was standing on the other side of the bars. "As okay as can be expected," Nik said, with anger in his voice.

"Gonzalez said he will release you when he receives official word of your authority to be in Mexico attempting to recover the lost silver," Roger said. "I will stay on him until that arrives."

"I doubt he is even doing that," Nik said.

"What do you mean?"

"They know I'm who and what I claim," Nik answered. "They're stalling for some reason."

"What about Morgana? Where is she?"

"They would not release her, claiming that she lied and that she does not have the authority that I have," Nik said. "Morgana thinks Bacca believes she is some sort of fortune teller who can guide his presidential aspirations."

"Nik, she doesn't do that. She's a spiritual guide for Apache beliefs."

"You know that, and I know that, but she is certain she can lead Bacca to believe that she does have those powers," Nik said. "And she, unfortunately, accused Bacca of killing her mother."

"That is unfortunate," Roger agreed. "So, how do we spring her?"

"I'm not sure," Nik said. "Maybe contact the local media and try to get them to help."

"The newspaper?" Roger quizzed. "What can they do?"

"Maybe they will apply pressure on Bacca," Nik said. "He's a political animal now and is tethered to the media."

"It's a thought," Roger said. "By the way, who is General Diaz? Do you know?"

"From what I know, I think he is in cahoots with Judge Kensington," Nik answered. "I think he was in on the silver heist. Why do you ask?"

"Ahh, let's just say a little fishy told me," Roger said, with a chuckle.

"A what?"

"Never mind," Roger said. "I'm going to look for Monclova's local newspaper."

Not mentioning his intentions of visiting the local newspaper to anyone in the sheriff's office, Roger went in search of a media outlet. A local store owner gave him directions to the Monclova Noticias, the town's newspaper. Upon entering the publication's office, he requested anyone who spoke English.

"Si, I speak English," said a middle-aged man with a pencil-thin mustache and graying, slicked-back hair. "I am Ricardo Romero, the editor-in-chief here."

"I have a juicy story for you," Roger said, shaking Romero's hand and offering a bright smile.

"Juicy?" Romero quizzed.

"A hot story. One I think your newspaper would like to print," Roger said, correcting his adjectives. "This might be one for your front page."

"Please, come into my office," Romero directed.

After entering a small room with a half door, Romero moved behind his desk and gestured for Roger to sit in one of the chairs positioned in front of the desk.

"Now, what can I help you with, Señor... Señor...."

"Señor Brinkman, Roger Brinkman," Roger said, straightening up in his chair. "I'm sorry, I should have introduced myself."

"So, Señor Brinkman, what story do you bring to my newspaper?"

Roger went on to explain that a United States task force, authorized by the Mexican Government, had ended up in Monclova in search of America's lost silver shipment. Roger finished his narrative by telling of Marteen Roberto Bacca's imprisonment of Nik and Morgana.

"Yours is an interesting explanation of your troubles," Romero responded, "but I am not sure how it becomes a story for the Noticias."

Roger leaned forward slightly and replied, "You don't see how this is a story? A group from the United States, authorized by your government to be here, is incarcerated by one of your country's most notorious outlaws and you don't see how that is a story? What exactly does your publication consider news?"

"Marteen Roberto Bacca is not considered an outlaw in Monclova, Señor Brinkman," Romero began. "I sympathize with your failed attempt to recover the silver your country has lost but I am not sure how your description of Señor Bacca exonerates your brother and his companion."

"Perhaps I'm not explaining it properly," Roger said. "You see, a group of Americans, in Mexico specifically to recover what belongs to the United States, is thrown in jail on some phony charges. In the U.S., that would be a major headline."

"I am afraid you are not in the United States. We are different here," Romero said. "Need I remind you that our two countries were at war not that long ago?"

"Look, Mr. Romero, I'm sorry about that conflict, but our two countries are intrinsically linked and at peace right now. I would hate to see that relationship damaged."

Romero sat staring at Roger for a moment and then said, "I will tell you what. I will assign one of my reporters to accompany you to speak to your Señor Nik Brinkman and see if he can come up with a suitable story for the Monclova Noticias."

"I will accept that," Roger said. "I do hope you have one that speaks English."

"I do have such a reporter," Romero said, rising from behind his desk. "Come with me and I will introduce you to him."

Romero took Roger into the main room and led him to a desk located in one of the room's far corners. Sitting behind it was a be-spectacled young man hunched over the desk furiously scribbling notes on a sheet of paper.

"Juan, I want to introduce you to someone," Romero said in Spanish.

The youth looked up, surprising Roger at how young he looked. The reporter referred to as 'Juan' stood up in response to Romero's request.

"Juan," Romero continued, only this time in English. "This is Señor Roger Brinkman. I would like you to accompany him in pursuit of a story. When you have something, bring it to me." With that, Romero returned to his office.

"Juan, may I call you that?"

"Si, Señor Brinkman," Juan Gutierrez said. "How may I help you?"

After briefly explaining the story of his brother's task force and the search for stolen silver, Roger asked Juan if he would start by interviewing Nik, who was in jail.

"Why is he in jail?" Juan asked.

"That's another part of the story," Roger answered. "He shouldn't be, but there is something very wrong going on here. I think this will make a great story for your newspaper."

"I see," Gutierrez responded. "Let me get my notes and I will come with you."

Roger and the Monclova Noticias reporter departed for the sheriff's office.

"How did you become a journalist?" Roger asked, as the two rode in tandem to the sheriff's office.

"I attended the Santa Fe University of Art and Design, in your country, where I learned to write in both Spanish and English," Juan said. "I then worked for a time with the Sante Fe Gazette as a cub reporter and then an editor because of my bilingual skills."

"So, how did you end up here at the Monclova Noticias?"

"My family was from Monclova," Juan said. "When my father lost his job in Santa Fe, we moved back to Monclova and I joined the Noticias."

"Did you find the Noticias to be like the Santa Fe newspaper?"

"No," Juan replied. "The Noticias is owned by Señor Marteen Roberto Bacca. We write what he likes to read. The Gazette tried to be more independent in its reporting, though that was not always easy either."

"Why not?" Roger asked.

"People are always beholden to someone," Juan answered. "Even newspaper people."

"I hope you're not going to let Señor Bacca influence you as far as this story is concerned," Roger said. "I need honest reporting."

"I am honest, Señor Brinkman, but I do not know that the Noticias will be. Señor Romero will decide what gets printed and what doesn't."

"Do you think it will get you into trouble doing this story?" Roger inquired.

"Señor Romero is fair and lets me be objective, but he is loyal to those who pay his salary," Juan said.

Roger didn't say anything more. His mind was racing to construct a story for Juan Gutierrez that would maintain his journalistic integrity but would be benign enough to make it into print.

"You know what?" Roger said, turning his horse in another direction. "I am going to take you to our camp first. I want you to learn about this story first-hand."

After arriving at the task force camp, Roger introduced Juan to everyone and then invited him to accompany him down to the river. On reaching the river, Roger picked out a spot where he and Juan could talk.

"Juan, I'm going to level with you," Roger began. "My story is not going to be flattering to Señor Bacca. However, I trust that you are a good writer and can structure this story so it gets into print, tells the truth as best we can, and does not get you or Señor Romero in any trouble."

"What do you propose?" Juan asked.

"I'm going to lay this story out just as it happened," Roger said. "Then we will work on the particulars so you can do a good job as a reporter, your newspaper will be willing to print your story, and no one gets fired… or worse."

"Now, let's go talk to my brother."

After Roger and Juan returned to the Monclova Sheriff's Office, they found only Sheriff Gonzalez's deputy on duty. When Roger asked to speak to Nik, the deputy turned to Juan Guitierrez and asked who he was.

"I am a reporter with the Monclova Noticias," Juan answered in Spanish. Juan and the deputy exchanged words and then the deputy took both back into the cell area to see Nik.

"Nik, this is Juan Gutierrez, he is a reporter for the Monclova Noticias," Roger said, turning to give the deputy a look of dismissal. The deputy scowled but returned to his desk.

After Nik and Juan shook hands through the bars, Roger explained that he had given Juan the honest truth about their mission and Marteen Roberto Bacca's incarceration of Nik and Morgana. And also, about the difficulty they would have getting the story into print unless they could give Juan a version that would not threaten the newspaper and Juan's job.

"Juan, I would suggest you write this as a potential situation that could cause strained relations between Mexico and the United States," Nik began. "No need to make it sound like sparking another war, but any mistakes made on either side would need to be resolved."

"I believe we could do that as long as Señor Bacca appears to be working toward that goal," Juan said. "If it looks like he might be committing a criminal act to further his political agenda that would not look good and not make it into print."

"We can do that, but we have to be careful," Nik advised. "I'm sure I can gain my release, but Morgana is another matter. Bacca doesn't want to give up Morgana because of her visionary powers. I can't leave Monclova without her."

"What about the silver?" Juan asked. "Are you willing to go back to the States without the silver?"

"If I know that Bacca indeed has the silver then that is good enough for me," Nik said. "I was not sent down here to fight for its return—only to find it."

"May I talk to Bacca about this?" Juan asked. "I might be able to get him to confirm his willingness to help recover the silver without admitting that he has it."

"Even better," Roger said. "If that was in print, Nik and the task force could return to the States with a public record that indicated every attempt was made to recover the silver, maybe even make Bacca look like he was willing to work closely with the U.S. Government to maintain good relations and perhaps help his campaign."

"That should take care of everything but Morgana's release," Nik cautioned. "I feel that is too sensitive to bring up right now. Juan, can you just come up with a good enough story to get me released and we will work on the silver issue and Morgana's release for another story?"

"Let me work on it," Juan said. "I will get my editor to secure an interview with Señor Bacca. I will make it look like I am oblivious to the deeper story."

"Excellent," Nik and Roger said in unison while glancing at each other.

"Juan, if there's anything more we can do for you, let us know," Roger said.

After Juan left to return to the newspaper, Nik turned to Roger and asked, "Can we trust him?"

"I cannot say for sure," Roger replied. "Juan's journalistic ethics seem to be intact, but only time will tell. But if he does what we asked, this could be our ticket out of here."

Chapter 24
General Diaz

D ressed in a red-and-blue-colored uniform with white, crossed belts across his chest, the captain strode into the general's office with his hat tucked under his arm. He approached the front of the general's desk, snapped his heels together at attention, and saluted.

"What is your report," the decorated officer behind the desk asked, returning the salute.

"We believe we have found where the United States' silver shipment has gone, sir," the captain said.

"Wonderful, where has it gone, Captain?"

"Our patrol found the balloon that was carrying the shipment near Ocampo, but the silver was missing," the captain continued. "The Tepehuan chief in Ocampo told us that it was taken by Marteen Roberto Bacca, sir."

"Are you telling me that outlaw confiscated that silver for himself?" General Porfirio Diaz said, rising to his feet. "I did not think he would be smart enough to go after it for himself."

"I am not sure how he found out about the lost silver, sir, but his hacienda is located in Monclova, not that far from Ocampo. Someone there may have alerted him."

"Thank you, Captain," Diaz said. "Is there anything else?"

"Yes, sir. The Tepehuan told us a delegation from the United States was also searching for that silver. They also are aware that Señor Bacca has it."

"What do you know about this 'delegation,' Captain?"

"Only that it is believed they have traveled to Monclova to confront Señor Bacca concerning the silver," the captain said.

"Very good, Captain," Diaz said, dismissing the officer. The general sat down behind his desk and called out, "You may come in now."

Judge Kensington and Sheriff Packard entered the general's office and sat down facing Diaz.

"We heard," Kensington said. "So, what do we do now?"

"We could march on Monclova," the general began, "but I am not sure how that would look in my quest for the presidency."

"We need that silver to finance your campaign for president," Kensington said. "We've spent a lot of money to confiscate it and we need to get it back."

"And we need to get it back soon," Packard said. "If the U.S. Congress moves forward, as many think it will, the value of silver will be raised to match that of gold. We're talking millions, my friends."

"I say, if we have to storm Bacca's hacienda then let's do it."

"Wait, there is another angle," Kensington said, leaning back in his chair with a pensive expression on his face. "The United States has not yet passed that legislation, but it did send a task force here to recover that silver. Perhaps we can work out something with them."

"I know of that task force," Packard remarked. "My boys in Texas informed me that it's headed up by Marshal Nik Brinkman. Brinkman knows both you and me. He'd never cooperate with us."

"That does complicate things," Kensington said. "That means we're going to need someone to pose as a front for us. It would have to be someone able to act as a representative from the States since Mexico's government isn't involved in this."

"And, also someone crooked," Packard said. "We're going to need someone willing to go along with our scheme."

"And expendable," Kensington commented in return. "We don't need to add any more dead weight."

"There is one possibility," Packard remarked, sitting up in his chair. "Wasn't there something else going on in Galveston about the time we were pulling off our heist?"

"I believe there was a counterfeiting ring or something like that," Kensington answered.

"That's right," Packard began, "and as I remember hearing the head of the ring fled to Mexico."

"General, is there any chance this guy may have been picked up by your navy? I assume he fled Galveston by boat."

"Even if we have him, what could he do?" Diaz asked.

"If we can find him, it's possible we could convince him to help us," Kensington added. "With our help, he may be able to print enough phony money to buy that silver from Bacca. I doubt Bacca's smart enough to detect the money as being counterfeit. They had a hard enough time doing that in the States."

"How are you going to convince Bacca to sell it to us?" Diaz asked.

"My guess is," Packard broke in, "if Brinkman went to Monclova to confront Bacca, Bacca must know that it is the United States that wants that silver."

"Precisely," Kensington added. "If he's a fugitive, we can make him an offer. First, to print the counterfeit money we need and, second, to pose as an envoy from the states."

"But wouldn't this Marshal Brinkman know who this man is?" Diaz interjected.

"That wouldn't matter," Packard chimed in. "Brinkman wouldn't know he was connected to us. And I'm willing to bet Brinkman would go along with the negotiations just to get his hands on that silver."

"But then, would not the silver be in possession of the U.S. task force?" Diaz questioned.

"Sure, but how difficult would it be for us to take it from them at gunpoint?" Packard said, with a chuckle. "As I understand it, they've got less than a dozen men in that group."

"I will contact the navy," Diaz offered. "I will put out a bulletin for this man's arrest. Do you have a description?"

"According to my sources," his name is Lester and he's probably carrying bags of money," Packard said.

"It's crazy enough to work," Kensington said, sitting up in his chair. "Let's get started."

***

"Gutierrez, get in here," Romero shouted from his office into the newsroom of the Monclova Noticias.

"Yes, sir, you wanted to see me?" Gutierrez said, entering Romero's office.

"I've secured that interview with Señor Bacca, Juan," Romero said, looking up at the reporter. "He will see you this afternoon. I caution you, be careful what you ask. If Bacca thinks you're going to make him look bad, I cannot guarantee your safety."

"I realize this puts you in a bad spot, sir," Juan said. "I will discuss any difficult matter with you before I submit anything for print."

"This could be a good story if we do it right," Romero said. "It could mean a promotion for you as well."

Yes, sir," Juan said, smiling. "Thanks for setting up this interview." Juan left the office and immediately headed off in the direction of the task force camp.

"I am on my way to Señor Bacca's hacienda," Juan Gutierrez said, as he dismounted near where Roger was standing. "Do you have anything you want to tell me before I go?"

"Yes, be careful," Roger cautioned. "Are you a man of faith?"

"Yes," Juan replied.

"Then, may God go with you," Roger added.

"Are you also a man of faith?" Juan asked.

"I am, Juan. I do not think I would have made it this far in the world had I not been. I can thank my parents for that."

"In that case, I'll be on my way," Juan said.

"Wait," Roger replied. "There are some things we should consider. One, do not suggest to Bacca that my brother, Nik, is innocent. Ask him the offense committed, giving Bacca the idea you are on his side and just doing your job as a reporter. Gather any information he will freely volunteer but do not probe for in-depth answers. All we are doing here is trying to draw attention to the situation."

"Also, make sure he is okay with printing what he has to say. If he is not, do not print it."

"You could pass as my editor," Juan said, with a smile. "I am dedicated to my calling as an objective journalist. But I've been told that a lack of discretion only suppresses the truth."

"An interesting way to put it, Juan. God bless you for this."

Juan nodded, remounted, and rode off in the direction of Bacca's hacienda.

Expecting his arrival, Bacca's guards ushered Juan onto the grounds. After being greeted by Bacca's assistant, the reporter was led into his office.

"To what do I owe a visit from a Monclova Noticias reporter?" Bacca asked, masking concern with a smile.

"It was reported to the Noticias that a dignitary from the United States had been incarcerated due to a criminal act on your property," Juan started. "I am here to follow up on a local story concerning Monclova's candidate for presidente."

Bacca's posture relaxed following Juan's explanation and he began thinking of ways he could use the story to his advantage.

"Si, Sheriff Gonzalez decided that the man claiming to be a representative of the United States should be held until his credentials could be confirmed," Bacca said. "I protested because I did not want to harm our relations with our neighbor to the north. However, the sheriff insisted."

"When do you expect that confirmation to be received, and are you confident the sheriff will release him when it arrives?" Juan asked, stalling for more information.

"I would think so," Bacca replied. "I could not allow the sheriff to hold an innocent man. I would have to insist the man be released."

"Was there anyone with this man at the time he was arrested?" Juan asked, almost instantly regretting that question.

Bacca stared at the young reporter for a brief minute before answering. "Señor Brinkman had an interpreter with him, but the interpreter was not arrested."

"Very good, Señor Bacca," Juan said, folding his tablet. "I believe that is all I need."

"I do believe your newspaper has a picture of me," Bacca said. "I assume you will print that, as well."

"Yes, most certainly, Señor Bacca," Juan said, detecting a softening of Bacca's tone. "By the way, there is one more question… if you do not mind."

"What is it?" Bacca said, hardening his tone again.

"Ahh… why was the American representative here?" Juan said, fearing that the question may have worn out his welcome—or worse.

Again, the reporter was given a cold stare before the answer. Bacca took a deep breath, smiled slightly, and said, "Apparently the United States has lost something they think is in Mexico and they wanted my help to find it."

"Are you at liberty to say what that 'something' was?" Juan said, giving in to his boldness despite his fear of reprisal.

This time Bacca's stare penetrated the reporter like an icy dagger. "Silver, will that be all?"

"Absolutely," Juan said, rising from his chair. "I have taken up too much of your valuable time already. I have all that I need," Juan concluded, nodding to Bacca's assistant to lead him out.

"One moment, Señor… Señor…" Bacca said.

"Gutierrez, Señor Juan Gutierrez," Juan replied.

"I have something you might be interested in seeing before you go. It is not related to this story, but it may be something else you would be interested in," Bacca said, pressing his hands on his desk as he got to his feet. "If you have time."

"I can make the time for you, Señor Bacca," Juan answered, his curiosity aroused. "It would be my pleasure."

"Please come with me then," Bacca stated, circling around to the front of his desk. "We must step outside."

Juan's fears began to return as Bacca led him onto the veranda and around to the back of the hacienda. The reporter was beginning to suspect that Bacca had found something he didn't like about his questions. He eased his anxiety thinking maybe Bacca was trying to distract him from his original story. They came to a heavy wooden door and stopped.

"You asked about the silver," Bacca said, turning to Juan. "Come, I have something to show you."

After opening the door, Bacca led the reporter down a long stairway into an empty room containing several doors. Bacca took some keys off a peg in the wall and opened one of the doors.

"Look at this," Bacca said, gently pushing Juan into the room.

"It's kind of dark. I really don't…" suddenly, Juan heard the door close behind him. A small viewing door opened revealing Bacca's face.

"I regret having to do this," Bacca said. "However, it is only temporary until I know what connection you have with this Señor Brinkman, whom I know you interviewed also. There are spies everywhere. I cannot take chances with an election coming up."

"But, Señor Bacca, this won't help…, the small door on the viewing portal closed and Juan could hear Bacca's footsteps ascending the stairs."

Chapter 25
Heading into Conflict

After going into town to pick up supplies, Roger Brinkman, Peter Zimmerman, and Carter Townsend rode back toward the task force camp outside of Monclova, silently lost in thought. As they rode past the small cathedral where Roger had gone to pray, Peter spoke up.

"What do we do now, Mr. Brinkman?"

"I wish I knew," Roger responded. "But what I think we need to do is assess what we're up against before making any rash decisions."

"What would you consider to be a rash decision?" Carter asked.

"Trying to use force to free Nik and Morgana and, perhaps, Juan Gutierrez if a similar fate has befallen him," Roger mused, since Juan was not at the newspaper when the three stopped to visit him.

"What is the alternative to that?" Carter continued.

"What I said at first," Roger repeated. "Instead of considering actions to attack the situation, we need to understand the situation before we do anything."

"Do we know anything more than those folks you mentioned are behind bars," Peter said, "or being held somewhere against their will?"

"Yes, like why are they being held against their will?" Roger instructed. "If we can figure that out, I think we can figure out what to do about it."

"You mean like lawyers and such?" Carter suggested.

"Not exactly, Carter," Roger answered. "Like you boys in the army assessing an enemy's strengths and weaknesses. Rushing into something could only make it worse but doing nothing would get us nowhere."

"Tonight, I intend to pray on it, and in the morning we'll gather with Lieutenant Gateway, Sergeant Davis, and Charlie Bluefeather to come up with a strategy that will get us all out of here safely."

"What about the silver?" Peter asked.

"They say money is the route of all evil," Roger said. "Just substitute silver for money and you may have come up with what we're really up against, Peter."

"I'm not sure I understand, Mr. Brinkman," Peter said.

"I think you will in the morning," Roger replied, as the three men entered the camp to find Gateway, Davis, Nantan, and Charlie sitting around the campfire. "Tonight, say your prayers and get some sleep."

After a lengthy discussion at the campfire, everyone retired for the evening with a lot on their minds.

✳✳✳

"I have received information that the Mexico Navy has arrested a man trying to enter the country illegally," General Diaz said to his friends Victor Giles Kensington and Curtis Packard.

"That is interesting. Is there anything else about him we should know?" asked former circuit judge Kensington.

"Just this," Diaz started. "He was carrying a bag filled with thousands of dollars in U.S. currency."

"Do you think he is the counterfeiter who escaped from Galveston?" Packard asked.

"There is every indication that he might be," Diaz said, breaking a smile and leaning back in his chair. "He was also carrying what looks to be a blueprint of United States' money."

"This sounds too good to be true," Kensington said. "Is there any way we can meet this person?"

"I have instructed the navy to hold him until we can interrogate him," Diaz said. "I believe I can have him released into our custody."

"But you are not a favorite of President Juarez," Kensington said.

"How will you do that?"

"I have friends in the navy who are not friends with Señor Juarez either," Diaz said. "We should have no problem, especially with the money that's available."

"Let's move on this," Packard said. "We need to send someone to Monclova to recruit this task force to help us obtain that silver."

"I have contacts," Diaz advised. "I have placed men in Monclova to keep an eye on Bacca's activities. But first, let's get our hands on that U.S. money."

***

The next morning, Charlie made plenty of coffee as the men of the task force began discussing their options for freeing their companions. While they were talking, five men on horses approached the camp. Roger, Gateway, and Davis walked out to meet them. As the riders drew near, the three men could see they were dressed as soldiers.

"Can we help you?" Roger called out, as the riders pulled their mounts to a halt.

"We are looking for your leader," the one dressed in an officer's uniform requested in English.

"For now," Roger began, "that would be me."

The officer dismounted, approached Roger, and offered his hand.

"I am Captain Andres de la Garcia. I represent Mexico's authorities and have heard you are here to recover some lost silver, is that right?" the officer asked.

"We are and we have written permission from your government to do that," Roger answered.

"We would like to help you to do that," Garcia said.

"I appreciate that, Captain," Roger responded. "But I am afraid the silver has been recovered by someone else."

"Do you know who?" the officer asked, narrowing his eyes.

"We think it is someone who lives here," Roger continued. "However, we have been unable to confirm that."

"Would this someone be Señor Marteen Roberto Bacca?" the officer asked.

"As a matter of fact, yes," Roger said. "But our attempts to speak to this... Señor Bacca, have met with more trouble than success."

"How so, Señor... Señor...?"

"Brinkman, Roger Brinkman," Roger replied.

"What trouble has befallen you, Señor Brinkman?" Garcia continued.

"I am afraid the true leader of our group has been placed into Monclova's jail, and our interpreter has been missing since visiting Bacca, as well as a journalist who was working on a story for us."

"You say your leader is in jail? Why?" the officer asked.

"We're not sure, Captain. We have been told that his authority to be here is in question until word arrives from our government to confirm that is the case."

"I may be able to help you with that," Garcia said. "What is your leader's name?"

"Brinkman, like mine. Nik Brinkman," Roger said.

"And is he an official of your country?" Garcia inquired.

"Nik is a United States marshal. He was present when the silver was stole... discovered missing," Roger offered. "The Texas Government felt he was the man best suited to create this task force to, hopefully, recover that silver."

"You say his name is Brinkman," Garcia began. "Are you related?"

"He is my brother, which is why I am here," Roger said. "These other men are..." Roger paused, not wanting to say soldier, "are qualified to help him complete this task."

"I do believe we can help you, Señor Brinkman. However, I must check back with my superior officer for instructions on how to best do that. Are you willing to wait until I come back?"

"Right now," Roger confessed. "It's the only thing we would have going for us. And the sooner, the better."

"I understand, Señor Brinkman," Garcia said. "I will return as soon as I have my instructions. Will you still be at this location?"

"We have nowhere else to go," Roger said, smiling. "And we really do appreciate your help. Thank you."

The officer mounted up and he and his men rode away in the direction of the Sierra Madre Oriental.

"Walter, Beau, I'm going to ride into town and let Nik know about this. I hate to have to drag the Mexican Army into this, but I'm beginning to feel a little desperate now," Roger remarked.

***

General Porfirio Diaz arrived at the Armada de Mexico outpost at the port city of Matamoros, Mexico, just across the Rio Grande from Texas. Keeping a low profile, he was ushered into the office of Captain Gustavo Mejia. "General Diaz!" the captain called out as Porfirio was introduced. Mejia snapped to attention and saluted.

"Por Favor, please be seated, Captain," the general answered. "I am here on official business and require some discretion, if I may."

"Whatever you wish, my general," Mejia complied. Mejia had fought alongside Diaz in earlier conflicts and supported the general's quest for president. "To what do I owe this honor?"

"I believe you have an American detained here, do you not?" Diaz inquired.

"We do," Mejia answered. "He was caught trying to enter the country illegally and placed under arrest. We are waiting for orders as to what to do with him."

"I am here to assist you in that matter," Diaz said, presenting a smile. "I have been asked to have this man placed in my custody. I will transport him to the proper authorities to decide on what to do with him."

"I understand he had some baggage with him."

"Si, my general, I have it here in my office," Mejia said, rising from his chair and retrieving the bag. "It is filled with American money. I can assure you that it is all there. At least, all that he was caught with."

"I'm sure it is, Gustavo. You always do such good work," Diaz said, leaning forward and lowering his voice. "When I am presidente, you shall be among my top generals."

"You are too kind, General," Mejia said. "There were also these blueprints. They look like something from the United States Treasury."

"Excellent, Gustavo. I am sure the Americans are anxious to get these back. I will see to it all is properly taken care of," Diaz said. "By the way, what is his name?"

"He has refused to give us his name, but through our investigation, we believe his name is Ronald Lester. We believe he was a former treasury agent and was connected to a criminal ring in the United States," Mejia explained.

"Please, keep this between us," Diaz cautioned. "I am afraid if too much information is released it could cause friction with our neighbors to the north."

"I understand, my general," Mejia said. "Nothing will go beyond the walls of this office. I will summon the guards to discharge him to your custody."

"But, just for protocol, would you mind signing this release form?"

"Not at all, Gustavo," Diaz said, standing up and smiling. "We must do this proper-like."

After the meeting, a shackled Ron Lester was turned over to Diaz. Lester was placed in a wagon with soldiers stationed on all sides. With Diaz leading the way, the detail left Matamoros with their prisoner.

Chapter 26
Money, Silver, and Morgana

Later, during the day after Roger first spoke with Andrew de la Garcia, Roger spotted the captain and his soldiers approaching the camp. Trying to stifle his enthusiasm in case Garcia wasn't bringing good news, he stood waiting for the small company of soldiers to approach.

"Let us not waste time," Garcia called out, without getting off his horse. "Let us go get your brother out of jail."

Roger broke into a wide smile and turned to see the others in camp clapping their hands and laughing with glee.

"As you can see, Captain. We've been beating ourselves up trying to figure out a way to get Nik out of jail."

"I understand," Garcia said, but without a smile, "but there is more that has to be done. I will explain when we get back with your brother."

After reaching the Monclova Sheriff's Office, Roger tried to suppress his 'in-your-face' feelings as he followed Captain Garcia into Sheriff Gonzalez's office. Garcia produced a paper that he placed on the sheriff's desk and spoke to Gonzalez in Spanish. The sheriff looked up with a somewhat grim expression but immediately rose to his feet and brushed past both men on his way to Nik Brinkman's cell.

Once released, Nik hugged Roger and immediately shook Captain Garcia's hand, following Roger's introduction. After entering the main office, Nik's personal belongings were returned to him, and he, Roger, and Andres stepped into the street only to see four of

Marteen Roberto Bacca's men on horseback waiting near the captain's soldiers. Garcia quickly mounted, followed by Roger. Nik mounted an additional horse that Roger had brought along to transport his brother. Garcia shouted something to Bacca's men in Spanish and then led his men in a gallop toward the task force camp.

After reaching the camp, everyone there congratulated Nik upon his return. Captain Garcia dismounted and asked all who were present to gather around to hear what had to be done next.

"An official notice has been sent to Señor Bacca of your release and that you would be renegotiating with him for the release of the silver. This notice comes with Presidente Bonito Juarez's signature and instructions that Señor Bacca accept you as an emissary for both Mexico and the United States," Garcia began. "You are encouraged to negotiate for a reasonable price but do not fail to accept the best you can get, regardless of the amount. It is important that Mexico retrieves that silver."

"I would also like to secure the release of my interpreter," Nik added.

"And a journalist from the Monclova Noticias, whom I believe is being held at Bacca's hacienda, as well," Roger interjected.

"I cannot guarantee the release of those through these same negotiations," Garcia replied. "However, you are welcome to try, but do not make it contingent on settling with Señor Bacca. Once we have the silver, these matters can be discussed later."

"We don't want any trouble," Nik said. "But that seems to be Bacca's method of operation."

"One last thing," Captain Garcia said. "When you have come to an agreement concerning the purchase of the silver, I and my soldiers will handle the transfer of the silver to you."

Nik and Roger looked at one another and simply nodded. "I would sincerely like to put this thing behind us and get these folks back home," Nik said.

"Here is a duplicate of Presidente Juarez's proclamation," the captain said, handing Nik the papers. "Just so you have a copy on you in case you run into any resistance."

Everyone again thanked Garcia for his help and the captain

and his unit rode off.

Early the next morning, Roger accompanied Nik down to the river while Nik washed up in preparation for his meeting with Bacca.

"Do you know what you're going to say?" Roger casually asked, as his shirtless brother splashed water on himself.

"Yes, I know what I'm going to say but I don't know what Bacca is going to say," Nik answered, his face and torso dripping with water as he reached toward Roger for his towel. "It's what that outlaw says that matters. Then I'm going to have to come up with the right words to try and swing him over to my way of thinking."

"What are you thinking?"

"I'm thinking, if he has that silver, I want it and Morgana's release," Nik said. "I've already lost one man on this expedition, and I do not want to leave another behind."

"If Bacca has that silver and agrees to your terms, what do we do then?" Roger continued grilling his brother, as the two began walking back to the camp.

"Roger, the more I think about this crazy trip the more I see the folly of it. Sure, even if Bacca doesn't have that silver, I plan to load up and go home," Nik said. "Right now, getting back to Esther and civilization is all that's on my mind."

"You're a very practical man, Nik," Roger commented. "I guess that's why you are such a good lawman."

As the brothers reached the wagon where Charlie Bluefeather had laid out clothes for Nik to wear, Nik stopped and looked at Roger for a moment.

"So were you, Roger," Nik began. "But you have a higher purpose now, a higher calling, if you will. You've been charged with saving souls and right now I'd be content with saving what's left of this task force—the silver be damned."

"I can see your point," Roger said as Nik began putting on his outfit for the day. "Trying to satisfy those in Washington, D.C., has turned this journey into a bit of a nightmare."

"Not to mention trying to satisfy Mexico," Nik remarked. "These people do not play by the same rules as we do in the States. They're not wrong, they're just different. I think the revival meetings we held early on did far more good than anything we've accomplished yet—or will accomplish."

"You know, I think you understand my job as well as I do," Roger said, smiling, as Nik placed his hat on his head and slid his hand across the brim.

"No, Roger, I know very little about your place in life, other than what our family taught us," Nik said, looking into a small mirror and stroking his mustache. "What I do know is the result of what you do. I just wish what I do made more sense."

"Well, I'll be praying for you, brother," Roger said, as Nik strode over to his horse and climbed into the saddle.

Nik looked down at the members of his task force and said, "Why don't the rest of you join Roger in praying for the success of this mission? But just in case, be sure to keep your powder dry."

Nik then turned his horse and rode off in the direction of Monclova.

When Nik reached the front gate of Señor Bacca's hacienda, the outlaw's assistant Francisco was there to meet him.

"Ahh, Señor Brinkman," Francisco said. "How kind of you to return. We have received word from Presidente Juarez that you have some information for Señor Bacca and he is anxious to hear what you have to say."

When Nik was led into Bacca's spacious office, Marteen was behind his desk waiting for him. Bacca exchanged a few words in Spanish with Francisco and the assistant left the room.

"Please, be seated, Señor Brinkman. I am happy that your confirmation finally came through and you could be allowed out of Sheriff Gonzalez's jail," Bacca began. "I am sorry you had to be detained, but as a presidential candidate, I cannot be too careful."

"I am in a forgiving mood, Señor Bacca, and I hope that we can come to an agreement," Nik stated. "I know you have been troubled by me and the task force that accompanies me. I assure you that if we can reach a deal, you will likely see no more of me."

"So, what is your proposal, Señor Brinkman?" Bacca said, leaning back in his chair.

"I am prepared to pay you, in American currency, for the return of the silver you salvaged in the Sierra Madre mountains near Ocampo," Nik said. "I think I can make it worth your while to turn that silver over to the United States."

"So, you are certain that I have the silver?" Bacca asked. "Why do you think that?"

"Because we have been to the site where the balloon crashed and there is no silver there," Nik started. "We were led to the site by Chief Pawhetah of the Tepehuan tribe, who informed us that your men gathered up the silver well before we got there."

"How do you know that this… Pawhetah is telling the truth?" Bacca questioned.

"Because we also got confirmation from a recovery party sanctioned by your country that your men had gathered up the lost silver," Nik said.

"And just who is this 'recovery party' you speak of?"

"I cannot give you those details because that information came through official channels from my country. They did not include the identity of the party but were convinced enough to send me here with a generous offer," Nik said.

"Do you have this money with you?"

"No, once we have agreed on a price, an envoy from the States will deliver the money and pick up the silver at that time," Nik instructed.

"If you want silver, I have a silver mine and can sell you silver from that," Bacca said.

"No, it has to be the silver shipment that was taken from Galveston Bay by a gas-filled balloon. The bars are marked for the United States Treasury," Nik stated. "My task force was not sent here to buy silver but to salvage the stolen shipment."

"You do not believe I stole your silver, Señor Brinkman?" Bacca asked.

"No, we believe we know who did, but we are not interested in him or his men. We just want the silver returned," Nik stated.

Bacca began to smile, leaned forward, and put his clasped hands on his desk. "I will level with you, Señor Brinkman, since you know neither I, nor any of my men, had anything to do with stealing that silver, I will level with you. We did see the balloon and later found out what its cargo was. I did send a party to get it and can honestly tell you that it is all intact."

"Wonderful," Nik said. "I am prepared to pay you seven hundred and fifty thousand dollars for it."

Bacca's smile widened into a laugh. "If that silver is so important to your rich county," he began, "I could not accept less than two million of your country's dollars."

Nik gazed at Bacca for a moment, then said, "I am prepared to go up to a million. That is considerably more than that silver is worth on the open market."

"This is not the open market, Señor Brinkman. This is silver precious to your country. I could not take less than… say, one million, plus your first offer of seven-hundred and fifty thousand dollars."

"I see what is going on here," Nik said, now also smiling. "Let's cut this poker game short, I can give you one million, five hundred thousand dollars. That's my top offer."

Bacca laughed out loud, "You know, Señor Brinkman, I like you. I will accept your offer to help you save face."

"Much obliged," Nik said, rising to his feet to shake Bacca's hand, but as soon as Bacca reached across the table Nik drew his hand back. "I'm sorry, Señor Bacca," Nik began. "I must also insist on the release of my interpreter, whom you have locked up in your basement, or whatever that is."

Bacca's face turned serious as he stared at Nik. "You mean Señorita Morgana Maria Cabezon? She is very valuable to me, Señor Brinkman."

"As a prisoner? What benefit do you derive from that?"

"She sees the future, Señor Brinkman. That is very valuable to a man in my position."

"She's a shaman, not a fortune teller," Nik said, trying to hide the sarcasm.

"For you, perhaps there is a difference," Bacca said, "but I'll make you this offer. If you tell me who was the thief of that silver shipment, I will consider releasing Señorita Cabezon when that envoy arrives with the money."

Nik thought for a moment but could not come up with a reason not to identify the judge. "The thief was Victor Kensington. He was a judge in our country until it was discovered he was corrupt. We believe he fled to your country. Do you know him?"

Bacca thought a minute and answered, "I have heard of him but did not know he was behind the theft of your silver."

"We have every reason to believe that he was," Nik said. "One of the members of his outfit was caught and confessed to Kensington's involvement."

"Gracias, Señor Brinkman," I will honor your request when your emissary arrives with the money. I assume that person will have the necessary papers to indicate I did not steal the silver, only recovered it."

"I'm sure you can have that included in whatever it is you think you will need," Nik concluded. "Good day, Señor Bacca."

After Nik left, Bacca called Francisco back into his office.

"Francisco, bring the mestizo shaman here," Bacca ordered. "I want to speak to her."

Chapter 27
The Showdown

Captain Andres Garcia was waiting at the task force camp when Nik returned. Nik dismounted and shook the officer's hand.

"It's going to cost a million and a half to get that silver back," Nik said, hoping the captain would not suffer a setback by the news.

"That is fine," Garcia said, noticing a hint of surprise on Nik's face. "We knew Señor Bacca would not be reasonable."

"There is one more thing," Nik added. "I made the exchange contingent on the release of Morgana Cabezon."

"Oh, I hope that does not complicate things, Señor Brinkman. Did Señor Bacca agree to that?"

"He did," Nik said. "Although reluctantly."

"Is that why the price was so high?" the captain asked.

"No, he said he would let Morgana go if I told him who the original silver thief was," Nik said. "I don't know if Bacca actually knew him or not, so I told him."

"Who would that be, Señor Brinkman?"

"Victor Giles Kensington, a former United States circuit judge," Nik said. "I believe he is living here in Mexico now."

If that news disturbed Captain Garcia, he did not show it. "That sounds like a harmless enough price to pay for this woman's release. I must be getting back now to let my commandant know what the offer is. Gracias, Señor Brinkman, and you too, Roger."

Everyone in the camp thanked Garcia for his efforts and the captain galloped away.

"So, you think this is all going to come together, Nik?" Roger asked.

"If Captain Garcia's superiors have that money, I think it will," Nik answered. "I'm still worried about Morgana, though. Bacca said he'd let her go once he received the payment, but I don't trust that man for a minute."

That evening, as the task force members sat around the campfire, Monclova Noticias' reporter Juan Gutierrez came riding up.

"Juan? So Bacca finally let you out," Roger greeted. "That's one less problem we have to worry about," Roger added, turning toward Nik.

"It is good to be free again," Juan began, "but I am not free to write the story you may have wanted. In fact, I was close to losing my job."

"I'm story to hear that Juan," Roger said, "but, as you can see, Nik is out of jail also."

"Juan, won't you join us?" Nik said, rising to greet the reporter. "We have some things to discuss, and we might just have an even greater story for you."

Juan obliged and Charlie greeted the young journalist with a hot cup of coffee. Nik remained standing, while the others sat on bedrolls, saddles, boxes, and small logs placed on end for seating.

"We now have to make plans for what may eventually happen," Nik began. "We have struck a deal with Bacca to turn over the silver, paid for by our Treasury and administered by the Mexican government. It's time we put our heads together as to what we know, what we can do, and how to prepare for it."

"Good idea, Nik," Roger said. "Why don't we start by finding out what Juan learned while he was incarcerated at Bacca's hacienda."

"I did not learn much from my interview with Señor Bacca, but I did learn a little while I was in his prison," Gutierrez began. "The mestizo woman in the cell next to me was eventually removed from her cell and taken to a place that I do not know. Presumably in the hacienda somewhere."

"Why do you say that?" Nik asked.

"I gathered from what little the guard would tell me that she would be given special treatment if she gave Bacca what he wanted from her," the journalist said. "I was told that if she did not cooperate, things could go very bad for her."

"If he harms her, I'm afraid I'm going to have to get involved in a way my calling would forbid," Roger angrily said.

"Hold on, Roger," Nik cut in. "Morgana is smart. She is going to outfox that charlatan outlaw. She might be enjoying his best hospitality by stringing him along."

"I'm sure you're right," Roger conceded. "She may be too bold for my taste but she's definitely smart and certainly smarter than Bacca."

"She is shaman," Charlie broke in. "She has the Spirit on her side to guide her. What is important is that we do not spoil her plan by allowing our plan to interfere with hers."

"That's right," Nantan said. "Shaman has a connection to the spirits that most of us do not possess. They do not predict the future, but they do see visions of it."

"What about you, Roger?" Lieutenant Gateway asked. "You're a man in a similar position when it comes to spirituality."

"Mine's a little diff…" Roger hesitated in midsentence, recalling the fisherman he had encountered down by the river. "Let's just say, my path is laid out before me. I think Morgana's is revealed as she goes along."

"So, what are we going to do, Marshal Brinkman?" Peter Zimmerman asked.

"Walt, I want you and Beau to form a garrison of sorts using Pete, Carter, Nantan, and Charlie," Nik stated. "Set up the chuck wagon as a battle wagon and disguise it. Inspect our weapons and go into Monclova and get more ammunition, even more horses, if necessary."

"Are you expecting a war?" Sergeant Davis asked.

"Trying to avoid one," Nik said. "But, depending on how this situation comes down, we may have to fight our way out of here. I want us to be as ready for that as possible."

"Juan, you can help us by writing up a story that says an agreement has been reached by the Americans and Señor Bacca. Try to appease Bacca as best you can," Nik added.

"Maybe even refer to Bacca as the next president. That ought to soften him somewhat," Roger suggested.

"As for Roger and me," Nik continued. "We're going to work on Morgana's release. When we achieve that, we're out of here."

"What about the silver?" Roger replied. "Aren't we supposed to receive that when the Mexican government seals the deal with Bacca?"

"I've got a hunch Bacca has no intention of letting us return to the States with that shipment," Nik offered. "I trust Captain Garcia, to an extent, but I don't trust those above him who are pulling these strings."

"Yes, Juan, what do you know about this General Diaz?" Roger asked.

"Although Bacca is an outlaw, he is more popular among the Mexican people than is Diaz," Gutierrez said. "Señor Brinkman is right, there is bad blood between those two men, and I would guess that either would do whatever is necessary to gain power."

After a short discussion of strategy, the reporter departed and the task force retired to their bedrolls.

After a good breakfast to give each member of the task force the energy to follow through on Nik's suggestions, the marshal and his brother set out for Dr. Alejandro de la Morales' office. The doctor examined Nik's back and, after removing a few remaining stitches, rendered the patient a clean bill of health.

"With the exception of a few scars, your back is strong again," Morales said. "But I cannot guarantee you won't have some back trouble as you age."

"Isn't that the case for just about everyone?" Nik remarked, flashing a smile at Morales.

"Those cuts ran deep, Señor Brinkman," Morales commented. "Some muscles may have been chronically damaged."

"Nik's future wife is a woman who will have his back," Roger joked. "And not one who will be on his back."

Even Nik had to laugh at the comment, as the brothers paid the doctor and stepped back onto the main street of Monclova.

"If you want to come," Roger suggested, "I want to talk to Father Benedict at the local mission."

"What about?" Nik asked.

"Benedict said Bacca attends mass there," Roger answered. "I would like to question him further on what he knows of the outlaw and his habits."

"Are you planning an attack?" Nik said, grinning.

"No, but he might give us a clue on how we can spring Morgana if we have to," Roger said.

Father Benedict was talking to a young man and woman at the front of the church near the altar when Roger and Nik entered. When the couple walked up the aisle past the two men to exit, Father Benedict followed behind them. After the man and woman departed, Benedict greeted the Brinkmans.

"Señor Brinkman," Benedict said, reaching out for Roger's hand. "What brings you back to my humble parish?"

"Father, this is my brother, Nik Brinkman," Roger began. "We have a dilemma you may be able to help us with."

"If it is within my power, I promise to do what I can," Benedict said, extending his hand to Nik. "You say you are brothers?"

Roger gave the priest a brief explanation of the brotherhood he and Nik shared, describing Nik's adoption into the family.

"We do not approve of slavery here in Mexico," Benedict said. "It is not something I admire about your country."

"Hopefully that's behind us," Roger said. "But we want to talk to you about Señor Marteen Roberto Bacca."

The father raised his eyebrows, as he answered, "My knowledge of Señor Bacca is limited, but I am happy to tell you what I know."

"You said he attends mass at your church," Roger continued. "Is there a usual time that he does that?"

"Each Sunday, promptly at nine o'clock," Benedict answered. "He brings many of his bodyguards with him. He may be a powerful man here in Monclova, but he trusts no one."

"Even better, Father," Roger said, "and how long does mass usually last?"

"At least an hour," Benedict said. "Then he and his men spend time in the local cantina, having breakfast and greeting people as a part of his campaign."

"So, he's in town most of the day?" Nik asked.

"At least for most of the morning," Benedict said. "He truly enjoys the attention, and the people give it to him to keep him happy. They know he can be trouble otherwise."

"Father, you have been most helpful," Roger said, again shaking the priest's hand. "And you're expecting Señor Bacca this Sunday?"

"Like I say, he is here promptly at nine, unless he is out of town."

"I know what you're thinking," Nik said after the two were alone outside. "With Bacca and some of his men in town on Sunday, we might be able to get Morgana out of that hacienda."

"Yes, but we don't know how long we'll have before it is discovered that she's gone," Roger added. "We'll have to move fast once she's free."

Roger and Nik returned to camp to find Captain Garcia waiting for them.

"We will arrive with the United States representative, who is to deliver the money to Señor Bacca," Garcia began. "We will supply the wagon to carry the silver and an escort. However, you are to meet us at the Monclova Sheriff's Office to sign some official documents releasing the silver into your hands. My unit will escort you back to camp with the silver."

"I just ask that you request Morgana be released," Nik said. "Bacca said he would do that, but I don't trust him."

"I will ask," Garcia said. "However, I am not authorized to force his compliance if he says no."

"We understand, Captain," Roger said. "We'll have to work something out on our end."

Captain Garcia then rode off while Roger and Nik looked on.

"He seems like a good man," Nik said. "Of everyone we've met so far, I would like to put him alongside Father Benedict and Dr. Morales as to those I would trust."

"I have to say that if he is involved in anything nefarious, I don't think he knows it," Roger said. "He's been a big help to us."

"So, what's our plan if Morgana isn't released?"

"We had better grab a pair of field glasses and find someplace where we can survey Bacca's estate," Nik said. "If we have to rescue Morgana, we'd better have some idea of how we're going to do it."

As they approached Bacca's hacienda, Nik and Roger spotted a tall bluff rising behind the grounds and made a wide circle around the property to come up behind it. After climbing to an area rising about thirty feet above the level of Bacca's fortress, they observed that the area was not heavily guarded.

The garden had a hedge around the landscaped area that nearly surrounded the hacienda.

"That hedge Bacca planted was likely to slow down intruders," Nik said, scanning the back of the estate. "The garden on the east side is also heavily covered in plants and several statues. That's where Morgana and I were when we were taken hostage."

"It appears to me that the grounds are not heavily guarded, which tells me most of the men are inside or in town," Roger said. "Like Juan said, if Morgana has been given some freedom, maybe they let her out to enjoy the garden. However, there's no way of knowing if and when that might be."

"I think there's a way to find out," Nik suggested.

"I'm listening."

"Morgana is a shaman," Nik started. "She is a sacred symbol in much of this country and Bacca believes in that. That's why he is holding her."

"I'm with you so far," Roger remarked, still scanning the property.

"Let's send Charlie and Nantan here asking that they be allowed to receive something spiritual from her, like a blessing," Nik said. "If they can get in to see her, they can find out where she is and where she could be Sunday morning."

"I like it, brother," Roger said. "If Bacca won't hold up his end of the bargain, perhaps you've found a way to hold it up for him."

Nik smiled as the two men climbed back down to their horses and rode back to camp.

The Brinkman brothers were pleased to find that both Charlie Bluefeather and Nantan were eager to put Nik's plan into action.

"What more can they do to us than say no," Charlie said. "They probably don't know anything about my background and Nantan is Apache. It would be seen as a gesture of goodwill."

"I suggest we do it now," Roger said. "If Bacca does not release Morgana along with the silver, the greater the chance he will think we might try to rescue her and increase the security around her."

"That's a good point," Nik said in agreement. "Charlie, Nantan, I don't think anyone in Bacca's clan would recognize you, although the sheriff was out here and might remember you. Just to be on the safe side, I will ride into Monclova ahead of you and occupy the sheriff. You two head over to Bacca's hacienda and ask for Francisco. He speaks English and is reliable."

Fortune was on Nik's side, as Sheriff Gonzalez was in his office. Nik explained how the silver transfer was going to take place and wanted the sheriff to help him understand protocol in the matter. Gonzalez was only too happy to oblige.

Staying clear of the sheriff's office, Charlie and Nantan approached the front gate and asked for Francisco. After explaining to the assistant their mission, Francisco approached Bacca.

"They are local natives?" Bacca asked.

"From the north," Francisco said. "They want to get the shaman's blessing on you as presidente of Mexico. Apparently, they are not fond of General Diaz or Presidente Juarez."

"Can you see any harm in this?" Bacca asked.

"Only if Morgana does not give them that blessing, holding back claiming that she is a prisoner here," Francisco said. "But if she is willing to do so, it would be good publicity for you, Señor Bacca."

"Tell you what, Francisco," Bacca instructed. "Tell Morgana in advance that if she does not give them the blessing they seek, they're dead men. Is that clear?"

"Very clear," Francisco said. "Is it too soon to refer to you as presidente?" he added with a broad smile that was not wasted on the outlaw.

After Morgana had been given the ultimatum, the two Indians were taken into the garden and told to wait. Francisco sent two guards to escort Morgana out to meet them. She wisely showed no surprise when she saw who they were. The shaman then told the guards that it was necessary to stand at a distance when the blessing was administered, or it could become a bad omen for Señor Bacca. The guards reluctantly complied and placed themselves out of earshot.

"What news do you bring me?" she quietly asked her visitors.

"Do you think Bacca will release you?" Nantan asked.

"No," Morgana said. "In fact, he has threatened to kill you if I do anything that would cause trouble for him."

"Nik has a plan to rescue you on Sunday," Nantan said. "Can you get permission to come to the garden in the morning?"

"You mean while Bacca is away at his church?"

"Yes," Nantan said.

"Then an attempt will be made to rescue you that day," Charlie advised. "If there is shooting, we have been told many of Bacca's men will be in town with him."

"I will ask the spirits for guidance," Morgana said. "And if anything goes wrong, tell Nik and Roger to be careful. I can be resourceful when I need to be."

"We will kneel now, and it would be good for you to make it look like you are offering us a blessing," Nantan concluded.

Morgana made several gestures as the men knelt down. She then had them rise and signaled to the guards to approach.

"Let them know I'll be ready," Morgana said softly and dismissed the Indians as she left the garden accompanied by the guards.

Nantan and Charlie were escorted off the grounds and made their way back to camp.

Chapter 28
The Exchange

The Saturday of the exchange of one-half million, five-hundred thousand dollars had arrived, and Nik and Roger Brinkman decided to go into Monclova to wait until Captain Andres Garcia and his detachment arrived to purchase the lost silver from Marteen Roberto Bacca. They stopped in at a small cantina located at the edge of town on the main street and sat down for coffee.

"I'm sorry I dragged you away from your gospel circuit, Roger," Nik said, pulling his cup closer from where the waitress had set it down. "If I'd known it was going to be like this, I never would have been so selfish."

"What, and miss all this excitement?" Roger said, gently blowing on the steam coming from his cup as he raised it to his mouth. "You said that same thing after our counterfeiting caper in Galveston. If that didn't deter me nothing would have."

"And what do you mean by 'selfish?'"

"I'm just more comfortable with you by my side when I'm in the middle of assignments," Nik said. "You're a preacher now. There's no reason for you to be putting yourself at risk doing a job I agreed to do."

"I'm not sorry that I gave up marshaling to enter the ministry," Roger said, as he put his coffee cup back down on the table. "But I do miss the Marshal Service. You're my touchstone who takes me back to the life I would have led had I not returned to seminary."

"I feel close to my family doing what I'm doing for the church, however God didn't call me to be a preacher because it was safe and comfortable. Although I can't be a marshal and a pastor at the same time, I do feel closer to God when I'm tagging along with you."

"What worries me is what would you do if you were confronted by someone intent on killing you?" Nik said, using a napkin to wipe the condensation from his mustache. "You used your gun just as I have when you were marshaling. Would you do it again?"

"Although God looks after me now, you know that I still carry my sidearm," Roger responded.

"But would you use it if you had to?" Nik questioned. "As much as I can't resist asking for your help at times, it's hard for me to think something dreadful could happen to you because you refused to use that sidearm if the occasion called for it."

Roger took a gulp of coffee and put the cup back down. "I'm not a killer, Nik, but I wouldn't be much use to the Lord if I were dead. Although I spread the gospel as my profession, I do it in an untamed land during dangerous times. I don't think about what I would do in all situations, but self-preservation is a strong motivator. There is no red line when it comes to forgiveness."

"I guess that's what my conscience hangs onto when I ask for your help," Nik began, leaning forward to sip his coffee while glancing out of the cantina window. What he saw caused him to nearly spit his coffee onto Roger.

"What the heck…" Roger exclaimed, grabbing his napkin to defend himself.

"Roger, look out the window. Do you see what I see?"

Roger turned to get a look at what had caused such a reaction from his brother. Captain Garcia's detachment was riding down Monclova's main street surrounding a wagon being pulled by two horses. Sitting in the wagon was Ron Lester. Nik pushed his chair back from the table and stood up.

"I've got a score to settle," he remarked as he moved toward the door.

"Nik, sit down," Roger ordered, as Nik turned to look back at this brother. "Don't do anything, at least don't do anything crazy yet. I'm guessing he's the so-called emissary who is going to deliver the money to Bacca. You don't want to interfere with that."

Nik slowly returned to his chair and pulled it out to sit down, all the while watching as the detachment went by.

"Roger, that man was going to kill you," Nik growled.

"And nearly did, but I'm still here, aren't I?" Roger said, leaning over the table toward Nik. "Don't you see what's going on here? They're going to pay Bacca in counterfeit cash. Lester is being used because he has the phony money and he's from the United States, not Mexico. Just look how they have him dressed."

"You're right," Nik said. "That means he's going to be driving back to the sheriff's office with that silver. There's no way Bacca is going to know that money is counterfeit. But Lester's bound to recognize us."

"Recognize you, yes, but not me," Roger said.

"How's that" Nik replied.

"Because I'm not going with you to the sheriff's office. You don't need me there, so I'm going back to camp to get everyone ready for... if you'll excuse me... all hell to break loose."

"So, you don't think I ought to shoot him when he shows up at the sheriff's office?" Nik said, with a puzzled look on his face.

"Nik, you'd be immediately arrested by Gonzalez, if Garcia didn't shoot you first. If Lester is mixed up in this thing, then I'm betting he's in cahoots with Kensington and Diaz. I have a hunch they do not intend for us to take that silver back to the States."

"Okay, you're losing me now," Nik said. "Why are they doing all this?"

"They used you to negotiate with Bacca, knowing you had credibility as an agent from the States," Roger said. "They're throwing funny money at Bacca to get their hands on that silver. They have no intention of letting us get away with it."

"Are you sure you don't want to go back to marshaling, Roger? You're really good at it, you know."

"You just go and sign those papers and take possession of that silver," Roger instructed. "I don't know if Garcia is involved or just doing his duty guarding that silver until it's in our hands. My guess is Diaz and his soldiers will soon be on our tail."

"Wait a minute," Nik said, contemplating Roger's deduction. "We'll likely have Bacca after us, as well. He knows we don't have the men to fight him and when he discovers Morgana is gone, he'll have a good idea who has her."

"That's the hell breaking loose I'm talking about," Roger said. "Bacca and Diaz meeting on the battlefield. It just might give us the opportunity we'll need to escape."

"You head over to the sheriff's office. I'm riding back to camp. I'll see you there when you arrive with that wagonload of silver."

Nik agreed with Roger's strategy, and both departed the cantina.

Roger returned to the task force camp and laid out the potential scenario of what was at stake.

"Walter," Roger said, addressing Lieutenant Gateway. "Prepare to abandon camp. I am not certain how we're going to make our exit just yet, but I can say we're going to have to do it soon and travel fast."

"Do you and Nik have a plan?" Gateway asked as the campers came out to greet Roger.

"I will give you a brief description of the details we discussed, but I cannot say how things will develop," Roger began. "Nik and I believe this silver exchange is a setup and we're the ones being set up. The only thing that would be in our favor is if Bacca releases Morgana along with the silver. But Nik and I do not believe he will do that."

"So, we'll have the silver but not Morgana?" Nantan asked.

"It's just speculation for now," Roger answered. "However, we do know that the money we've been told the United States is offering for the silver isn't worth the paper it's printed on."

"What do you mean?" Gateway interjected.

"Nik and I have seen the 'emissary' sent to deliver the cash and he is a known fugitive from Texas, a former counterfeit operator," Roger said. "We believe the money they deliver to Bacca won't be U.S. currency at all."

"Do you think Bacca will be able to detect that?" Sergeant Davis asked.

"No, it's an extremely sophisticated forgery, but if we have to rescue Morgana by force that will likely be enough to put Bacca and his bunch on our tail," Roger replied. "Tonight, I'm suggesting the rest of you depart with the silver following the river east. I'm guessing

Nik and I will have to liberate Morgana tomorrow morning while Bacca and his men attend mass in town."

Roger continued explaining the tentative plan to the men and encouraged them to be ready to go once the details were finalized.

"Meanwhile," Roger continued, "I have some personal business to attend to."

Roger returned to the river wondering if he'd see the fisherman again, but there was no one on the river but himself. He then found a quiet place to get down on his knees and begin to pray.

"Roger," said a voice coming from behind him. Roger jumped to his feet, looking for whoever had addressed him.

"Yeah, what do you need?" Roger asked, recognizing the voice and thinking it was someone from the task force. Then he spotted the man in black attire decorated with silver conchos and wearing a large sombrero standing near the river.

"You, you're the man on the train in Galveston," Roger said. "Do I know you?"

"That's not important," the man replied. "What is important is that you take Captain Garcia into your confidence and do as he tells you."

"I appreciate the advice, but I'm not sure the rest of the task force feels the same way,"

"They will because they trust you," the man replied.

"But who are you?" Roger said.

The man pushed back his sombrero and smiled.

"Pa!?" Roger cried out, recognizing the face.

"Pastor Brinkman," said another voice from behind, causing Roger to wheel about, only to see Peter Zimmerman standing behind him. Peter held up abruptly when he noticed tears running down Roger's cheeks.

"Pastor Brinkman, are you all right?" Peter said.

"Peter, look who is here," Roger said, extending an arm back toward the man by the river and turning to face him.

"Who?" Peter asked, seeing no one.

The figure had vanished and Roger lowered his head and quickly wiped away the tears. "Oh, no one," he said. "I guess I was just so deep into prayer I kind of felt someone was there with me. Pay no attention."

"I'm sorry to bother you, Pastor Brinkman, but the men want you to give your approval," Peter said. "We've got everything ready to go."

"Thanks, Peter, let's get this show ready for the road."

***

Nik Brinkman decided to stop in at the Monclova Noticias to see Juan Gutierrez.

"Juan," Nik began, "I think I have just the story you need to secure your career as a reporter. I need you to come with me. I will explain along the way."

Gutierrez gathered his writing material and followed Nik on his way to the sheriff's office. Nik explained to Juan who Ron Lester was and the crimes he was wanted for. He also told the reporter of his suspicion that Señor Bacca was likely being paid in counterfeit money in exchange for the silver.

"Use discretion before you print anything about the money being counterfeit," Nik cautioned. "If the money being exchanged is legitimate, it could come back on you. I think if you merely explain who the real Ron Lester is, that will be enough to raise suspicions."

"What is all of this about, Señor Brinkman?" Juan asked.

"It comes down to my task force and me getting out of here alive," Nik answered. "There are two great forces that want the silver that's going to be placed in our possession. That means we'll become a target and our best chance of survival is for those two forces to be distracted by opposing each other."

"How do you intend to do that?"

"I don't know just yet," Nik answered. "I'm just hoping you will figure that out and help make it happen. All I can do is give it to you straight."

When Nik and Juan arrived at the sheriff's office, Sheriff Gonzalez was waiting with the legal paperwork in his hand.

"When the United States emissary arrives and signs this document, you are free to take the silver and go," the sheriff said.

Nik looked over the contract knowing it was likely real enough and would be enforced by both sides. He was also certain the contract would in no way guarantee the silver would ever reach the United States.

"Looks good, Sheriff," Nik said, handing the document back to Gonzalez. "I brought along a reporter so things will be public and legal-like."

Gonzalez puffed a muzzled laugh as he took the paper from Nik with a sly smile. It was then that Captain Garcia's unit rode up surrounding the wagon loaded with silver.

"The guy in the fancy duds riding the black horse is Lester," Nik whispered to Gutierrez, while Gonzalez walked over to open the door for the U.S. 'dignitary.' Nik smiled as Lester walked in and nearly froze in his tracks, recognizing the Galveston marshal.

"Señor Brinkman, may I present United States Treasury Official Sebastian Mason," the sheriff announced, puffing out his chest.

Nik held back his laugh when he heard the name Lester was using for a cover. How clever, Nik thought, to use the name of the marshal's longtime friend, Sebastian Mason, since it could be traced back to the United States government as legitimate. No one in Mexico knew that except Kensington and Lester himself.

"Señor Mason," Nik said, extending his hand to Lester, who immediately put on a pleasant face to shake Nik's hand. "How nice of you to come all this way to help us secure the silver that rightfully belongs to the United States."

"Just doing my sworn duty," Mars… er, Señor Brinkman," Lester answered, catching himself in mid-sentence. "Shall we dispense with the formalities, sign the agreement, and be on our way?"

"The sooner the better, Ambassador," Nik said. "My men and I will be anxious to see to it that this shipment is returned to its rightful owner."

"Don't let temptation get the better of you," Lester said jokingly, smiling contemptuously.

Nik and Lester signed the document and Lester quickly departed. He mounted his horse and, followed by the soldiers assigned to him, galloped out of Monclova.

"Señor Brinkman, my men and I will escort you to your camp," Captain Garcia said. "You may drive the wagon carrying silver that is now in your country's hands."

Nik thanked the captain, Sheriff Gonzalez, and Juan and climbed onto the driver's seat of the wagon.

As Lester and his escort rode away, Nik looked over at Captain Garcia. "No sign of Morgana, I take it?"

"Sorry, Señor Brinkman. I did mention to Señor Mason to ask but I do not know if he made the request to Señor Bacca. He seemed to be in a big hurry."

"Not surprised," Nik commented. "Thanks for trying, Captain."

Once they reached camp, everyone came out to greet Nik and the accompanying unit of soldiers.

"Congratulations, Señor Brinkman, I applaud your efforts to secure your country's silver," Garcia said, looking down at Nik from his horse. "I assume you will soon be on your way back to America. I am sorry about Señorita Morgana."

"You did what you could, Captain. However, we plan to leave tomorrow morning," Nik said. "We appreciate all the help you have given us."

"It was our duty..." Garcia was suddenly cut off in midsentence as Roger approached.

"Captain, could I have a word with you?" Roger said, reaching out to grab the reins of Garcia's horse.

"Certainly," Garcia answered.

"Roger, what's up?" Nik asked.

"Nik, I'll explain later, but I am compelled to discuss something with Captain Garcia."

Recognizing the conviction in Roger's voice, the captain dismounted and joined Nik, who climbed down from the wagon. Roger led the two men to the back of the camp.

"Captain Garcia, can I trust you to hold in strictest confidence what I am about to tell you?" Roger began.

"I am a man of honor," Garcia said. "It is not my position to betray a confidence."

"Captain, this whole issue is not as it appears. This silver exchange is not on the level," Roger said.

"Roger, I don't think …," Nik cut in.

"Nik, I will explain later, but for now let me speak my mind."

Nik's puzzled expression also held some fear as he listened to Roger, who told Garcia that General Diaz, Judge Kensington, and Lester were up to no good.

"Lester introduced himself as Sebastian Mason," Nik said, looking at Roger with a knowing glance.

Roger shook his head in disgust and continued with his monologue for Captain Garcia's benefit.

"So, you are saying that my commanding officer is corrupt?" Garcia said.

"Roger, let's not hang ourselves…" Nik interjected, worried at what Garcia might do.

"I had my suspicions all along," Garcia said, cutting off Nik's response. "I owe my allegiance to the country of Mexico, and I am afraid the general does not do the same. He is out for Porfirio Diaz and always has been."

Nik's expression turned into one of elated surprise,, as he smiled at the captain.

"We do not want any trouble to fall on you," Nik said. "But what my brother said is true. It is best that you know what you are up against when you return."

"The fellow you knew as Sebastian Mason was a phony. His real name is Ron Lester, a fugitive felon from the States."

The captain looked at both men for a moment and responded, "I cannot return with what you have told me and maintain my honor," he said. "I feel I must now do what is right, no matter the consequences."

Roger and Nik looked at each other as if a great weight had been lifted from their shoulders.

Chapter 29
The Getaway

After listening to what Roger and Nik Brinkman had to say about General Diaz and his association with Judge Victor Giles Kensington, Captain Andres Garcia went back to speak to the small detachment of soldiers who were with him. After a brief explanation, the soldiers departed without him.

"Aren't you going with them?" Roger asked the captain.

"My duty is to my country and, as I see it, a little bit to you and your country," Garcia replied. "If I may, I would like to make a little suggestion."

"By all means, Captain," Nik said. "We'll take all the help we can get."

"Please, let us dispense with the captain reference and call me Andres instead," Garcia said, removing his cap and jacket. "I believe it is important that we move out tonight if we are going to get ahead of what is to follow."

"We plan to do that," Roger remarked. "But Nik and I cannot go until we try and rescue Morgana from Bacca's hacienda, and we cannot do that until tomorrow morning."

"Perhaps I can help with that as well," Garcia offered. "Do you have a plan as to how you will carry out this rescue?"

"We do," Nik said and explained their plan to secretly meet Morgana in Bacca's garden and escape with her while Bacca and his men were away at mass.

"You are going to need a distraction," Garcia said. "I can do that since Spanish is my native language and they know me at Señor Bacca's."

"What will you tell them that will hold their attention?" Roger asked.

"It is obvious, I will explain that there may be something wrong with the money turned over to Bacca," Garcia began. "That will cause a panic, drawing Bacca's men remaining at the hacienda to hear what I have to say. It will be easy enough to keep them occupied while you spirit your companion away."

"Meanwhile, your men can begin following the Nazas River toward the mountains in the east tonight," Garcia instructed. "When you escape from Bacca's, head northeast until you come to the river. I will catch up to you and show you the shortest route to the Rio Grande and Texas."

"We're grateful to you for this," Nik said, still uncertain as to where Garcia's loyalties lay. "Are you sure you want to do this?"

"I cannot be a part of what you have told me," Garcia said. "Unless you are deceiving me for some reason, I cannot see doing anything any other way."

Nik looked at Roger to let him know he still held some anxiety over putting their trust in a man they only knew as a captain in General Diaz's army.

"It's okay, Nik," Roger said. "I'll explain it to you later."

Nik put Gateway in command of the overnight trek to get the task force and the silver as far away from Monclova as possible before morning.

"Make sure everyone is armed," Nik instructed. "I do not see this as a clean getaway. We may have to fight our way out of here."

After packing up all but the horses Nik, Roger, Garcia, and Morgana would need, Gateway took the lead driving the chuck wagon, while Sergeant Davis followed in the wagon containing the silver shipment.

The next morning, Sunday, Garcia again donned his uniform and joined Nik and Roger as they approached the outskirts of Monclova.

"Roger and I are going to have to circle around behind Bacca's estate," Nik said. "Give us about a half hour and then approach the front gate with your story. We do appreciate your help."

As Nik and Roger rode off, Nik turned to Roger and said," What if Garcia isn't on the level and exposes our plan?"

"Let's just say an angel told me Garcia was on the level and to trust him," Roger answered.

"We could use an angel about now," Nik answered. "I hope the one that spoke to you wasn't a devil in disguise."

"I'm trained to know the difference," Roger said, laughingly. "There is no turning back now."

After reaching the bluff, Nik and Roger climbed up to where they had surveyed the estate the day before. Morgana was walking through the garden and Nik could see two guards talking among themselves and paying little attention to her.

"I'll go down behind that hedge that surrounds the garden," Roger said. "I will look for a signal from you if Garcia's diversion works well enough to distract those two guards."

"If they turn their backs on her, I will hold up two hands," Nik said. "If they don't, you're pretty much on your own. I'll have the horses ready at the end of the hedge. Just call Morgana over and we'll make a run for it."

After working his way over to the hedge, Roger was able to get close enough to Morgana to toss a small rock in her direction. She turned to see him but held up her hand for Roger to stay back and keep quiet. Roger set his gaze on the bluff to see if Nik was signaling him—nothing yet.

Suddenly, shouting came from in front of the hacienda. Nik could see the two guards in the garden run for the front of the estate. Nik immediately raised both hands, while resisting an urge to call out.

Roger signaled for Morgana to hurry over to the hedge. Seeing the guards running in the opposite direction, the shaman ducked behind the hedge and followed Roger to where Nik was waiting with the horses.

In Bacca's absence, Morgana had dressed in her blouse and trousers and slid easily onto the mount that was waiting for her. Roger did the same and the three set out on a gallop circling north around the estate. They kept out of sight and were soon riding at full gallop in the direction of the Nazas River.

Once they reached the river, they turned east, picking up the tracks of the two wagons. They rode hard and near nightfall caught up with the task force that had stopped near the river.

"We'll have to stop here for the night," Nik said, as they pulled up to the others. "Our horses cannot continue at this pace without some rest and nourishment."

"We've had enough rest to continue traveling through the night," Lieutenant Gateway said, helping Morgana off her horse and expressing his joy in seeing her, as did the others. "You can rest here and when you're ready, we won't be hard to find. We thought it too risky to build a campfire, so if you're hungry, Charlie has cold beans and rice to help tide you over."

"That sounds as good as a juicy steak right now," Roger said, sliding from his saddle. "We have no idea if Bacca and his men are on our trail. Captain Garcia provided an excellent diversion for our rescue but we don't know how long it was before they noticed Morgana was missing."

"If he tipped off Bacca as to the possibility the money was counterfeit," Nik said, "even if he's not after Morgana, he may be after the silver."

"We've been able to make good time, even with this load of silver," Sergeant Davis said.

"Do you think Garcia is going to catch up with us?" Gateway asked.

"It's hard to tell," Nik answered. "We don't know how much time he spent at Bacca's estate or if they even let him go."

"Let's hope so," Roger said. "He might be in trouble with General Diaz as well."

A few hours into the night, Gateway and the task force again continued their trek up the Nazas River, heading for the southern end of the Sierra Madre Occidental mountains. Nik, Roger, and Morgana took care of their horses, helped themselves to some of Charlie's cold rice and beans, and stretched out to get some rest before moving on.

A little after midnight, Nik sat up, listening intently. He could hear the sound of a horse walking slowly in their direction. He got up and drew his pistol, peering into the darkness trying to make out where the noise was coming from.

"Hold it right there or I'll shoot," Nik said, as soon as he saw the horse and rider.

"Señor Brinkman, is that you?" said the rider.

"It is… Andres?" Nik said, recognizing the voice.

"Si," Garcia replied, dropping down out of his saddle. "Is your task force still here?"

"No, they've moved on," Nik answered, as Roger and Morgana had also stirred from their slumber and joined Nik.

"Good, they must continue on the move if we are to stay ahead of those who would attack us."

"Is Bacca on your tail?" Roger asked.

"He probably is, but I tried to create a diversion by crossing the river and coming up the other side," Garcia said. "I'm hoping he would think I crossed the river to go north. It would be hard to follow in the night."

"Excellent," Nik said. "We are resting our horses, as well as ourselves. We plan to continue trailing the task force before daybreak. Join us for a few hours of sleep before we set out again."

"Gladly," Garcia said, unsaddling his mount and putting it with the other horses. He set down the saddle for a pillow and was soon asleep.

Well before daybreak, Morgana woke up and called to the others.

"It is time to get up and get on our way," she said, as the others started to stir. "They are coming. We must stay ahead of them."

"Did you hear something?" Nik said, rising quickly.

"I have seen them," Morgana said. "They are well behind but are traveling fast."

"How many would you estimate?" Roger asked, rising to his feet and groping for his gun belt and hat.

"They are coming in two different directions," Morgana said. "One group from the west and one from the south."

"It is Diaz who comes from the south," said Garcia, sitting up and trying to shake the sleep from his head. "They are trying to head us off at the pass."

"At the pass? What pass?" Nik asked.

"The Nazas River passes through the Sierra Madre but is not easy to follow," Garcia said. "There is an easier and quicker pass that leads directly to the Salado River, where we turn north. Diaz will try to block that pass."

The conversation died down as the four saddled their horses, checked to make certain nothing was left behind, and rode out following the Nazas River east.

The riders kept their horses cooled down by walking them in the river, while restraining them from taking on too much water. Later that afternoon, they came upon the task force and the two wagons. They were moving slowly.

"The heat is taking a toll on the horses," Gateway said, as Nik rode up to his position. "We hope to reach those mountains by nightfall."

"I'm afraid I have some unpleasant news," Nik said. "We have two groups after us. I figure it is General Diaz and Marteen Bacca. They are approaching from two different directions."

"My guess is neither has loaded wagons slowing them down," Gateway lamented.

"Not hardly," Nik said. "My guess is the general wants that wagonload of silver. I'm not sure if it's Morgana that Bacca's after or the silver, perhaps both."

"We've seen no sign of anyone yet," Gateway said. "Perhaps we've gotten a good enough head start."

"Considering that we have caught up to you twice," Nik stated. "I'm not feeling optimistic."

Now moving slower, the task force followed the river into the lower foothills. As the evening shadows began to cover them, Gateway rode back toward Sergeant Davis, observing the progress. He continued back to where Nik and Roger were riding next to the chuck wagon.

"As soon as it's dark, we're going to have to stop," Gateway said. "If we don't rest these horses, they'll never make it through those mountains."

"Instruct the others to make camp," Nik said reluctantly.

"Do you think that's wise, Nik?" Roger asked.

"You heard the man," Nik answered. "We don't have a choice. We can only hope we have enough head start to break through before our pursuers catch up to us."

"And if they do?" Roger asked.

"We'll have to figure that out if, and when, it happens. There's no way we can fight our way past Diaz's army," Nik said. "We may have a chance to hold off Bacca, but it depends on the size of his band of outlaws."

Gateway had the wagons form a V shape, far enough away from the river so the horses and riders could get behind them.

"This won't offer us much protection, but it gives us a defensive position," Gateway said. "My guess is, if there is shooting, they won't shoot the horses. They're too valuable, especially pulling wagons."

"What do you suggest, Roger?" Nik asked, turning to his brother.

"Rest and prayer is the best I can offer, Nik," Roger said. "Maybe the Good Lord will delay those who are after us. Our other option is to try and cross the river to the other side, but I don't think our wagons would make it."

Nik rode over to the wagon of silver, reached down, and picked up a silver bar. He put it into his saddle bag and rode back.

"Hoping to keep that as a souvenir?" Roger asked.

"More like proof that we gave it our best," Nik said, "if we don't make it to Texas with the rest of it."

"The place to cross the river is two to three miles farther ahead," Garcia offered. "If we can cross there before Diaz reaches us, we will at least have reached the pass I spoke of."

"Charlie, build a campfire behind the wagons and cook us up something appropriate for a last supper," Nik said.

"Are you that pessimistic?" Roger asked, with a slight grin.

"Just a figure of speech," Nik said. "Even if we escape across the river, I'm not sure when we'll get to eat again."

In spite of the somber situation, Nik's comment drew a laugh from everyone. Charlie, Pete, and Carter built a fire and began putting together the evening's meal while the rest of the group took care of the horses and prepared to get some rest.

Chapter 30
Crossfire

No one in the task force got much rest during the fitful night, but no one complained. All anyone could do was hope that the horses would be rested and ready for a long day's ride.

"Let's add two more horses to the silver wagon," Nik said, as the group readied the animals for departure. "A couple of us will have to ride in the wagons but we'll be able to move faster with more horsepower pulling the silver."

Once the extra horses were harnessed to the wagon, Peter rode with Charlie in the chuck wagon and Carter accompanied Sergeant Davis on the silver-laden wagon. The group rolled up the Nazas River making good time when Captain Garcia called out.

"Hold up," he shouted, as he rode up front where Nik and Gateway were riding. "Lower the brims of your hats against the rising sun and look ahead in the distance."

The wagon train came to a halt and Nik reached into his saddlebag for his field glasses. "We're too late," he said in a hollow voice. "There are mounted soldiers lined up about a mile ahead."

"I was afraid of this," Garcia said. "That is where we need to cross the river. I knew if Diaz got ahead of us that is where he would cut us off. He knows the pass like I do. It was used during our wars with Spain and France."

"What do you suggest?" Nik asked. He still couldn't get past his nagging suspicion that Garcia couldn't be trusted.

"Remain here and wait for them to send a unit out to meet with us," Garcia said. "Let us hear what they expect from us."

"There's no way I'm going to risk any lives fighting the Mexican Army," Nik said. "What do you think they'll demand of us?"

"I assume they want the silver, but you can negotiate to keep the horses," Garcia said. "I do not believe we have anything more that they want, other than me."

"What will they do to you?" Nik asked.

"Court martial, jail," Garcia speculated, "perhaps even a firing squad."

"As far as I'm concerned, you're being held as my prisoner," Nik said. "I think I can make that stick and they know we're from the United States. I don't think they want an international incident on their hands."

"Why would you be holding me as a prisoner?" Garcia said, smiling uneasily.

"You tried to steal some of our silver. Now we're using you to get back to Texas," Nik replied.

As Nik was speaking, five riders from among the line of soldiers could be seen approaching. One was holding up a white flag.

"They do not want trouble," Garcia said. "Let two of us approach with a banner of peace and hear their terms."

"Charlie, get me a strip of white cloth and a rifle to tie it to," Nik called out. "Roger, I'm going to need your company."

"I could go with you," Garcia said.

"Will they be speaking English?"

"Yes, they know English."

"Then you stay here. You're my prisoner, remember?" Nik said, with a straight face.

"Roger let's go out to meet this 'negotiating team,'" Nik said, as Charlie handed him a rifle with a white flag tied to it.

Gateway and David gathered near the chuck wagon and its ordnance, in case there was trouble. The remaining members of the group stood with them, watching Nik and Roger as they proceeded toward the military unit.

Suddenly, the detachment's lead horse reared up and the rider began firing past Nik and Roger. He then turned around and rode back in the direction of where the other soldiers were waiting.

"What the…" Nik said, as bullets began whizzing by in the direction of the retreating unit. Roger and Nik turned to see Marteen Roberto Bacca's band riding hard toward them and the wagons. Everyone in camp gathered beneath the two carts, lying on their stomachs, rifles and pistols in hand. Leaping off their horses, Nik and Roger joined them.

The cavalry line charged from the east, as Bacca's men pulled up and dismounted, taking cover wherever they could. The military soldiers did the same with the task force caught in the middle about one hundred yards from each.

"We're caught in a crossfire," Garcia called out.

"Hold your fire," Roger yelled out to the others as he sprawled out under one of the wagons. "I just hope no one shoots our horses."

"This situation is hopeless, but I have an idea," Garcia said.

"What is that?" Roger asked.

"First, where those soldiers were lined up is where you want to cross the Nazas River. Follow the Nazas to where it feeds into the Rio Salado. Turn north and follow the Salado to where a small stream flows into it. Cross both and head into the rising sun and it will take you to the Rio Grande. The village of Piedro Negras lies north on the Grande and across the river from there is your Eagle Pass."

"That's wonderful," Roger said. "I'm familiar with Eagle Pass and Fort Duncan. But, in this situation, how are we going to get there?"

"I will show you," Garcia said, as he crawled up onto the driver's seat of the silver-laden wagon. He took hold of the reins, snapped them, and shouted. The horses took off in a southern direction, already excited by the gunfire. As suddenly as it began, the shooting stopped.

After recognizing what was happening, riders from both sides of the skirmish took off after the wagon of silver.

"What is he doing?" Gateway asked.

"He's luring both sides away from us," Roger said. "I suggest we follow his lead and get out of here as fast as we can."

Everyone scrambled out from under the wagons and ran out to gain control of the horses. They froze when they heard another shot much closer to them. Bacca and two of his men had closed in on them. Nik walked around to the other side of the chuckwagon to confront them.

"What do you want?" Nik shouted. "The wagon of silver is headed that way," he added, pointing in Garcia's direction.

"Yes, my men will get that, but you have something else that I want," Bacca said.

"What?" Nik asked.

"The mestizo shaman," Bacca said, smiling.

"I paid you for her," Nik said. "Setting her free was part of the bargain."

"I was told the money might not be good, so there is no bargain," Bacca said, turning to his escort. "She stays with me. Boys, get what is mine."

The simultaneous sound of Winchester rifles injecting shells into their chambers was heard as Roger, Gateway, Davis, and Morgana emerged from behind the wagon with barrels pointed at the intruders.

"It looks like you're outnumbered," Nik said, with a slight smile. "Besides, I didn't give you that money. Take it up with the United States Treasury."

"Oh, and by the way, these folks are excellent shots. Would you like a demonstration?"

Bacca looked at the four rifles pointed and him and his men. He then gave Nik an angry look and turned his horse to ride after the wagonload of silver. His men lit out after him.

"Let's not waste time," Nik shouted. "Get that chuck wagon rolling and let's head for the spot on the river where Garcia said we could cross."

Within minutes, the task force had reached a crossing point on the Nazas River. The waters were still running high.

"The horses can make it but not the wagon," Charlie Bluefeather called out, as he surveyed the stream.

"Then cut those horses loose," Nik ordered. "Grab what you can from the wagon and leave it behind. We do not have a lot of time to waste."

With everyone on a horse, bareback or otherwise, the task force plunged into the river, making it safely to the other side. They turned upstream and put as much distance as they could between themselves and the raging battle going on behind them.

Once satisfied they were out of danger, Nik ordered a halt.

"I don't think there's anything more those folks want from us," he said. "I just hope we didn't start another war in this country."

"Like any other country, there's always going to be someone at war with someone else," Roger said, offering a sigh of relief. "Our best bet is to follow Andres' directions and get back to safety as soon as possible."

"Charlie, what did we salvage that we have to eat?" Nik asked.

"Mostly dried meat," Bluefeather answered. "All else was no good."

"There is much to eat here," Morgana cut in. "Many plants in Mexico are edible, as well as deer and many birds."

"Okay, I guess we shouldn't starve," Nik said.

"What do you think is going to happen to Captain Garcia?" Lieutenant Gateway asked.

"I hate to think about that," Roger answered. "I'm afraid he probably didn't survive the gunfire once those two hostile outfits caught up with him. I can't help but thank the Lord for him. I'll always remember what he did for us."

"It's too bad," Gateway said. "To us, he's a hero. To Mexico, he's somewhat of a traitor."

"Maybe we ought to have his name engraved on that silver ingot you saved, Nik," Roger suggested. "Then enshrine it somewhere."

"I forgot about that," Nik said, flipping open his saddle bag to inspect the one souvenir the task force had to commemorate their expedition. "I almost wish I hadn't taken it."

"No, it is good that you did," Morgana replied. "We may have caused more trouble than we intended, but that bar of silver will serve as good medicine. It symbolizes the real enemy here—greed."

"Well boys, let this be a lesson to you," Roger said, turning to Peter and Carter riding behind him. "We started out in peace to recover something of minimal value, only to have it turn out to be unrelated to peace or value."

"I think we all need some time to heal," Nik said soberly, looking ahead as each rider became lost in their thoughts.

The rest of the trip up the Nazas River to the Rio Salado continued without incident, as did the journey north reaching the confluence Andres Garcia had described.

"This is where I get off," Morgana announced, much to everyone's surprise.

"I don't understand," Roger asked. "Where will you go?"

"My grandfather is not well," Morgana said. "He lies west of here and I had a vision that he will not last long."

"Who is your grandfather?" Gateway asked.

"He is Cochise, chief of the Chiricahuas Apache," Morgana answered. "His daughter was my mother."

"That's quite a trip to take alone," Sergeant Davis said. "Are you sure you want to take that chance?"

"No chance," Nantan offered. "I will go with her. Cochise is an honored name among the Apache. I would like to pay my respects as well."

"Don't you have to report back to Fort McRae?" Roger asked. "You're still United States Military."

"I'll take care of that," Gateway said. "I'll give an order for Nantan to accompany Morgana on her trip back. Just make sure you report back to McRae once you've paid your respects, Nantan."

"Are you sure the two of you will be okay?" Nik asked. "That's extremely rugged country you'll have to travel through."

"Not to us," Morgana assured Nik. "It is the country we are familiar with."

"Well, before you go," Roger began, "I suggest we have a little ceremony to see the two of you off. I will ask my God to bless your journey and the two of you can combine that with the power of your Great Spirit."

During the suggested ceremony, tribute was also paid to Kelly Laumpagh and Andres Garcia for their services. The task force said its farewells as the two Apache travelers followed the tributary north and Nik, Roger, Gateway, Davis, Charlie Carter, and Zimmerman crossed through the Salado headwaters on their way to the Rio Grande.

Chapter 31
Roger's Calling

The task force, now consisting of seven men on horseback, rode into the small village of Piedras Negras, just across the Rio Grande from Eagle Pass and Fort Duncan.

"I think I'm done with Mexico," Nik said. "Let's find out if they have a ferry across the Rio Grande to Eagle Pass."

The seven men stopped in front of the local cantina and waited for Nik to inquire inside. After several minutes, he emerged with a señorita carrying a tray of tequila, limes, salt, and seven glasses.

"We're in luck," Nik said. "Most of these folks speak English so I thought we'd have a round of drinks before making our way across the river."

"I guess a little bit of Mexico is still in your blood," Roger said. "I think a farewell toast to this country is in order. Peter, don't tell your mother about this," Roger added with a laugh.

The ferry on the Mexico side of the Rio Grande was nothing more than a raft. Nik and Roger decided to cross first to Eagle Pass and secure a ferry in Texas large enough to accommodate the horses. Roger also offered to go on ahead to Fort Duncan and solicit the help of Colonel Shafter in setting up billets for the seven men.

Once the men and horses were inside Fort Duncan, Lieutenant Gateway helped to administratively end the volunteer status of the task force's four military men and return them to semi-active duty. He also formally confirmed the orders he gave to Nantan.

Roger and Nik entered Shafter's office and gave the lieutenant colonel a briefing explaining their mission into Mexico.

"That's quite a story, gentlemen," Shafter said. "I know you're anxious to get back to your homes but remain here as long as you like until you feel ready to travel again."

"Thanks, Colonel," Nik said. "Now, if you'd tell me where I can send out a telegram, I have a few people that I need to inform of our arrival back in the States."

"You're in luck," Shafter said. "Eagle Pass was recently connected to the Texas telegraph network."

Nik, Roger, and Gateway all went into Eagle Pass to inform by telegram those who might be anxious about their return.

Nik sent a telegram to Esther Boatman to let her know he was coming home soon. He also telegraphed Judge Conklin and his deputy marshal, Ambrose Tucker, of his arrival in Texas.

"Walt, would you ask Captain Horne at Fort McRae to inform the Paul Zimmerman Family that their son Peter is doing well and I will soon be bringing him home?" Roger asked.

"Anyone else?" Gateway asked.

"No, that should do it," Roger answered.

"Aren't you going to send something to that lady from Philadelphia that you met?" Nik asked.

"No, I think I'll pen a letter to her," Roger said. "I don't think she's waiting for a telegram. In fact, I'm not sure she's even expecting to hear from me."

"I guess you have a stronger constitution than I do," Nik said, grinning.

"I have to," Roger answered, with a smile. "Between my traveling clergy duties, and you dragging me across country, I don't have that much leisure time."

"I'll try to go easier on you," Nik said. "I don't suppose you'd want to preside over my pending nuptials?"

"You mean head back to Galveston with you?" Roger said. "What about Peter Zimmerman? I need to get him home to his folks."

"Have you forgotten," Gateway chimed in. "Pete's in the army now. He'll be heading back to Fort McRae with me and the next detachment out of Fort Duncan."

"He's right, brother," Nik said, chuckling. "I would bet your circuit in the New Mexico Territory has found someone to take your place. Besides, you've traveled this path before, when you came to Galveston."

"You're going to get me excommunicated," Roger said, halfheartedly.

"Not for answering another call," Nik added. "There is almost nowhere in the Old West that your services aren't needed."

"You know, if you weren't my brother I'd think you might be related to the devil," Roger said, laughing. "I think we'd better be getting back to Fort Duncan."

After dinner on the post, Roger excused himself to take a walk and think things over.

"Would you like some company?" Nik asked.

"No, I need to sort some things out. I don't think well when I'm talking," Roger said, grinning at his brother.

"Take all the time you need, Roger," Nik answered with a smile, hoping his brother would choose to return to Galveston, Texas, with him.

There was a trail not far from Fort Duncan that led down to the Rio Grande. It was quiet and certainly a place where a man could get lost in his thoughts. Roger had a lot to think about and sat down on a fallen tree that had lost all its bark. Before long, he was whispering prayers for assistance with the decisions he had to make.

"Mister, could you help me?"

Roger looked up, thinking he was alone but certain he'd heard a voice.

"We could use your help, sir," the voice continued.

As Roger looked around, he saw a small boy standing nearby. Roger could tell the lad was an Indian, but his pleading face told him the child needed help.

"Certainly, son, what can I do for you?" Roger asked.

"My people need help," the boy continued. "There were some white men helping us, but they're all gone now."

"Your people need help?" Roger said, thinking the lad's request a little odd. "I'll do what I can. Where are your people?"

"In the Wyoming Territory," the boy said. "By the river you folks call North Platte."

"Wyoming?" Roger exclaimed, trying to maintain a calm demeanor. "You're a long way from home, aren't you? What's your name?"

"Little Bone," the boy replied. "The white folks called me Paul."

Roger scanned the Rio Grande to see if there was a boat or canoe that the boy may have been riding in and had become separated.

"Look, why don't you..." Roger stopped in midsentence, as he looked back to see where the boy had been standing, but he wasn't there. "Wait, where did you go?" Roger called out as he quickly moved to where the lad had stood.

"Looking for someone?" Nik asked as he came strolling down the same path Roger had taken to visit the river.

"Ah, hey, Nik, did you see a small boy here a few seconds ago?" Roger inquired as he continued to look about.

"A small boy? What was he doing, fishing?" Nik said, stopping just short of where Roger stood.

"An Indian boy, he couldn't have been more than nine or ten years old," Roger explained.

"Well, unless he decided to go for a swim, I didn't see anyone on this trail," Nik said. "Sorry to bother you, but you've been gone quite a while."

"My apologies, Nik, ah... no, you're not bothering me, but I would have sworn there was a young Indian lad here a minute ago."

"Seeing things again?" Nik asked. "What did this one have to say?"

Roger looked a little exasperated. He knew Nik was growing suspicious of his 'visions,' but Roger had always been reluctant to speak to anyone about it, even Nik.

"Nik, as you've probably guessed, I have visions that inform me of certain things or lead me in different directions."

"I had guessed it but I'm glad you've finally decided to tell me about it," Nik said. "This way I don't have to think you're completely crazy."

"It was a vision I had of Pa that told me to trust Captain Garcia," Roger confessed.

"Pa! You had a vision of Pa?" Nik said with some concern. "Have you been seeing members of our family?"

"No, that was the first time I envisioned anyone one from our family and it was only for an instant," Roger explained.

"Pa," Nik muttered shaking his head. "No wonder you were so sure about Andres. I wish I had known sooner. Perhaps I wouldn't have distrusted him like I did."

"I'm sorry about that," Roger replied, "but that brings me to my next question. What do you know about the Wyoming Territory?"

"Rough country, why do you ask?" Nik questioned.

"Ahh, let's just say…" Roger stammered.

"A little birdie mentioned it?" Nik cut in, with a slight laugh.

"Yeah, something like that," Roger replied. "A birdie whose folks in Wyoming are having a hard time of it."

"Who doesn't have a hard time of it in Wyoming?" Nik said. "Wait, don't tell me, instead of coming with me to Galveston to enjoy a fabulous wedding by the ocean, you're thinking about going to Wyoming? Roger, you barely made it out of Mexico alive and now you're thinking about going to Wyoming?"

"I know it sounds crazy, Nik, but I'm subject to go where the Good Lord calls me."

"And in this case, the Good Lord took the form of a little birdie to call you? Or was He a little Indian boy, who just happened to be passing through Eagle Pass, Texas?" Nik said, half joking while feeling a little exasperated.

"I knew you'd understand, Nik," Roger said, putting his arm around his brother's shoulders and grinning from ear to ear. "I'll be expecting you and Esther to come and visit me from time to time. I hear it's beautiful in Wyoming this time of year."

Nik let out a laugh, as the two brothers walked back to Fort Duncan, each with an arm around the other's shoulders, laughing and talking all the way.

Author's Note

I hope you enjoyed this book. Please consider giving it a rating and add a few words about your reading experience at your favorite online retailer.

The link below with a QR code will take you to the book's web page. From there, you can follow links to various online retailers.

Giving my book rating and writing a short written review about why you enjoyed it will help me immensely.

Thank you!

Tim W. James

www.sastrugipress.com/iron-spike-press/borderline-justice/

Use your smart device to scan the QR code for the book's webpage.

About Tim W. James

Tim W. James has been a writer since grade school. When not writing, he continues his passion for athletics by playing golf and watching his favorite sports teams. He and his family live in California.

Additional Books by Tim W. James

THE ROGER BRINKMAN SERIES

BLOOD JUSTICE

Two brothers, one a preacher's son, the other an adopted would-be slave, set out in opposite directions to avenge their family's murder only to cross paths in pursuit of the killer.
www.sastrugipress.com/iron-spike-press/blood-justice/

COUNTERFEIT JUSTICE

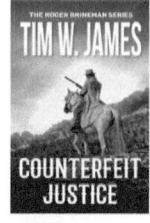

Preacher Roger Brinkman takes his crucifix and his Colt to fulfill a promise and help his lawman brother battle thieves, counterfeiters, and murderers in the Old West.
www.sastrugipress.com/iron-spike-press/counterfeit-justice/

BORDERLINE JUSTICE

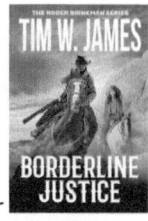

Pursuing outlaws into Mexico, Preacher Roger Brinkman and his brother Nik team up to recover a stolen U.S. Treasury silver shipment only to find the truth they wanted was borderline at best.
www.sastrugipress.com/iron-spike-press/borderline-justice/

Standalone Books

THE BLIND MAN'S STORY

While on vacation, journalist Beau Larson encounters a blind man high on a forested bluff. This leads him to a brewing war between conservationists and the timber industry, resulting in a mysterious murder.
www.sastrugipress.com/books/the-blind-mans-story/

Enjoy Additional Iron Spike Press Books

THREADS WEST (LARGE PRINT EDITION)
   Immigrants from Europe discover more than
they bargained for when landing on the shores
of America.
www.sastrugipress.com/iron-spike-press/threads-west/

MAPS OF FATE (LARGE PRINT EDITION)
   The European settlers embark on their ex-
pedition west, only to discover their fates are
inextricably linked to an unexpected map.
www.sastrugipress.com/iron-spike-press/maps-of-fate/

UNCOMPAHGRE (LARGE PRINT EDITION)
   The European immigrants are now wise to the
ways of America but they soon find out what
their knowledge is worth in the Rocky Mountains.
www.sastrugipress.com/iron-spike-press/uncompahgre/

MOCCASIN TRACK (LARGE PRINT EDITION)
   A new generation of children finds that their
parents' immigration to America created more
than they bargained for.
www.sastrugipress.com/iron-spike-press/moccasin-track/

Visit www.ironspikepress.com to learn more
about these and other exciting titles.
Thank you for your purchase!

Enjoy Additional Sastrugi Press Books

ANTARCTIC TEARS BY AARON LINSDAU

Experience the honest story of solo polar exploration. This inspirational true book will make readers both cheer and cry. Coughing up blood and fighting skin-freezing temperatures were only a few of the perils Aaron Linsdau faced.

www.sastrugipress.com/books/antarctic-tears/

JOURNEYS TO THE EDGE
BY RANDALL PEETERS, PH.D.

What is it like to climb Mount Everest? It requires dreaming big and creating a personal vision to climb the mountains in your life. Learn directly applicable guidelines on how you can create a vision for your life.

www.sastrugipress.com/books/journeys-to-the-edge/

SHAKE YOURSELF FREE BY BOB MILLSAP

Learn how to overcome difficult encounters with misfortune, tragedy, and loss. Emotional recovery is a journey requiring a mindset shift. Get this book now and take control of your life.

www.sastrugipress.com/books/shake-yourself-free/

THE MOST CRUCIAL KNOTS TO KNOW
BY AARON LINSDAU

Knot tying is a skill everyone can use in daily life. This book shows how to tie over 40 of the most practical knots for virtually any situation. This guide will equip readers with skills that are useful, fun to learn, and will make you look like a confident pro.

www.sastrugipress.com/books/the-most-crucial-knots-to-know/

Enjoy Sastrugi Press Zane Grey Editions

RIDERS OF THE PURPLE SAGE

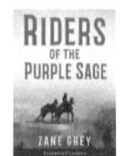

Zane Grey's classic cowboy story set the stage for an entire genre of books that continues today. Grey's story of fighting prejudice touches hearts and compels readers to examine how they deal with an internal struggle. www.sastrugipress.com/classics/riders-of-the-purple-sage/

THE RAINBOW TRAIL

Set ten years after *Riders of the Purple Sage*, Jane must decide between the fate of her adopted daughter Fay and the life of Lassiter. Grey's follow-up classic is a must-read for those who enjoy the western genre. www.sastrugipress.com/classics/the-rainbow-trail/

THE LONE STAR RANGER

His father was a gunslinger and the Texas Rangers declared him an outlaw. How can Duane survive to clear his name in this Zane Grey classic? Starting life has an outlaw's son had certain disadvantages in the Old West. www.sastrugipress.com/classics/the-lone-star-ranger/

THE LAST TRAIL

Renegades kidnap a young Mexican woman from a frontier fort and two men set out to rescue her. Faced with impossible odds and conflicting motives, can they set aside their differences for a common goal? www.sastrugipress.com/classics/the-last-trail/

THE U.P. TRAIL

Intertwining lust, violence, greed, love, bigotry, sacrifice, heroism and depravity, Zane Grey's *U. P Trail* dissects the impacts of economic and social change on a romantic background. www.sastrugipress.com/classics/the-up-trail/

The Mysterious Rider

Full of romance, mystery and adventure, Zane Grey's *Mysterious Rider* is an Old West classic where the desire to settle an old score threatens the existence of a business and a family founded on murder and mayhem. www.sastrugipress.com/classics/the-mysterious-rider/

The Light of Western Stars

Ride through danger, mystery, romance, betrayal, and sacrifice with the wealthy and sultry easterner Madeline Hammond, trying to eke out a life in the wilderness of New Mexico. www.sastrugipress.com/classics/the-light-of-western-stars/

To the Last Man

Based on the real-life story of a long-running bloody family feud in Arizona, Two families have been fighting for a generation. Is it ever possible for the bloodshed to end? www.sastrugipress.com/classics/to-the-last-man/

The Heritage of the Desert

Pushed to the fringes of death, Jack Hare faces demons he never expected. An entire wavr between cattle rustlers is brewing and Jack is unexpectedly thrust into the middle of it. www.sastrugipress.com/classics/the-heritage-of-the-desert/

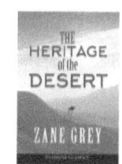

The Man of the Forest

Through the character of a lone man in the forest we are introduced to hard facts of the Wild West. A solitary cowboy overhears a kidnapping conspiracy and has to decide if saving the victim is really worth the risk. www.sastrugipress.com/classics/the-man-of-the-forest/

Read additional Sastrugi Press Zane Grey titles here: https://www.sastrugipress.com/classics/zane-grey-books/

Zane Grey is considered to be one of the original Western authors.

www.ingramcontent.com/pod-product-compliance
Lightning Source LLC
Chambersburg PA
CBHW022010010726
47494CB00003B/970